'My breath turned to mist as I read. *Begars Abbey* takes its reader to a sinister place and locks them in, all alone. A dark, gothic delight best enjoyed by the light of a single, flickering candle'
JANICE HALLETT, author of *THE APPEAL*

'An inventive, lavish, twisty ghost story that will keep you guessing and turning the pages until the very end. Atmospheric and hugely enjoyable'
ALISON LITTLEWOOD, author of *MISTLETOE*

'An atmospheric, spine-tingling page-turner packed with curious characters and sinister twists. Light your candles for a historical thriller that'll keep you gripped all night'
JENNIFER RYAN, author of *THE CHILBURY LADIES' CHOIR*

'A shiver-down-the-spine jaunt into the gruesome past, with a deliciously creepy finale'
C.E. ROSE, author of *THE HOUSE OF HIDDEN SECRETS*

'As a gothic novel *Begars Abbey* has it all: remote and storm-bound Yorkshire, hidden diaries and keys, locked doors and long corridors, even a wicked old woman... But V.L. Valentine provides the reader with something more, through her appealing, nail-biting heroine, Sam'
ALIX NATHAN, author of *THE WARLOW EXPERIMENT*

BEGARS
ABBEY

Also from V.L. Valentine and Viper

The Plague Letters

BEGARS ABBEY

V.L. VALENTINE

First published in Great Britain in 2022 by
VIPER, part of Serpent's Tail,
an imprint of Profile Books Ltd
29 Cloth Fair
London
ECIA 7JQ
www.serpentstail.com

Copyright © V.L. Valentine, 2022

Text design by Crow Books

1 3 5 7 9 10 8 6 4 2

Printed and bound in Great Britain by
Clays Ltd, Elcograf S.p.A.

A CIP catalogue record for this book is available from the British Library.

ISBN 978 1 78816 4566
Export ISBN 978 1 78816 4573
eISBN 978 1 78283 6575

FSC
www.fsc.org
MIX
Paper from
responsible sources
FSC® C018072

For Sylvan, Mom and Dad

BEGARS
ABBEY

Prelude

5th February 1954, York train station, England

A gust of gritty wind and Sam closes her eyes. The scene comes forth, unbidden. The grate and metal whine of the trains transform into the lilting flurry of a winter's ball. Ancient, dark-panelled walls close in. A chandelier lowers like a midnight sun. The air is warm – teasing her with its spicy scents of juniper and pine boughs, the Yule log on the fire.

Sam sees the swirl of old-fashioned heavy velvet and wool skirts mixed with those as light as air – chiffon, silk. She puts a hand to her head to try to slow it all down. The movement of the dancers is so swift around her, she can't see the too-heavy rouge, the blistered fingers, the ragged nails. The fiddler is so lively, the great hall so crowded, that the frozen smiles are unseen, the forced laughter covered. Her forehead starts to pound at the rhythmic click of the shoes kept and polished beyond their years; the unsteady clink of crystal and cutlery by the table of jellies and pies. The younger guests can't stop staring at the table; they take only small plates of food, but she knows they want more. The eagerness and hunger in their eyes, the fear that makes them hold back, it makes her feel sick. She knows their giddiness, their desire to lose themselves in the moment, to forget.

She wants to look away but she can't. She feels their longing, feels them pull her in. She wants to sweep up her hair and slip into a dress of never-ending tulle. Dab her neck and wrists with her grandmother's jasmine perfume. She wants to take one of the delicate little cups of punch, sip it slowly, then take the hand of that smiling man and be led onto the dance floor. But over there, by the arched entrance to the hall, Sam sees the young lady of the house. A girl of about seventeen. Dressed in a black silk sheath threaded with metallic green and gold, she smoulders in the candlelight. One moment dark ash, then with the slightest movement, an ember come ablaze.

Sam sees one of the guests studying the young lady, trying to read the frown on her face. Sees the young lady rub her arms as if she were cold; the guest matches her frown and quickly leaves the ball.

Sam shakes her head and mercifully, the vision is gone. Instead, she sees Alec, standing by the train that will take them to London. He's frowning, too. He's always frowning, always impatient. He waves a folded-up newspaper at her. He wants her to hurry up. She can't tell if the clouds of steam are coming from him or the train idling behind him. She smiles. He's reassuring even when he's annoyed.

Sam Cooper is twenty-six. She forced them to bring her here, from America to York. Arrived at this very train station on 2nd January.

Alec calls to her again. She pauses, pretends to check the back of her nylons for a run, just to annoy him more. He blows out an exasperated sigh, pulls the brim of his fedora down even further over his dark brow. He wants a cigarette, she can tell.

'By god, if you don't…' he hisses through his clenched jaw.

She does a slow little two-step as she walks towards him then gives in, reaches to take his outstretched hand. Stops cold. Behind Alec, down the platform, Sam sees someone rushing towards them. Her wool coat is plain, like Sam's; the dress underneath is probably not her own. Sam knows her. She is clutching a wine-coloured carpet bag, the pattern faded, muddled.

'Miss, may I come?' she asks.

1

Two Months Earlier, 5th December 1953, Brooklyn, New York

A goddamn miracle worker. How had Sam's mother done it? How had Vera Cooper kept them alive all these years? Sam chewed on her thumbnail as she stared at the light bulb in the shadeless lamp by her mother's bed. The bare bulb made the walls – yellowed from decades of her mother's cigarette smoke – seem even dirtier. Sam and her mother used to whitewash the rooms every few years. But the stains from the cigarettes quickly built back up, almost as if they had just seeped through the paint. Eventually, her mother gave up.

This two-room walk-up in Bensonhurst, Brooklyn was the only home Sam had ever known. She slumped down the wall onto the sticky linoleum floor, pulled her knees to her chest. Vera Cooper was gone now. She had died nearly a year ago. Wherever she was, Sam hoped she couldn't see her, crouched next to the dresser. She spit out a bit of fingernail, rubbed at an eye and got on with her search.

The dresser drawers were laid out around her. They were almost empty; Sam wasn't proud and tried not to be sentimental, so right after her mother's death, she'd taken for herself any blouses or nylons that were in decent shape. What was too holey or threadbare she used as rags. The pink button-up vest with prancing circus ponies she cut up and stuffed into the cracks around the windows. Vera's tiny, tacky red feathered fedora she stuffed around a pipe under the kitchen sink, hoping the cheap glue would prove toxic to the visitors gnawing a hole there.

All that was left in the drawers was a hatbox, some purses and three stained blouses. Sam had meant to see if she could get the stains out so she could wear those too. Vera had been the same height as her, both unusually tall for women; Sam felt like a giraffe when she passed the Italian grannies in the dark halls of their tenement. She and her mother had been roughly the same weight, too; if anything Sam weighed more, because her mother had eaten nicotine for breakfast, lunch and dinner. They were both pale, with dark, deep-set eyes and thick black brows. Sam's were more arched though, with a noticeable point like the wispy tufts at the peak of a kitten's ears, or so her mother used to say when Sam was little.

Their similarities had ended there. Her mother had smoked, Sam chewed gum – or her nails. Her mother had hated to go into Manhattan; Sam spent as much time at the Met museum as possible. Vera's dark hair had been thick and unruly; Sam's dead straight. In the New York summer, the humidity had made Vera's hair bush out to three times its size. When Sam was a kid, she thought she'd die from embarrassment walking next to Vera; her mother stood out in their neighbourhood. 'Eccentric,' the neighbours – always polite about Vera – had put it. More like a bag lady, Sam had thought. It wasn't that Vera was dirty or mumbled to herself; though she did talk differently than everyone else – she was from England.

She had just never tried to fit in, and her outfits were so god-awful loud. Vera would wear a heavy pink knitted cap on a sweltering summer's day, or she'd go outside in January in nothing more than a floral print house dress, hand-knitted woollen socks her only nod to the cold. Her mother had loved splashes of colour, but did not care about coordinating her outfits, or the cut, or dressing for the weather. She had worn camouflage rain boots found at some army surplus store no matter the time of year. Who other than a crazy bag lady would have gone out in such get-ups?

Sam, astoundingly, had been alone in this view. One day, when she was about twelve and standing at the street corner with her friend Donna, she saw her mother coming home in a particularly embarrassing outfit – a yellow raincoat and a polka dot rain hat. There wasn't a cloud in sight. Sam had muttered, 'Christ. Room for one at the funny farm, please.'

'You don't know shit,' Donna had replied, taking out a wad of stale bubble gum and sticking it to the stop sign they were standing by. 'I'd give my baby brother to have your ma.' Donna held out her hand for another stick of gum.

'That's not much of a trade.' Sam slapped her hand away.

'Fine. My Shirley Temple doll then.'

'You tore her hair out.'

Donna Sedano was Sam's best friend; she had always been about a foot shorter than Sam, with a head of close-cropped black curls. When they were little, Donna had reminded Sam of a bowling ball. As Donna got older, a wrecking ball.

'You hear that thump yesterday? Sounded like a bag of books hitting something?' Donna continued. Sam nodded. Donna lived one floor down but the walls in their tenement were about as thick as toilet paper. 'That was my old lady. I'm just sitting at the table, doing my homework' – Sam snorted at this ridiculous claim – 'and out of the blue, she throws the Bible at my head. Said she was trying to get Jesus into me. Said if she didn't do something quick, I'd be knocked up by fifteen. I laughed, only because I was thinking about the boys around here, and how I'd be crazy to get with any of them, and then she did it again. Now your ma, she don't even own a Bible does she?'

Sam had rolled her eyes, not following Donna's logic, but didn't say anything. She had been surprised that Donna was sticking up for Vera – or anyone's mother – because trashing parents was a favourite pastime in the tenement.

Donna's family was Italian, like most of Sam's neighbours in Bensonhurst; Italian or Irish immigrants. As Sam got older, she realised they saw something in Vera that she didn't. Sometimes she'd pass by the women, smoking cigarettes on the front stoop before their husbands got home from work, and they'd smile at her and say what a nice lady her mother was. Sam could tell by their tone they meant it with a capital L – not the whiny twang the delivery boys gave the word when they thought you were being a pain in the ass. Sam had asked her mother once why everyone called her a Lady; her block was not a place where compliments were heard much. Vera had frowned and said, 'They don't know what they mean.' Sam had agreed. She'd been to the movies enough to know that real ladies don't wear the things her mother did or give their kids powdered milk to drink.

'So why do they say it?' she'd persisted, chewing harder on her thumbnail, thinking she was about to learn something profound.

'I'll tell you when you're older, darling,' Vera had said – her most common response to Sam and something Vera rarely delivered on.

Another time, the year before they went to high school when Donna was being a real pissant about everything, she had tried to get Sam to steal a roll of Life Savers from the corner store. 'I'll do your homework. Or how about I cut your bangs? Or your nails. You pick.' Sam had sat quiet on the park swing, ignoring her, then Donna let loose with a gurgled roar, her mouth open so wide that Sam could see her tonsils vibrating. 'Christ! Ask Vera then!' (They had both recently started referring to Sam's mom as 'Vera', because she was so unmotherly – she didn't hug and she didn't hit.) 'Get the money from her! She's one of them Romanov princesses. You know she is!' She pushed Sam off the swing. 'Where's her stash of jewels?' Donna had yelled as she twisted Sam's arm behind her back. 'Why are you holding out on me?'

Sam shoved Donna off and scrambled up. 'Vera's not Russian, you idiot!' she said as she kicked Donna in the tail bone then ran home.

Vera had laughed her head off when Sam told her what had happened, but Sam didn't think any of it was funny.

Donna still lived below her, though she had some kids now, and this late, even on a Saturday night, she would be asleep. Sam sighed, recommitted herself to the dresser drawer before her. She took out the hatbox and examined the horror within. It was an old neon-green pillbox with a monstrous fringe at the back. Her mother had worn it to Sam's fifth-grade recital.

The other mothers in the tenement were earthy, crude. Sweat stains on their house dresses, under their arms, down their backs. They shuffled in and out of each other's apartments in slippers squashed at the heel, asking what kind of shit they had cooking, or what they got from their husbands the night before. 'Something good?' they'd snicker. They liked to talk, to share. They were fleshy, uncomfortably warm. Vera had been cold, hard bone.

Sam tore the lining out of the hat and coming up empty, tossed it across the room. She knew why Vera had worn these things. To scare people off.

Sam pulled out the purses and stuck her fingers through the holes in their frayed creases. One was electric blue and covered with ducks, the other purple velvet with red soap bars. She threw them into the trash pile, too. She put the turned-out drawer back in the dresser and started on the next. It was useless, she knew it. She'd gone through them all before. Right after her mother died, then a few months ago when Sam got fired again. She'd had a series of jobs as a typist. For a while, she managed to stick at the Brooklyn port authority, which was a good place, but her last job had been at a dingy fly-by-night insurance agency. She always got fired, and for the same reason: she was too slow. She wasn't really; when she put her mind to it she could type as fast as anyone. But she had a really bad habit of spacing out and not realising it till another girl poked her or, worse, the boss rapped a hole punch hard against her desk. With no good references, she had decided to go back to the job she'd had in high school, down at the corner grocer's. Less pressure, nowhere near as dull, but the pay was bird seed.

So she was back looking one last time for false bottoms or dimes squirrelled away inside linings or shoved in cracks. Her mother had a habit of hiding inconsequential things in odd places, but right after that fight with Donna at the park swings Sam had thought she'd finally struck gold. Stuffed up in the sofa frame, she had discovered a small square box, only about four inches wide and embroidered with flowers. They had faded from yellow, red and purple to something murkier, but the box was still beautiful. Inside, there was a soft sage-coloured velvet lining and to her utter amazement, jewellery. A tiny amethyst brooch; a ruby and gold ring; earrings with dazzling clear teardrops that must have been diamonds. There were five pieces in the box – possibly more but that's as far as she had gotten when Vera came through the door. She wasn't mad at Sam; Vera rarely lost her temper or raised her voice. Sam was mad, though. Donna had been right: Vera was some kind of runaway princess. She pointed to the jewellery and asked why her mother had lied to her, made a fool of her? 'And why have you been feeding me nothing but oatmeal all this time?' she yelled. Vera stared flatly at the box then said that the jewels were fake, she got them from a local theatre junk sale. Said they wouldn't even buy a week's worth of fried-chicken dinners. 'So why hide them?' Sam had asked, completely fed up with Vera's secrets and her inconsistencies, that Vera had refused to ever answer any of the questions Sam had about their life. Like who Sam's father was – Vera wouldn't even tell her if she'd been married or not – or who Vera's father had been, for that matter.

Sam had known for some time that Vera and her story didn't

add up. *But what in God's name could this woman be hiding?* Sam had seen a good deal of life by this point, all themes and variations on fathers and mothers and families, or lack of. Fathers passed out in their own vomit in the alley. Husbands who were really brothers (down in 3B, ugh). Mothers who ran away, sisters who were the real mothers, grandmothers with their minds long gone, strapped down in their own beds to keep them from wandering out in front of a bus. It was inconceivable to Sam that Vera could've been hiding anything worse. So why wouldn't she tell Sam anything? Ever?

Vera didn't answer her this time, either. Only closed the box and put it up on the shelf over her bed.

When Sam went looking for the box again – she was going to take it to the pawnshop to see what they said – it was gone from the shelf. She found it later under a floorboard, but each time she went back for it, it was in a different place and with one less piece of jewellery.

Up until that box, it had always been a game for Sam – to find what her mother had hidden. But she decided she didn't care anymore. Vera could keep her stupid secrets.

Sam used one of the stained blouses to unscrew the hot light bulb from the lamp and returned it to the socket over the kitchen sink. It was the only bulb she had left. She turned around, hands on hips, to face her remaining possessions. The small, plain kitchen table and two chairs. A pine side table next to the sofa that doubled as Sam's bed. The draughtsmen lamps. Her mother had hated frilly or ornate furniture. Liked it cheap and straight, she had said. *And beat up*, Sam thought. She would be lucky to get ten dollars for all of it; the wood was so scraped and wobbly. Even after she sold it, she wouldn't be able to afford to sleep on the floor. She was four months overdue on rent. Not unusual – but she didn't have her mother's powers of persuasion and she was sure the building superintendent would kick her out come January. She eyed the sofa. Time for a farewell look in the springs. With a great thud, she dumped the whole thing over onto its side. A baby started wailing in the apartment below, followed by several big pokes of a broom handle on the ceiling. *Guess Donna's awake now*, she thought. She wound her hand up through the springs and in between the frame and upholstery. Peanut shells. Paper clips. Faded receipts. She pulled out a piece of old popcorn and put it in her mouth – it tasted soft and stale.

There was a tin box in the back corner of the frame. It had been there for years; it was one of the last things Sam had found before she'd given up the game of figuring out Vera. She'd never come back to it. There was no promising jingle or heft to it and a surprisingly unrelenting lock had defied her attempts to pick it. She assumed it was filled with stupid things like old crossword puzzles or stamps or matchbook covers – things she had found elsewhere in Vera's hiding spots – and had forgotten about it.

She pulled the tin box out once more and braced herself for whatever bizarre remnant of her mother's anxiety she'd find this time – felted balls of cat fur? – and took it over to the kitchen table. She took out the cleaver – her mother had enjoyed butchering her own meat when she got a hold of any – and brought it down hard on the clasp. The box skittered away. She didn't want to risk her other hand by holding the box in place, so she started hacking wildly around the lock plate. Below her, Donna was pounding on the ceiling again with something bigger this time – the baby's head? Sam grimaced but kept going. It felt good to vent her anger. At her situation. That her mother had shut her out. That she was alone.

It didn't take long to cleave open the thin metal. She looked inside, then shook her head in disgust. This was not going to pay the rent. A stack of small, thin envelopes. Addressed to Vera, but sent to a PO box instead of their apartment. And judging by the return address, these weren't love letters from her absent father.

Bell & Sons Solicitors
Grave House
Blake Street
York, England

She took out the letters and spread them over the table. There were about two dozen of them, and several had postmarks dating back to right before Sam was born. Well, someone had been persistent. Why had a law firm been writing to Vera for over twenty-six years? Some of them hadn't even been opened. What had Vera done? What was she ignoring? What *wasn't* Vera ignoring was more like it.

If the envelopes had been fatter, Sam might have been more curious. But she didn't really want to discover that her mother was a fugitive or that she owed money in another country. Or both. Vera, a criminal. That would explain a lot.

She held up the most recent letter to the light, felt a small catch in her throat. It had arrived the week before her mother died. She pulled out the single sheet of notepaper, unfolded it.

Dear Miss Cooper,

In answer to your query, Lady Cooper is still with us.

Your most obliged & obedient servant,
Roger Bell

Lady Cooper? Who was Lady Cooper? She had to be a relative, right? And what exactly did 'still with us' mean? Every phrase in the short letter was a mystery. What query? What exactly had Vera asked Roger Bell? She screwed up her face even more as she looked at the last line – Vera had an obedient servant? Huh? What kind of new craziness was this? She started opening the rest of the letters. Each one arrived around the same time every year and was a near copy of the next, except half the letters – those dated before 1942 – were signed by a Henry Bell and – Sam blinked hard as she re-read them – these did not refer to a 'Lady Cooper'. Instead, Henry Bell wrote: 'In answer to your query, your mother is still with us.'

Sam felt hot, dangerous – like she could explode. Lady Cooper. Lady with a capital L. The neighbours had been on to her mother, all right. Maybe Vera wasn't a Lady, but her mother certainly was. So why had they been living in a fourth-floor walk-up in Bensonhurst? Why had Vera raised her daughter this way?

The letters were all postmarked December or January; a time of year, Sam recalled, when her mother was even more tense than usual. On some of those dark winter evenings, Vera would dump a pack of cigarettes into a bowl and use the glowing end of one to light the next until she had smoked them all. Once Sam had been old enough, she would leave the apartment during these toxic rituals. Had the letters been the cause of them?

Lady Cooper. Vera's mother. Sam's grandmother. *And there's a good chance she's alive*, Sam thought as she threw the ruined box in the trash can. She put the letters back in their envelopes, then stacked them in piles on the table. Why were there no letters directly from Lady Cooper? Or had Vera hidden them? Were there hiding spots yet unknown to Sam? Impossible.

Why had Vera kept this from her? They had a living, known relative, and a rich one at that, it seemed. At least one with money enough to have lawyers write on her behalf every year for decades. What awful thing had Vera done? Or... what awful thing had happened to Vera? She went to the stove and turned on the burner, opened a can of chicken soup and poured it into a pot. She had a few dollars left. She'd go to Western Union on Monday and send a telegram. To York, England.

There was a pop, a flash of light, then the room went black. The light bulb had blown. Sam gave up on the chicken soup and put it – pot and all – in the icebox. Then she went into her mother's bedroom and took Vera's faded red chenille bathrobe off the hook behind the door. She wrapped herself in it and curled up on her mother's bed.

2

6th December 1953

'Christ almighty, I told you!' Donna cursed in that deep, gurgling yell of hers. She'd come upstairs at five in the morning to ruin Sam's sleep as payback for the night before. Donna's short black curls were dented in on one side and she had the baby on her hip. Her quilted pink robe hung open and showed a belly that always looked pregnant even when she wasn't.

Sam put a mug of instant coffee in front of her friend and pushed the letters towards her.

'You owe me half!' Donna hissed as she read a letter, her baby trying to grab it out of her hand. 'You wouldn't be in this mess if you had listened to me.' Sam arched an eyebrow in disbelief. 'You snoozed your way through all of it!' Donna cackled. 'Keeping your head down, little Miss Goody Two Shoes. Never wanting to piss off Vera. Well you could've been living on Park Avenue instead of this pig puddle! I told you she had a stash! I knew she was loaded!'

'No you didn't.' Sam gave her a dirty look. 'You made that all up and you know it.'

'What was there to make up?' Donna barked as she leaned down to pick up several letters her baby had sent cascading off the table. 'That fancy accent and those big words of hers? You don't talk like that unless you've got money somewhere.'

Sam rubbed at her temple. 'So what was Vera hiding then? What was so bad in England that she kept it all a secret?'

'You, you idiot. You're a bastard. She was cut off!' Donna said this with a little too much glee.

Sam scowled. 'Knock it off. So I'm a bastard and they wanted nothing to do with me. But that doesn't explain why Vera never told me about them.' Sam reached for the baby, who was trying to crawl across the table towards her. It was a little girl, only about fifteen months old, with hair just like Donna's. 'Why did Vera come to America? Why didn't she want me to know about my grandmother?'

Donna drummed her fingers on the table. 'Who cares, go over there and get the loot.'

'Don't be so crude.'

'Listen, stupid. Those bedroom eyes of yours?' She waggled a finger at Sam's face. 'Too bedroomy! Wake the hell up!' she growled. 'You got nothing here. I'm gonna kick your bony butt if you don't get going. You and Vera, sitting up here, year after year, doing nothing. Never going anywhere, never seeing nobody. Aren't you tired of it?'

'The thing is,' Sam said slowly, 'Vera knew she was dying. She knew we didn't have any money. I still had the job at the port authority then, but she knew it didn't pay much. And this' – she picked up a letter and tapped it against the edge of her empty coffee mug – 'this means, all along, she knew there might have been another way for us.'

'Are you listening to me? They cut her off! Vera was a *Lady*. Her mother was a *Lady*. No bastards allowed!'

'You don't know that. Any of it. The letters are addressed to *Miss* Cooper; she's never referred to as a Lady. And maybe there was a guy. Maybe Vera had a husband. There or here. Maybe he died.'

Donna looked at her. 'I didn't know they stacked shit that high. This Roger Bell. He says he's waiting to hear from Vera. Vera keeps asking 'em if her mother's dead. She needs her mother dead so she can inherit. Well it didn't go like that. So that means when Lady Cooper kicks the bucket, *you* inherit.'

'Huh? Why would Lady Cooper change her mind now? If she cut Vera off, that means I'm cut off too.'

'Whatever! Get over there and start begging.'

'It's not about the money,' Sam said, burying her nose in the sweet scent of the baby's curls and taking the coffee mug out of her little hands.

'You got a brain the size of a chicken's. If you're gonna sit there and be stupid' – she nodded towards the baby – 'she's good company. I'm going back to bed.' Donna pulled a bottle out of her robe pocket as she got up from the table and plunked it down in front of Sam. 'Just think' – her eyes glittered mischievously – 'if you get up off your ass, you won't have to wear that same dumb orange sweater every day... and you might finally get laid.'

'Jesus, Donna,' Sam said as her friend high-tailed it out the door. She looked down at the baby, the child's eyes wide in confusion at the sight of her mother leaving. The baby started fussing so Sam gave her the bottle Donna had left. She kissed the little girl on top of her head, then flinched as a memory rushed in – one of the last times she'd seen her mother, over there on the couch, trying to smile at Sam through the pain. She stood up and turned away from the living room, started pacing across the small kitchen with the baby on her hip. Vera had left nothing and Sam hadn't expected differently. They had scratched by – everyone did in Bensonhurst. But Vera must have thought about what having a family would've meant to Sam after she was gone. Even if the family had disowned Vera, why hadn't her mother left the door open even a crack for Sam? She looked at the baby and said in a sing-song voice, 'I think your mama's right. There's only one way to find out.' The baby squealed, then threw her bottle down.

3

7th December 1953

The Western Union on 18th Avenue opened at eight on Monday morning. By six, Sam had combed her hair and pulled it back into its usual low ponytail, drunk two cups of black coffee and chased them with peanut butter straight from the jar. She put on a dark brown corduroy skirt and the burnt-orange sweater Donna apparently hated. Sam wore it all the time not because she didn't have options, but because Vera had knitted it. Though Sam didn't know why she was putting it on now, she was so mad at her mother.

It was a frigid morning, the puddles turned to ice, but she didn't notice as she stood outside the telegram office waiting for it to open. Her mind was going crazy with the possibilities. As she watched the milk trucks disappear for the day, the paper boys head to their next jobs, she shrank back into her old green wool coat.

A clerk came from the alley and wound the metal shutters up, unlocked the door. He looked at Sam with a toothy grin then whistled in approval. She brushed past him without a word and went up to the counter, the first in line. She handed

the telegraph operator one of the envelopes sent by Roger
Bell with the address circled, and her message.

MR ROGER BELL

FOUND YOUR LETTERS STOP MY MOTHER VERA
ISADORA COOPER IS DEAD STOP URGENT THAT I SEE MY
GRANDMOTHER LADY COOPER STOP DYING WISH OF VERA
STOP I HAVE NO FUNDS PLEASE HELP

SAMANTHA JANE COOPER

'You don't need the stops,' the operator smirked as she typed
up the message. 'You get charged per word these days.' She
handed the message and solicitor's envelope back to her,
looked at her sideways. 'Dying wish, honey? Good luck with
that.'

Sam exhaled, blowing her bangs straight up in exasperation.
At the last minute she had changed 'money' to 'funds' to try to
give it some class. But she could see it read like a scam.

'When will he get it?' she said, trying to keep the worry out
of her voice. 'When will I hear back?'

'You don't know this fella?' The operator had bleached-
blonde curls, a beauty mark next to her ruby-red lips and one
of those nasally put-on, fast-talking accents like Sam heard in
movies.

'No.'

'You know what kinda telegram never gets a response?'

Sam gave her a sour look as she turned away. *Wise ass*, she
thought.

'Shoulda asked me before you sent it, honey.'

She headed for the door, but the clerk from earlier stepped in front of her, a wide, cocky grin on his face. 'What's the rush, sweetheart?'

Sam paused. She knew she was not attractive. Her most prominent features were her long, pointy nose and thin but jutting chin – kids used to call her Gulch, after Almira Gulch in *The Wizard of Oz*.

She moved to walk past him but he blocked her way with his body again.

She met his eye briefly; he winked and made a show of adjusting his pants.

'*Spit. That's all they are, spit on the sidewalk.*' That's what Vera used to tell her about guys like this. '*So spit on them. Just a wee bit, mind you. No need for dramatics. They shall be quite confused, the poor brutes, and then off you go!*' But Sam just shook her head and quickly walked away.

*

Sam went to her shift at the corner grocery and at the end of the day, bummed a light bulb off her boss. She took her time heading home, shuffling her feet slowly through the slush because she enjoyed the sound it made and had nothing better to do anyway. There'd been a brief whiteout during the afternoon, enough to put a few inches of snow on the ground that had since melted into a pasty grey sludge. She chewed her way over to the nail of her little finger, wondering if there might have been a better way to word the telegram, and had just arrived at her apartment building when she heard someone shout her name. She looked up and saw old Mrs Catania sitting on a chair next to the stoop; she was always out at dusk, being pretty gone in the head and waiting for her sons who were never coming home from the war. Sam's jaw nearly fell off when she saw who was standing next to her. The oily clerk from the telegram office.

'For crissakes,' she yelled. 'Get out of here!' That little sneak. He'd stolen her address. She'd get him fired.

'Got something for you, sweetheart.' He waved an envelope in front of her face.

She reached out to grab it from him but he whipped it behind his back.

'What are you gonna give me for it?'

Sam wasn't going to let him get away with it this time. She threw her head back and hollered, 'Help! He's hitting Mrs Catania! He's beating her! He's stealing her purse! Help!' Half the windows in the buildings around her flew up, and she felt the ground shake as neighbours pounded down the stairs. The clerk looked around in a panic, and Sam swiped the letter from his hand before he tore off down the street. She watched for a moment as a stampede of her neighbours chased after him, then ripped open the envelope and pulled out the telegram:

MISS COOPER

MY CONDOLENCES. WILL WIRE FUNDS BUT A VISIT IS
NOT ADVISABLE. I SHALL EXPLAIN VIA POST.

ROGER BELL

They don't want me. They'd rather buy me off than see my face. She let the telegram fall to the gutter.

4

8th December 1953

MR ROGER BELL
MUST COME NOW CANNOT WAIT VERA INSISTED
WITHIN THE MONTH
SAM COOPER

Donna had helped her think through what to say. She was better at these things. Being pushy. After Donna got a husband, she had insisted they move in with her mother, who was a widow now. One, to save money. Two, so Donna could torture her mother for all the years she'd tortured her.

Sam headed over to a different Western Union, the one on 86th, to send the telegram. She didn't ask around about what happened to that kid last night, but she didn't want to give him an excuse to come back, either. As she handed over the message, she told the operator to tack on a final line:

FLAT BROKE NO MORE TELEGRAMS

That was Donna's idea too, but Sam did not find it easy to be so forward and couldn't commit the words to paper.

'Flat broke, it makes me sound pathetic. Grubby,' she'd told Donna.

'No, it makes you sound honest,' her friend replied. 'You got any other options you ain't telling me about?'

After she left the telegram office, she headed for her job at the grocer's, chewing one piece of gum after another as she went. *Vera insisted.* The lie was a believable one, that Vera's dying wish was for her mother and daughter to know one another. That whatever hatchet had been thrust into whoever's back be buried. Vera would be climbing out of her grave if she knew what Sam was doing. *I don't like it, either, Vera. Do you think I like begging? Do you think I like it that you're dead?*

The lawyer's telegram was shaking loose too many unwanted thoughts. Vera was dead and Lady Cooper didn't seem to care. How was that possible? Wouldn't she have some remorse over the rift after hearing this? Wasn't she curious at all about Sam? Because Sam was dying to know more about her. Sam had never picked up much gossip about Vera from the neighbours. The other women gave Vera her distance – there was something about her that kept any viciousness in check. Her height, her manner, her accent. Not even a snicker behind her back about Sam's absent father. Then again, families without dads weren't that unusual in Bensonhurst, especially after the war. And it wasn't a middle-class neighbourhood. People here liked the thought of being respectable, prided themselves on clean children and clean homes, but no one worked too hard at hiding the other messes. *Another way Vera stuck out like a sore thumb*, Sam thought glumly.

Just before noon, a delivery boy – sweet as pie, this one – showed up at the grocer's with another telegram. Sam had been careful to change the return address on her last telegram to avoid any more run-ins at her apartment building.

MISS COOPER
WILL BOOK PASSAGE TO ENGLAND FOR END OF
DECEMBER. MORE TO COME
ROGER BELL

It felt like Sam was taking her first breath in days. She couldn't believe it. She was going to meet her grandmother.

*

The telegrams flew back and forth over the next few days. Mr Bell arranged for an agent in New York to verify Sam's identity and book her ship's passage to Liverpool. A holiday crossing, New Year's at sea; the very idea made Sam dizzy. Mr Bell would meet her at the dock, then accompany her by train to York and on to a place called Begars Abbey, where her grandmother lived.

The agent pronounced it like beggars. *Beggars Abbey?* she wondered. *This just gets weirder.* Her grandmother lived in a convent? Was she a nun? Was that what this was all about? Was Vera also a love child? Was Vera the dirty little secret, not Sam?

Mr Bell had also wired Sam a considerable amount of money, more than she'd ever seen in her life. All his agent had said was that the funds were for 'your affairs and incidentals on the crossing'. The man was a Manhattan lawyer and she hated how stinking new and shiny his suits were. At their final meeting, after clearing his throat several times, he'd said: 'The North Atlantic in January, it's ah... chillier than what you're used to. You might want to purchase a few... warmer things before you board.'

But she had seen the blush in his cheeks and realised he wasn't being a jerk about the shoddy state of her own clothes, he was attempting to be kind. So she took a risk and asked, 'Is my grandmother a nun?'

The man cleared his throat again. 'Ah. No, I don't think so.'

'Then why does she live in an abbey?'

'I believe it was an abbey once, but it's been a private home for some time now.' He then looked down at her shoes, suede winter boots that had been a Vera find. But they looked older than Sam and barely reached above her ankles. 'Macy's. You've been there right? Tell them where you're going and they'll set you up.'

Sam knew Macy's. Vera found department stores suffocating, said they made her feel like she was being clobbered by a hippopotamus. So once, when Sam was sixteen, she had gone in on her own. It was after school and she had the night off from the grocer's – but the minute a sales lady approached her, she turned beet red and ran from the store. She didn't belong there and they both knew it.

It might be nice, she thought as she left the lawyer's office with tickets for the RMS *Parthia*, a new passport and a final envelope of cash, *to go back and let Macy's turn me into a new person*. But her legs kept on towards the subway station. She did slow down when the window of a small shop caught her eye, its mannequin wearing one of those smart, cinched-waist, full-skirted dresses. It was dark red, a silk-wool with a slitty boat neck and three-quarter sleeves. A black patent leather purse was elegantly perched in the mannequin's hand. Sam instantly wanted it; it would hide her tomboy figure. She could get some padding for the bra... Her mind started to play 'what if' again, but a wave of nausea pulled her back. *Don't go there, Sam.*

She had already decided what she would do with the money. A lot of it had gone towards the rent she owed. This would pay off several months in advance; she was sure she'd end up back in Brooklyn before long. The building super had smirked – a greasy, lewd smirk – when she had handed him that first thick envelope of bills. Like she had finally messed up, as he knew she would. 'No,' she had said, wanting to cut off the look on his face with a knife. 'My mother had family. They sent it to me.' She could tell he didn't believe her. She wished she hadn't said anything; it made her sound weak, delusional.

The grocer did not smirk when she told him, but it was clear he didn't believe her, either. 'Who did it? Who hurt my Sammy?' He thought she was pregnant and slinking away to hide it, or worse.

'I'm telling the truth,' she had said. 'Really.' Then she gave him a quick salute goodbye and ran out because she could tell he was about to burst into tears.

*

A little over two weeks later she found herself at a ship terminal in Manhattan, a single suitcase in one hand. She clutched her green coat tight with the other – she had sewn back on the missing buttons for the trip but that didn't stop the icy wind from finding its way in. She had on her mother's camouflage rain boots – her ankle boots were in the suitcase – as she thought Vera's would do a better job keeping her feet dry on the ship. Sam knew she looked a dope, but she was also perversely counting on the boots to do their magic and keep other passengers and their questions away. Sometimes it wasn't anyone's business, that's what Vera used to say.

She regretted that decision by the end of the first day. She had retreated to her cabin, petrified, chiding herself for not listening to the agent and buying better clothes. She was sure she was the poorest person on the ship, poorer than even the cleaning ladies. The *Parthia* was a small ship, a seahorse next to the *Titanic*, but even more opulent, if that was possible. There appeared to be only one class aboard: filthy rich. The other passengers seemed to change their clothes non-stop, getting fancier by the hour. Eyeing Sam's boots and drab coat, the staff kept directing her to housekeeping. By nightfall, everyone but Sam was tipsy, and they stayed that way for the rest of the voyage. Sam was riotously nauseous once they hit the open ocean and its heaving winter seas, and as the waves splashed high against her cabin window she was sure they'd capsize. But to her amazement, she eventually found her sea legs and spent as much time as she could on deck – ignoring the disapproving looks – so she could watch the fathomless, volcanic ocean.

5

The ship docked early Saturday morning in Liverpool. Sam wondered if anyone would notice if she stayed on board; what really was so bad about turning with your tail between your legs, back to your imperfect but familiar dog hole? She could go back, find that Western Union clerk. Get him to marry her. God, what a hideous thought. *Knock it off, Sam*, she said to herself.

She leaned over the deck rail and peered down over the crowded dock. Mr Bell had said he would meet her off the ship. But where exactly? How would she know him? She picked up her suitcase and made her way down the gangplank. At the bottom, she still didn't see anyone obviously looking for her, so she approached the ship's steward who was saying goodbye to the passengers.

'I'm meeting someone. Where should I wait?'

'Where you were told to wait,' he said dismissively, turning to the passenger behind her. He had clearly never forgiven her for the camouflage boots.

Sam didn't let it go. 'Is there a common meeting point?'

'You might try the clock.'

She walked over to the giant wrought-iron clock and stood underneath. The ship had been on time, and it was now half past eight. She stood there for a while, catching herself chewing on her nails, then forgetfully starting again. The crowd had thinned, the debarking passengers were down to a trickle. She watched as men and cranes unloaded freight from the bowels of the ship. It was cold and Sam was now wet from standing so long in the mist. She looked up at the clock – quarter past nine. Sam laughed, despite herself. She was a young, working-class woman, travelling alone. The super had thought she was a fallen woman; waiting around on a dock like this would prove his point.

She made her way over to the liner's offices, realising she should have done this sooner. Mr Bell was probably inside. *What kind of idiot waits outside in this weather?* A beggar held out his cap as she walked by. At least she had more going for her than he did – at the moment anyway. She slowed her step, thinking of Begars Abbey. *Beggars.* Why was her grandmother's house named after homeless people?

The office was largely empty, and no one even looked up when she entered. There were no older, distinguished-looking lawyer types waiting for her. She saw a sign for the passenger lounge and headed there. An elderly woman was sweeping the floor, and Sam nearly cried when the woman asked her if she'd like a cup of tea. She was starting to feel desperate. Had she screwed something up somehow? Had Mr Bell changed his mind? Or merely forgotten that Vera's poor, bastard daughter was arriving today?

She gladly took the tea, even though it wasn't something she usually drank; it gave her a headache. Vera had disliked tea, too. Anyone else, Sam would've used the word hate. But Vera avoided strong emotions as much as possible. Sam had once asked her mother if that was the reason they lived in an Italian neighbourhood, because everyone drank little cups of black coffee all the time. Sam had thought she'd get a smack for saying something so dumb, but her mother had looked at her, eyes filled with intrigue, and said, 'Could be.'

'Would you like some help, miss?' The cleaning lady watched as Sam took a sip. 'Are you waiting for someone?'

Sam didn't answer right away, she didn't trust herself to speak yet.

'A bloke stand you up?' The cleaning lady laughed, showing Sam a mouth of brownish teeth. She could also smell gin on her breath. 'Seen it myself, too many times, luv! How do you think I got stuck here?' She laughed even harder at this. 'It's all right, luv, you'll get through. Do you have someplace to go?'

Sam shook her head, still afraid she'd cry if she spoke. Finally, she said, 'Not a boy. A lawyer. He was supposed to meet me here.'

The woman chuckled again. 'Man or boy. You never can trust 'em, can you?' Her laugh turned into a phlegmy cough, then she softened her tone and nodded to a clerk standing behind the counter. 'That lad over there, tell him what you need. He'll sort you out.'

Sam showed the clerk her ticket – she should have pinned it on her jacket that first day on the boat to prove she wasn't a stray – and one of the telegrams and he immediately put a call through to Bell & Sons.

'It's a Saturday, miss,' he said sheepishly, as if he regretted having to tell her. 'There probably won't be anyone to answer.'

Sam's heart dropped as she watched him place the call. After a few agonising minutes, he suddenly smiled and nodded at her. 'We have a Miss Samantha Cooper here. Just off the New York boat. She says a Mr Roger Bell was meant to meet her?' He listened for a moment, nodded his head, then handed Sam the phone.

'Hello?' she said tentatively.

'Roger's not there?' said a voice on the other end.

'Roger Bell? No.'

'Are you sure? Of course you are. Put the clerk back on.'

Sam handed the phone back. Who was that? The voice was decisive and direct, the voice of someone in a rush and out of patience. She stared at the clerk, tried to make out what was taking place. 'Right,' the clerk said. 'Not to worry. We'll get her on the next train to York.'

*

The whistle blew and the wheels screeched against the track as the train came to a halt at York station. The damp mist of the Liverpool docks had changed to a dry, icy air as the train crossed inland and by the time it reached York, a light snow had begun to fall. Sam looked out of the window. A man was on the platform, pacing such a fast, short track she was sure he would leave scorch marks. He appeared preoccupied and impatient, taking quick drags on his cigarette. *I'd bet a boot that's him*, she thought. The two-word Charlie she'd spoken to on the phone in Liverpool. She couldn't see his face; he was looking down at the platform, a fedora pulled down hard over one eye. He was tall, over six feet, and angular, his

34

suit hanging off him like a scarecrow. *Mid to late thirties*, she thought. Sam took a deep breath and tried to calm herself; she could feel the anxiety rolling off him and flooding into her carriage.

By the time she stepped down onto the platform, he had walked to the next carriage over and she could see him scanning the crowds. He did a quick pivot towards her just as she reached him, the abruptness of the motion causing her to take a step back and into the path of another rushing passenger. She quickly recovered herself.

'Are you with the law firm? Bell & Sons?'

His shoulders dropped in relief and the squint of his black eyes eased, but not by much.

'Miss Cooper? Miss Samantha Cooper? Good.' He shook her hand and then took her suitcase and with a curt nod motioned her forward.

'Yes,' she said, not moving. 'But I go by Sam.'

'Sam. All right then,' he said with a tight smile. 'I'm sorry my brother couldn't meet you. You must forgive us. A very shabby welcome indeed. I assure you, this is not how we normally treat our clients.' The words were hollow, said in the same brusque manner she had heard on the phone. His whole manner was one of irritation, as if she were no more than the office coffee pot found empty. He gestured once again for her to walk.

'Roger Bell is your brother?' Sam was about to ask if he was okay – because even by Brooklyn standards where no one was ever on time it seemed odd – but the man's response came rapid fire.

'Yes. Now. No doubt you would like a bite to eat, you must

be famished, but there is a rather bad storm on the way. I packed some sandwiches – something light to keep you going till we get to Begars. Any sensible person would keep you in town – or have persuaded you not to come at all – but I'll not cross Roger. Not today anyway.' He tossed his cigarette and headed towards the station exit. Sam still didn't budge. She was used to rude, bossy people. That didn't mean she liked it.

The man had almost left the station before he realised she wasn't behind him. He lit another cigarette while walking back towards her. 'Did I miss something?' He looked around. 'What? Is there another bag?'

Sam didn't move. 'Who are you?'

He gave her a crooked smile and tilted his hat back so they could see one another more clearly. 'I'm terrible, aren't I? And likely to not improve on further acquaintance, I regret to say. I've let this business get to my head. It's not like my brother, not at all, to forget a client and I'm distracted by what could've happened to him.' He paused while a train whistle blew, stamped his cigarette out under his shoe – it wasn't even half gone – then said, 'I am Alec Bell, solicitor at Bell & Sons. Roger would tell you I am his baby brother. Now let's go.'

'Why isn't Mr Bell here? Why should I not have come?'

This time, he put his hand on the small of her back and pushed her forward.

'Why are you in such a rush to get me somewhere you think I shouldn't be?'

'You see my dilemma, don't you? I'll tell you in the car. Now. Please?'

6

Alec Bell held open the car door for her. It was a black two-door, rather hunched and dour. An older model. It reminded her of little old Mrs Catania. Not that Sam spent much time in cars – there hadn't been that many in her neighbourhood until a few years ago. But if you were lucky enough to have a car in Brooklyn these days, you got a mint-green or cherry-red one with a white top and a big snout and a big rear. Not this grandma car.

Mr Bell kicked the car into gear and pulled away from the yellow-bricked station, his tyres slipping a little in the thin layer of snow that covered the street. He cursed under his breath, but slid the car into an even higher gear. Sam wanted to ask him to slow down – she'd never seen anything like the city around her. They passed under an arch and drove alongside a medieval stone wall that Mr Bell told her had once surrounded the whole town, then crossed a bridge guarded on its four corners by ancient stone sentry posts. They drove down a quaint street hemmed in by low brick and stone houses, and up ahead Sam spotted the biggest cathedral she'd ever seen. Alec revved the engine as if he were aiming to drive them through its front door. Sam grabbed the door handle as he took a sudden left and the back of the car fishtailed around a corner before he shot them out through a stone gate.

'A quick tour, you understand. At least you can say you've seen York,' he said by way of explanation.

'Can't we go back?'

'Not possible.'

Soon they were skidding down a narrow country road. Sam tried not to gawk at the unfamiliar patchwork of fields and low stone walls that were just as foreign to her as York's ancient gate towers.

Mr Bell rolled down his window and lit another cigarette, then offered one to Sam. 'No thanks,' she said.

'Suit yourself,' he retorted through a cloud of smoke, then coughed.

Sam grimaced then rolled down her window, too. She leaned into the frosty air, hoping it would slap her out of the bad mood the Bell brothers had put her in.

'How far?'

'Half-hour or so. We'll make it in time I think.'

'In time to beat the storm?'

'In time to get you there, and then with a bit of luck, convince you to turn right around and come back to York with me.'

'Why would I want to do that?' she said as she motioned for him to slow down. They were passing through a village – 'No, a hamlet,' Mr Bell corrected her – a desolate line of queer old stone buildings, each connected to the other and all on one side of the road. The windows were dark, the homes appearing deserted, but she could see smoke puffing out of the chimneys and wanted a closer look, but within a minute they were back out in the open countryside; the solicitor had no time for her curiosity.

Mr Bell threw his cigarette out of the window then reached into a cloth-covered basket that was between them and handed Sam a parcel wrapped in wax paper. Before she could take it, she was forced to grab the dashboard and door handle as the car swerved; he had suddenly braked to avoid some small animal that had darted across the road.

She opened the wax paper; the sandwich inside did look good – cheese and ham between thick brown bread. But she held it in her lap for the moment; she knew she should eat but also suspected he was trying to shut her up.

'Why would I want to leave after ten minutes?' she repeated. 'Are there no beds?' She understood why they might not want her at Begars. A relative of questionable background, come nosing around the family silver. But why would *she* not want to stay?

'It should be condemned as a ruin. A nice place to picnic. That's all it's good for.'

'I find that hard to believe.'

'Well, it does have some historic merit, I'll give you that. Used to be a nunnery. The family will tell you there has always been a monastery on the grounds since the sixth century. Constantly being sacked by some marauding band or other. All the nuns locked inside and burned to death at one point, the story goes. Then nuns from some very severe order came over from France in the twelfth century and rebuilt. Those are the ruins you see today. Though my father said it was never an abbey, it was only ever a priory – a very small and minor one. The real abbey – Bégard Abbey – is back in Brittany, but someone here adopted the name after Henry VIII kicked out the last batch of nuns. Makes the place sound more important, which I'm sure Lady Cooper appreciated. She very much liked the idea of those great and noble medieval lady abbesses. Her people were Beauforts, *the* Beauforts, she'd have wanted you to think.

'The Beauforts?' Sam asked vaguely, chewing on a nail. She was trying to follow his story, but something wasn't adding up.

'Yes. Lady Cooper would have said she is of noble blood. If you'd caught her on a sad day, she'd tell you about John of Gaunt and Margaret Beaufort, the Tudor grand dame. I'm surprised Lady Cooper didn't change it to Beaufort Abbey. She might have if she'd had more time. Or she might have even—'

Alec stopped abruptly; Sam had grabbed his forearm. 'What do you mean, "If she'd had more time"? The agent in New York, your brother, they told me she was still alive. She's died?'

Mr Bell glanced down at her hand with a strange smile, then back up to the road. 'No, sorry. Bad habit. She's very much alive. Unfortunately.'

Sam pulled her hand back, embarrassed and angry. 'You're doing this on purpose. Why are you trying to confuse me? What do you mean, "unfortunately"? That's a rotten thing to say about someone.'

'She's bedridden. You'll see. I only meant—' His tone softened. 'You're right. It's not kind. I'm not thinking about the right things.' He gave her a quick look. 'I heard about your mother. I am sorry. I knew her when I was a little boy. She had no time for me of course – quite smart of her. She was much older than me, closer to Roger's age. I was only eight or so when she left, but she was…' He laughed a little. 'I was rather scared of her.'

Sam took in the sharp edges of his cheekbones, made all

the more prominent by the gauntness of his face and a long hawkish nose. Already she could see he had a mouth that preferred to stay in a scowl and dark eyes that were quick to flare. There was such an intensity and tightness to his features that she found it hard to imagine he had ever been scared of someone.

'Why?' she asked.

'She was a very serious young lady; she had no time for silly little boys. She had this way of looking right through you, as if you didn't exist. That if she needed a hammer, and there wasn't one around, she'd pick you up and use you.'

Sam thought about this. It was true. Well, it wasn't that Vera used people. It was more that she rarely noticed what was right in front of her.

He jerked the car into a lower gear as they came to a crossroads, then jerked it back up – he had a pretty twitchy hand, as impatient with the car as with everything else. She waited until he had settled on a gear, then asked, 'Mr Bell. Why did my mother leave England?'

'Call me Alec.'

'Alec,' she said in an annoyed tone. He was delaying again.

'She never told you?'

'No. She never mentioned a word about Begars or her family. I didn't know anything until after she died.'

'Not a word?' He paused. 'I don't blame her.'

Sam wasn't one for theatrics. Vera had told her they weren't worth the energy. A flat stare, followed up with a long silence was just as effective. That's what she did now in response to his flippant remark.

'I did it again, didn't I?' he said offhandedly as he lit another cigarette, sounding not the least bit chastised. 'Sorry. Begars. It's not a pretty story. Or a happy place. I knew that even as a child. I have four older sisters, each as impatient with me as Vera was. All of them quick to pinch. One even gave me a black eye once. Think of how much worse I'd be if they hadn't kept me in check.' He laughed. Sam didn't join in.

'But they loved to make up stories about Begars,' he went on. 'Naughty little boys and girls locked in its dungeons. God, how they adored all those lurid gothic tales about trapped virgins.' He grimaced. 'And they loved to show me where they'd been sealed up alive in the walls, or they'd say a howl of wind was really a nun moaning about the place, trying to take her revenge. They were trying to frighten me, of course.'

'Are there dungeons there?'

'No. But there's a crypt.'

'So your sisters liked to scare you. What does that have to do with Vera? Or why she left?'

He jerked the car through another crossroads. 'There's some truth to their warnings. It used to be that my father would take some of us along if he was there on business, or sometimes if we were invited to a garden party, we'd run about. But shortly before your mother left, us children stopped going. My father... was increasingly uncomfortable with the place.'

'But why?'

Alec took a long drag on his cigarette. 'It's... difficult to explain. It's nothing to do with Vera.'

'I see,' Sam said drily.

'It's personal, to my family.'

She reddened, was taken aback by this – he had such a

casual way of talking about her family, and yet here he had just thrown up a big wall. Then again, she thought, he was being paid to discuss her business. She wasn't.

'I will say,' he went on, 'there's something ugly about the place. My father had its care for forty years and always kept it at arm's length, very much unlike his other clients. Roger, too, once the portfolio passed to him.'

Sam fell silent for a few moments, frustrated that he wouldn't just come out with it. 'When exactly did she leave?'

He drew in a sharp breath. 'When she was seventeen.'

'And she wasn't sent to America, for school? An arts programme maybe?' Vera's main source of income had been giving drawing or music lessons to children in the better part of Brooklyn. Some tutoring too. She also did some accounting for the grocer, but that was in exchange for food – and cigarettes. 'An extended stay with distant cousins, and she decided to stay put?'

'Not that I'm aware of, I'm afraid.'

As if he sensed her rapidly declining mood he added, 'I was shocked when Roger told us that Vera had gone before her mother. I am sorry.'

Sam picked at the sandwich in her lap, not at all appeased. She wanted information, not condolences. 'If my mother wasn't nice to you, I'm sure you deserved it.'

'Agreed.' He didn't say anything for some time, seeming to concentrate on the road. The snow was falling harder now and several inches already covered the tops of the hedges. Eventually he flicked his cigarette out the window and rolled it up. 'Miss Cooper. What did Roger tell you?' He looked at her again nervously.

This is it, she thought, *he's ready to drop the bomb.* 'It's Sam.

Nothing. He told me nothing. I never spoke to your brother. It was all through a few telegrams and then through an agent in a Manhattan law firm, who didn't really know anything either.' Or had been instructed to say nothing.

'Look out there,' Alec suddenly said, nodding to her lap; her sandwich had been about to slide off onto the floor. She mumbled a thanks, then wrapped it back up and put it in the basket. She had no appetite.

'I would've handled it differently,' he said, as he quickly checked to make sure Sam had wrapped her sandwich tightly enough and then tucked in the cloth covering the basket. 'You. All of it. I don't think how my father and Roger proceeded all these years was fair to anyone. What I said earlier – about Vera – that I didn't blame her for not telling you. I didn't mean it. I can't understand why Vera never mentioned a word to you about Begars. But I suppose I shouldn't be too surprised. Because she never told anyone here about you. We didn't know you existed until you telegrammed Roger.'

Stunned, Sam turned to look out her window. She had considered this back in Brooklyn; Donna had come up with it in one of her wackier theories about Vera's behaviour.

They'd been out on the stoop one day, when Donna blurted out, 'She was afraid! That's why!'

'Huh?' Sam had replied.

'Maybe,' Donna went on, her eyes flashing with sinister delight, 'they never asked about you in the letters cuz Vera never told 'em about you.'

'What?'

'Yes, Vera was afraid of what they'd do to *you* if they found out!'

44

'That doesn't make any sense.'

'Think, numbskull! They'd need to cover up the scandal, protect the family name. Maybe your father was the stable boy! Vera knew she couldn't let 'em find out... they'd put her in a nuthouse to hush it all up, and pack you off to an orphanage. She had to keep you a secret from them.'

'If that were true,' Sam had said, annoyed, 'if they didn't know about me, then Vera would've found some way to still get money out of them all those years. She would've come up with a good lie or something. And it doesn't explain why she never told *me* about *them*.'

'She was worried you'd go looking for them and then ka-blam! She's in the nuthouse.'

'This isn't a soap opera,' Sam had said, then tuned out the rest of what Donna was saying.

But now, she had to consider if there was some truth to Donna's theory.

She faced forward in the car again, stared at the long stretch of road before them and pulled her coat tighter around her. 'We thought... I thought Vera had been disowned. Because of me.'

'No.' Alec said it so quickly she knew he'd been trying to puzzle through it too.

'Would she have been, if Lady Cooper had known about me?'

'No, there was no such provision. By the time you were born, Lady Cooper was no longer in a fit state to take any sort of legal action.'

'What about my grandfather? Lord Cooper?'

'Sir Thomas,' Alec laughed slightly. 'He wasn't a lord. Bought his title, a knighthood.'

'Oh,' Sam said, biting back her irritation at Alec's manner. 'So he's dead too then.' She could feel his eyes on her, his turn to take in her profile, size her up more. Figure out how fragile she was, or how much trouble she was going to be. She angled her face back towards the window, as far away from him as she could. *He can look at my ear if he wants to. Decode that, Mr Bell.*

The car rocked as a blast of wind hit it and Alec, eyes back on the road, clenched the steering wheel tighter. 'It isn't right,' he said. 'Roger should have settled all these questions before you came over, so you would know more about what you were walking into.'

Sam felt sick to her stomach. She wasn't used to riding in cars, especially down narrow country lanes in a rising wind. Or perhaps it was the feelings the conversation was dredging up. She'd spent years stuffing away her emotions about Vera's silence, her moods. And now she was here, demanding information from people as baffled as she was. *Vera didn't want them to know about me at all, money or not.* Was her mother that ashamed of her? Sam couldn't believe it; Vera just didn't seem the type. She wasn't one to apologise and she had never felt the need to fool the neighbours with some sob story about a dead husband.

'My mother was still cut off.'

'What do you mean?'

Sam thought for a minute. 'When I was little – this was during the Depression, when things were really bad – there was a boy in my building whose nickname was Boots, because he was the only kid whose parents could afford to buy him new ones. The rest of us, if we had a hole, we just padded the sole with some folded-up newspaper.' She pulled the cuff of her coat sleeve over her hand and rubbed at the fogged-up window. 'The point is, my mother had this habit of sending me downstairs to play at my friend Donna's every day at five-fifteen. I was about six or seven and I'd show up and her dad would be washing up, just home from work – he was a mechanic, so he still had his job – and Donna and I would play a little bit and her mother always asked me to stay for dinner. I didn't think anything of it; Donna's mom was a good cook. She made real meals.'

Sam paused a moment to linger over the good part of the memory. Mondays was bean soup with fresh, crusty bread. Tuesdays there was homemade pasta. Sunday's dinner was her favourite: a ragu with a little bit of beef, simmered for hours.

'Later, during the war, I remember Vera was so excited about us having ration books – all the mothers were. They were out on the fire escapes, pegging up clothes on the lines across the alley and they were saying that if things got bad the ration books would keep them out of those god-awful breadlines, the ones they had in the Depression, and I heard Donna's mom say, "Don't you worry none, Ms Cooper, your Sammy's always welcome, she don't eat much. Now my Donna, they could feed an army on what she eats," and the women all laughed. Donna and I didn't think it was funny. But it was only then that I realised how close we'd been to the edge, and that no matter what, Vera had made sure I was fed. And I thought about my bones-for-a-body mother. I had always thought she just wasn't a big eater. But suddenly I realised that probably wasn't true at all and I felt like the biggest idiot.'

'Christ, Sam,' Alec said. 'I'm sorry. My father didn't know.

47

I'm sure if he had, he would've done something. I know he would have.' He lit another cigarette and she quickly rolled back down her window, glad to let him think it was the icy wind making her eyes sting. *What's with you*, she thought, *dredging up that crap?* She hadn't thought about those dinners at Donna's in years. What it must have felt like for Vera not to be able to feed her own kid. How she kept them out of the breadlines. The women shared their cigarettes during the worst years; it was only later, when things weren't as tight, that her mother traded some of her work for the grocer for cigarettes. But now it occurred to Sam, maybe Vera *had* stood in those lines, and kept it to herself. Sam had been so young, she wouldn't have noticed; she'd never gone hungry.

'Don't worry about it,' she said to Alec. She wiped at her eyes, forced a laugh. 'It was better at Donna's; Vera could ruin a can of corn,' she lied.

Sam was grateful just then to see a crumbling yellow stone arch ahead. A wrought-iron gate was set into it, and after they passed through it, she could tell by the crunch of the tyres that the road had turned to gravel. They headed into an alley of old oak trees, its thick, skeletal canopy turned nearly black in the darkness of the storm. Sam held her breath as they drove through, but as they came out the other side, the view expanded to reveal a long and low ancient house. This must be her grandmother's home.

'You talked about this place like it was Dracula's castle,' she said, her voice full of confusion. She had expected to see a black and white cardboard cut-out straight from a horror movie, with towers and turrets and a lightning bolt tearing the sky behind it. But instead she saw something more like

Irving Berlin's Holiday Inn. Snow-kissed and lights twinkling from all the windows, smoke twirling like sugar twists from the chimneys. A house bustling with life. Not a sepulchre.

Alec stopped the car at the foot of a picture-perfect stone bridge, its walls topped with puffy mounds of fresh snow. 'You realise of course,' Alec said as he opened his door, 'that once Lady Cooper dies, Begars will be yours. I suggest you burn it.'

He was gone before she could protest and she watched in angry dismay as he strode up to the bridge to check it for ice, the wind knocking him about as he went. She hoped for a big enough gust to lay him flat.

The snow was building to a whiteout but she could still see the house, the warm tint of its tawny stone. It was a curious building, as if someone had attached an old barn or warehouse to a majestic home. The windows at the furthest end were irregular in size – fat, skinny, squat, rounded – and set so haphazardly she couldn't fathom their purpose or how the floor levels matched up. But the house suddenly changed in character a little past the halfway point. The windows became larger and more proportionate, the architecture increasingly decorative. It appeared more like a home, albeit a very grand one.

Alec had returned and tipped his hat to dump the snow off before closing the car door. 'Why does it look like that?' She pointed to the plainer side of the house. 'Like a barn or something. Are there cows in there?' Sam liked that idea, imagined the heat of the animals, the sunny smell of the straw.

'No, it's not a barn. It's the prioress's house; that particular structure dates back to the fourteenth century I think. The walls anyway. The foundation is much older. It's where the prioress worked and slept, and where the guests stayed. The nuns lived in a dormitory behind the church – you can see some of those ruins there.' He gestured to the back left of the house. The roofless church was the only recognisable structure; the rest was a series of walls and many of those were being swallowed up by an encroaching wood.

'Henry VIII broke with the Catholic Church in the 1500s,' Alec continued. 'Took all the church lands and gave some of them to his friends. The poor fools who got this patch converted the prioress's house into a manor house and at some pointed renovated part of it... that's the south wing. Not sure why they left the north wing alone. Perhaps they ran out of money and told their friends it was more charming that way.'

To the left of the front door, massive diamond-paned windows stretched the height of the house. Despite the onslaught of the snow, Sam could see a brilliantly lit chandelier through them and the hint of flames from what must have been a large fire; and another tall column of lights tapering at the top – a huge Christmas tree? She scanned the other windows to see what they might reveal, stopping on an upper floor in the southern, renovated wing of the house. She saw a silhouetted figure there, almost as if they were watching out for Sam. Her grandmother?

'It's straight out of a storybook,' Sam whispered.

'Not bloody likely,' Alec snorted in reply.

A terraced hill of snowy shrubs and ornamental grasses led up to the house; an even bigger hill reared up immediately behind it, the bare branches of its trees rendered glorious with the fresh lick of snow.

Alec nudged the car carefully over the icy bridge, but

coming down the far side the tyres lost their grip and the rear of the car swung forward. The snow had suddenly changed to sleet – ice fragments ricocheted off the metal roof; it sounded like she was in a rocket ship hurtling through an asteroid belt. Alec managed to steer out of the small spin and the car bolted forward again as he worked the gears to tackle the last climb of the drive.

Just then, Sam spotted a figure. Someone was walking quickly towards them, a woman in a long coat, holding something tightly under one arm.

'Watch it, there! There!'

'What? What is it?' Alec shouted back.

'There! You're going to hit her!'

The woman's head was down in driving sleet, her hands buried in her pockets and her thick hair swirling in the wind. She didn't move off the road – didn't she see them?

'For god's sake!' Sam yelled – both at Alec and the woman. The car was heading straight towards her, and Alec seemed oblivious. Sam yanked at the wheel and had one last glimpse of the woman – she had finally looked up and was staring straight at them, her eyes unflinching in the headlights – before the car veered into a bigger spin across the drive and crashed up a bank, its tail end slamming into a tree.

Sam sat there numb, her mind split over what she had just seen. She could hear Alec panting next to her, then a long, low intake of breath, like waves receding before a tsunami.

'What the devil is wrong with you?' he yelled.

The windows were fogged over; Sam rubbed her sleeve against the windshield but couldn't get a clear view. Alec was still yelling, but she ignored him. She kicked the door open and stumbled out, searching for the woman. Had they missed her?

Alec staggered after her. 'What's going on? Are you all right? Did you hit your head?'

Sam slid to a stop in the middle of the drive and looked around. 'Where'd she go?'

'Who?'

'That woman you almost hit, you idiot.'

'What?'

'She was coming down from the house. She was walking down the drive. She didn't see us until…'

The sleet and wind were howling around them; Sam turned her back to it to keep from falling over. Alec took a few steps up and down the drive, searching for signs of the woman. He shook his head, then lurched back towards Sam, fighting against the wind with one arm up to shield his eyes from the sleet – but she could still see into them. There was something new there. His irritation replaced with concern. Worry. For her. Like she was no longer a mere inconvenience but had become real. She didn't like it. He was the first to break their gaze, turning to get their things out of the car. Despite the furore of the storm, his mood had changed. He was calmer and uncharacteristically patient.

'Let's get you—' He stopped himself when he saw the challenging set to her jaw. 'Let's get inside.' He gestured for her to go first.

She turned wildly about; the woman couldn't have disappeared that quickly. She was about Sam's age, maybe younger. Had she run off? Afraid she'd be blamed for the accident? Sam doubted it; she remembered the look in the woman's eyes. Like she dared them to hit her. Like she wasn't afraid of anything. Sam felt a fog descending, blotting out everything around her. She knew those eyes. Knew that look. That thick, unruly hair. Vera. The woman looked like Vera. But much younger, much more intact – the deep lines from chain-smoking not yet etched in her face. Sam wanted to sit down, a sense of dislocation settling over her; she was numb to the cold, the sleet. In the distance she heard someone shouting, felt a tremor – like the vibrations of a subway train coming in. Suddenly she reeled forward and a face came into focus. It was Alec, calling her name and pulling her up the drive.

That wasn't Vera. Vera wasn't a ghost. Her mother wouldn't have consented to such foolishness, and Vera, wasted almost down to nothing by her illness, had made it abundantly clear she had been ready to die. 'We can't leave that woman out here!' Sam shouted at Alec through the wind. 'She'll lose her way, she'll freeze to death.'

Alec put a hand on the small of her back and pushed her forward. 'Miss Cooper—'

'Sam!' she yelled back, eyes tearing in frustration and confusion.

'Sam, there wasn't anyone. There were no tracks. Come on. You're tired. You've not eaten anything. We need to get inside.'

'No. You're wrong. It's you. You hit your head.' She pointed at Alec's forehead. 'It's bleeding. We need to get *you* inside.'

They were still a few hundred feet away from the house. Sam's mind was slowing; she wasn't sure what to do. *Someone there can help us*, she thought. Then she did a double take, wiped the snow from her eyes and looked again. Despite the welcoming glow she had seen before, no lights shone now;

the windows had gone dark. Had she imagined it all? The candles and the chandelier? She blinked again, and to her relief she saw a small flicker of light on the porch. Someone was waiting for them, holding up a lantern, its golden light beckoning them in.

7

By the time they reached the house, the door was closed and lantern-bearer gone.

'Where'd she go?'

'Who?'

'The woman on the porch. She was standing right there, waiting for us. Was it Lady Cooper?'

'Sam,' Alec said, irritation and impatience returning to his voice, 'there was no one there. No one in the drive and most certainly not Lady Cooper.'

Sam rushed up the steps and onto the enclosed stone porch; she looked down for footprints, but all she could see was fresh snow. 'You think I'm seeing things, don't you?'

Not answering, Alec pushed past her to rap the iron knocker on the wide oak door, then knocked the snow off his shoes against an old boot scraper before stamping right in. A thick curtain separated the entryway from the house; he pulled it aside to let Sam walk through.

It wasn't much after two in the afternoon, but Sam's first glimpse inside Begars Abbey was one of near darkness. *Magnificent darkness*, she thought. The front hall was not particularly wide, with much of the space taken up by a square staircase rising along the right side. The main light – diffuse and silvery – came from two deep-set windows above the stair landing. The walls were panelled in dark wood, and the grey stones of the floor were large and unevenly worn. Another curtain was drawn across a double arched doorway on the left side of the hall, and further back along that same wall was a bench and a low, squat door. Opposite that door, another one was cut into the wall beneath the stairs. To Sam's left, beside the arched doorway, was a small table set with a vase of flowers and a plain black telephone.

The silence of the house was surreal; Sam had never known anything like it. Her life in Brooklyn was nothing but noise – women yelling all day, the men yelling all night. Always some baby crying, some door slamming, sirens whining past.

Alec called out and Sam heard a screech – something like a parakeet right before the cat pounces on it – coming from deep inside the house, then a faint, rhythmic jangling. A broad-set, elderly woman hobbled in from the squat door tucked away at the back left corner of the hall. She stopped when she saw them, squinting as if they might be robbers. *Not the one with the lantern then*, Sam guessed.

The woman dabbed at her nose with a crumpled-up handkerchief, then like a change of film reels, she smiled warmly and stretched her arms wide as if to hug them both to her breast.

'Oh my,' the woman said in a high-pitched, melodious voice. 'Oh my stars! As I live and breathe!'

Was this her grandmother? She was very friendly-looking – not at all intimidating – in her blue button-up dress and well-worn cardigan, its sleeves pushed up to the elbows. For a second Sam let herself believe it to be true, that Alec had been exaggerating and 'bedridden' was his sarcastic substitution for old age. The woman started towards them again, but she did not walk easily, as if her hips and knees hurt. Sam was ready to go help her, but Alec cut in.

'Mrs Pritchett,' he said with the same curt nod he'd first given Sam. 'I trust you're in good health.' The tone of his voice was perfunctory; he was back in solicitor mode.

'Mr Bell! What a pleasure! What a pleasure! It's been ages! Look at you! So handsome! And still with all your hair!' Mrs Pritchett had made it to the front of the hall and reached up to touch his hair; Alec stepped away to avoid her hand. 'And who is this? Who is this fine young lady you've brought with you? I tell you, she's an improvement on your last, she is!'

The woman grabbed Sam by her hands and stretched her arms out to take better inventory. Sam smiled wryly – the woman must be joking. Surely she knew who Sam was. She looked over at Alec for reassurance. He wasn't smiling. He was tapping his hat against his hand and looked pretty stern.

'None of your games, Mrs P. You know who this is and that she's had a long journey. And a bit of a fright out there. I think straight to her room and send up some food.'

'What?' The elderly woman took a step away from Sam, looked at Alec in dismay. 'What do you mean? I know her? A fright? What?' Sam's thoughts turned to pity; this poor old woman looked genuinely confused. Sam guessed Mrs Pritchett was well on the other side of seventy. Her hair was dyed a flat burgundy and clipped up in the back; her eyes were small but bright; they belied the pain the woman must be in, Sam thought. In addition to her limp, Sam could see that her knuckles were swollen and her fingers deformed by rheumatism.

'Mrs P,' Alec's voice was rising – unnecessarily, Sam thought. 'I don't have time for this.' He picked up Sam's suitcase and started up the stairs.

Mrs Pritchett went after him. 'Mr Bell, I do wonder! What is it you're up to now?' She put a heavy-shoed foot on the first step, thought better of the climb, then turned back to Sam, eyes wide in shock. 'Do you mean to say...?' She looked again at Alec, raising her handkerchief to her mouth. 'Why your brother said she wouldn't be here till Tuesday!' She hobbled back to Sam, grabbed a hold of her arms again. Sam felt relief wash through her, the awkward shame of being forgotten – by everyone! – dropping away. So that's what had happened. Somehow Roger Bell had the dates wrong. That's why he hadn't been in Liverpool to meet her. But why hadn't Alec said so? It was an easy enough explanation – though Sam didn't see how someone could mix up a transatlantic arrival.

'This is Miss Samantha?' The old woman smiled at her in pleasure. 'Vera's daughter?'

'*Miss* Vera's daughter,' Alec corrected.

Mrs Pritchett ignored him. 'Why, look at you! Yes, of course! Those high cheekbones, those eyes... Why, you're like that film actress, what's her name?' She pivoted back to Alec as if she expected him to know the answer. He came back down the stairs and lit a cigarette as a response. 'The one in *Casablanca*! Lauren Bacall! She looks just like her, doesn't she?'

'You mean Ingrid Bergman,' said Alec.

'I mean nothing of the sort!' she huffed then smiled again at Sam. 'Yes, so tall! So pretty! Why I thought I'd seen a ghost just now, Lady Cooper as a girl!' She put a dramatic hand to her heart and took a deep breath, as if she'd truly been frightened. 'Oh what a relief! Oh how good it is to see you! I'm Mrs Pritchett – she patted a ring of keys hanging at her waist – 'the housekeeper, for my sins.' She then made a great show of slapping her hands against her sides as if she didn't know what to do with herself, she was so overcome with excitement.

Alec took a drag on his cigarette, his dark eyes locked on Mrs Pritchett. 'When did Roger tell you that?'

'Hmmm?' asked Mrs Pritchett, still smiling and cooing over Sam.

'Don't play daft. When did Roger tell you Sam was to come on Tuesday?'

'Oh.' She fluttered her handkerchief, then gave him a dirty look when she realised he was smoking. *An ally perhaps*, thought Sam. 'I can't be expected to remember that! A letter? Or did he ring?' She suddenly frowned. 'Where is he? Is he still outside? What?' She looked past Alec, confused. 'He shouldn't be out there, not in weather like this. Go on, now!' She started shooing Alec with her handkerchief. 'Bring him in, before he catches his death of cold!'

'My brother's not here,' Alec said flatly.

'What? Why ever not?' Mrs Pritchett said, her voice reeling higher with alarm. 'Why have *you* brought her?'

'The truth is,' Alec said, his voice now anxious, 'I don't know where Roger is. Our office is closed for the holidays, and I've been laid up with a touch of bronchitis. I was only there this morning to catch up on some work when I got the call from a clerk at the docks. Roger would have taken the train to Liverpool, so I can't think what might have delayed him.'

'Ah well, you're here now.' Mrs Pritchett glowed at Sam. 'But you've caught us out! We're not ready for you! And what with this storm! Most of the staff, what little we have these days' – she threw another dirty look at Alec – 'stayed away or have left already. Didn't want to get stuck here, did they?'

'Mrs Pritchett,' Sam said, 'we nearly hit someone out on the drive. A woman. Did someone just leave? I'm worried about her, out there in the storm.'

The housekeeper dabbed at her nose again. 'Now which of them would've left it this late? Such silly-headed things. Don't know how they manage to survive a summer's day let alone this.' Her tone had quickly turned cold. Then she noticed the disapproval on Sam's face.

'Oh don't worry about them, Miss Samantha. I can't believe any of them are still out there. Might have been a girl from Bagshot's farm, searching for a lost sheep.'

'He thinks I saw a ghost,' Sam said, still angry at Alec for dismissing her. 'That I got us into a wreck over a figment of my imagination.'

'What? A wreck?' Mrs Pritchett cried then started to frantically check them for blood. 'You foolish boy!'

Alec ignored the woman; instead, he said softly to Sam, 'I never said any such thing.' Then quick as a wink, he was back ordering the housekeeper about. 'Stop that. No one's hurt. Sam needs warming up and some food. Now. As do I.' He headed for the stairs again.

'You won't find it up there, Mr Bell. I told you, we weren't ready for her. And oh my, the boiler's been out since yesterday; the electric's gone out as well and the generator does nothing but smoke! Much like you, eh? I expect you think we normally stand around in the dark? Well, with what you give us to run the place, you shouldn't be surprised. If you want heat, you'll have to suffer my sitting room for the moment till we get something arranged.' Mrs Pritchett smiled conspiratorially at Sam. 'It backs on to the kitchen range; it's as toasty as a basket of kittens.'

'Is that what you're serving these days?'

Mrs Pritchett looked at him as if he had aliens sprouting from his ears, then said, 'You always were an idle boy. The generator. Might I trouble you to take a look?'

The two walked through the curtained archway, sparring as they went, Sam all but forgotten. Again.

She lingered for a moment, tried to pick out through the gloom the details of the room around her. The walls were lined with portraits; Sam searched for her mother as a young girl and tried to identify the elusive Lady Cooper. It was odd, thought Sam, that the housekeeper hadn't really asked about Vera or her death. Mrs Pritchett hadn't said much about her grandmother, either, other than to say that Sam looked like her.

Sam pulled back the curtain hanging over the archway that Alec and Mrs Pritchett had disappeared through; beyond was a grand room with the same dark wood-panelled walls as the front hall, but these stretched high to the top of the second storey. The room was long but shallow; dull white light streamed in from the great bank of latticed windows and fell upon a much-polished old table that nearly matched the length of the space. All told, the room wasn't more than fifteen feet front to back, but the height of its ceiling, the size of its windows and a fireplace on the back wall big enough to cook a family in gave the impression of a larger-than-life space. She recognised the vast chandelier and realised that she had seen into this room on the drive up. But its candles were unlit, and the fireplace was empty, and there was no Christmas tree. The wishful projections of a tired mind, she admitted reluctantly.

Sam sighed and let the curtain drop. She went back to scanning the walls of the hallway for a portrait that might be her mother. Surely she would have had a portrait painted...

The front door blew open, its heavy curtain kicked up by a hard gust. The wind wound around Sam's legs and arms – almost like it wanted to pull her to the floor. She ducked and covered her face at the sound of glass shattering.

Then as quickly as it came, the squall stopped. The room darkened as the curtain fell back across the front door and the wind released her. Sam patted herself down, expecting to find pieces of glass stuck in her legs. To her relief, she was intact, save for a snag in her nylons. The vase on the side table near the door, however, lay broken on the floor. She shivered; she'd never felt anything like that. It was a cold wind – but it was almost as if it carried something with it, something vile, something indecent. She walked over to close the front door and by the time she reached it, she was already chiding herself. *Ridiculous, Sam!* Nothing like being left alone in a dark old house during a storm. She smoothed out her coat and skirt. It was time to find Alec and the housekeeper. She started for the arched doorway but stopped at a sudden noise from above. She took a step back and looked up the stairs.

On the small landing stood a woman in a black dress with a white collar, holding an old-fashioned tin lantern. A single candle flickered inside. This must be the woman who had been waiting outside on the porch. *Screw you, Alec*, she thought. The woman's hair was cut bluntly at her shoulders. Backlit as she was by the deep windows, her features were nearly indistinguishable. But there seemed to be a patchy, rough texture to her face, as if her skin was severely chapped or blemished by a rash. Her eyes were lost to Sam behind small round glasses. But if they hadn't known Sam was coming today, why had the woman been out on the porch? Oh, Sam realised, she must have been seeing the other girl off. The one Alec had nearly hit. *There was no one waiting for me at all then*, she thought with some disappointment.

'This way, miss,' the woman on the stairs said in a low voice.

Sam picked up her suitcase to follow her, but just then Alec returned.

'How can anyone confuse solvent with oil?'

'What?' Sam asked.

'And the vents in the shed were blocked, to keep the generator warm, she said!'

'Who? Mrs Pritchett?'

Alec grabbed the suitcase from her and put it back down on the floor. 'It's a wonder that no one's died of asphyxiation. I expect she puts laundry flakes in the soup.'

'I don't understand,' Sam said.

Alec frowned at her. 'Someone put solvent in the generator motor instead of oil. This place is a disaster.' He saw the shattered vase on the floor and looked at Sam. 'What happened?'

'A gust of wind.' She shrugged.

He shook his head, disturbed by the chaos of the place. 'I'll sort it. All of it. Let's see what harm we'll find in Mrs P's sitting room.' He opened the curtain over the archway and nodded for her to go through.

'I don't mind the cold, I'm used to it. I'll go upstairs with her and get out of your hair for a while.' She turned towards the woman with the lantern, but was surprised to see she was gone.

'Go with whom, Sam?' Alec stepped forward, following Sam's gaze.

Sam sighed in exasperation. The simplest things had become hard. 'Whoever *that* was.' She pointed to the landing. 'She was the one on the porch outside, with a lantern. A maid I guess?'

'Sam—'

She saw it in his eyes again. Concern. Worry.

'Don't look at me like that,' she said. 'This is your rodeo. Not mine. I'm just visiting.'

Alec glanced up the stairs, then back at Sam. 'Lady Cooper's nurse, then. Though I don't know why she's left her to bother with us. Now come on.'

So damn bossy, Sam thought. *Worse than Donna.*

8

'I've asked the girl to make up a room for you.'

Sam couldn't help but give Alec a smug look as Mrs Pritchett said this.

'Fresh linens and such. No time for a proper airing, but you'll be comfortable.' Mrs Pritchett poured Sam a cup of tea and handed it to her. They were in the housekeeper's sitting room. Through the arch next to the fireplace in the great hall – the name of the high-ceilinged room she'd seen earlier, Alec told her – was a passage that led to the housekeeper's domain: the kitchen and larders, her sitting room, and the hall where the servants dined.

'I sleep down here, too, these days,' Mrs Pritchett prattled on as she settled into a chair across from Sam. 'When we lost the butler I decided to put his parlour to good use. Easier on me old legs, not having to go all the way up to the attic every night.' She leaned over and said to Sam in a low voice, 'That's where the servants usually sleep. You'll need to know these things, dear.'

She straightened back up and smoothed out her dress. 'A bit of economy on my part, it was, changing rooms like that, you see. As Mr Bell and his brother would be the first to tell you, there's always need for economy, for one reason or another.'

Alec let the jab roll off, added an extra spoon of sugar to Sam's tea.

'Oh don't fuss, Mr Bell,' Mrs Pritchett said, dabbing at her nose with her handkerchief and watching him. Alec stepped away, and satisfied, she clasped her hands in her lap and said with a broad smile, 'Now, I want another good look at you and then you should go for a lie-down... Are you warm enough, dear?'

Alec had come back and draped a blanket over Sam's legs and Mrs Pritchett suddenly looked very distressed, as if she had somehow failed Sam.

'How is Lady Cooper?' Alec said.

'Well enough.' Mrs Pritchett sniffed.

'Might you be more specific? I recall Roger saying she had a bad go of it recently...'

'Recently? Perhaps *you* could be more specific? Narrow down the timeframe? For I'd say she's had nothing but a bad go of it since... Well.' She threw a quick look at Sam then changed the subject. 'Now what do you propose to do about the generator? We can't go on like this. I can't imagine you mean for Lady Cooper to suffer so.'

Sam leaned back in her chair and got to work on a thumbnail as she took a look around; she had no desire to get in the middle of what seemed to be a long-running campaign. The sitting-room ceiling was unusually low; they were now in the northernmost part of the house, the wing that Alec said had largely remained untouched since the days of the convent. The walls and ceiling were plaster shot through with visible wooden beams. The sitting room's brick fireplace with its pale stone mantel seemed outsized for the space, however;

especially since the fire was relegated to a small grate inside it. A Turkish rug covered the warped floorboards, and an old desk stood in one corner; against another wall was a cupboard and a radio in a handsome cherry-stained case. Sam wondered what Mrs Pritchett liked to listen to. Cooking programmes? *War of the Worlds*?

A set of small windows let in only the faintest of northern light and to banish the chill, Sam reluctantly took a sip of her hot, sugary tea. The housekeeper had also put out a plate of bread and butter, and some cheese. 'I'll make a better show of it at dinner.' She winked at Sam and gestured towards the bread. 'Made it myself. Still like to put these hands to some use, when I can. I used to be the cook here, once upon a time. I was born on the estate you know, 1880 or thereabouts.' She smiled as she watched the coals glow in the fire. 'Worked my way up, I did. Not like some people.' She shifted in her chair, a small tilt of the head in Alec's direction. She held up her crooked fingers, examined them in the firelight. 'They put you to work early in those days; any little bit helped! I was scrubbing pots before I could walk, wasn't I? Seems like it anyway.'

Sam heard Alec snort. He was stewing on the edge of the desk across the room and now it was Sam's turn to give him a dirty look.

The housekeeper shifted in her chair again. 'Now that was *real* work. Scrubbed the nerves right out of my fingers.' Then she laughed, as if she found these memories comforting. 'A blessing, really. Or these might give me more bother.' She rubbed at her knuckles a moment, then gently folded her hands in her lap, looked up to smile at Sam. 'I had my wits about me, I did. No one needed to worry about me. Not Mary Pritchett. Wasn't long before I left those pots behind. Except I'm back at it again, aren't I, Mr Bell? Day like today and who do I have to help? No cook. No scullery maid.' She sighed dramatically, then she suddenly asked, 'Don't you like your tea, Miss Samantha?'

Sam quickly took another sip, not wanting to offend the housekeeper, but Alec jumped in.

'She's a Yank, she prefers coffee.'

'Do you now?' Mrs Pritchett lifted her chin in disapproval. 'We'll have to see about that. I dare say you've never had a proper cup of tea.'

Irritated, Sam said, 'Vera hated the stuff.'

Mrs Pritchett took a deliberate sip of her tea, then said, 'Well *you're* here, aren't you, not Vera.'

Sam blinked in shock and Alec bolted up from his perch on the desk, clapping his cup down in its saucer so hard Sam thought it would break.

'It must be time for your rest, Mrs Pritchett,' Alec said in a voice so cool it could freeze blood. 'We'll leave you to it.'

'These boys,' Mrs Pritchett whispered to Sam, as if she had already forgotten her own poisonous comment, 'they do like to feel important, but I'll let you in on a trick—'

Sam couldn't stay quiet. 'Mrs Pritchett, did they tell you that my mother is dead?'

Mrs Pritchett looked at Sam in surprise, then leaned over and put a hand on her knee. 'Why yes, yes of course.' Her face fell, a far-off look came to her eye. 'I was the one who had to tell Lady Cooper. I don't think she's recovered from the news, though I couldn't say…'

Sam was about to ask her what she meant but Alec cut in again.

'Which room, please, Mrs P?' Alec said.

'Yes, of course,' Mrs Pritchett said, not bothering to look at Alec. 'I would show you but…' She smiled wistfully. 'These bones of mine are good enough, it's the joints that give me such trouble. Mr Bell, do you think you might manage? Vera's room. I thought you might like that.' She patted Sam's knee.

'*Miss* Vera's room,' Alec hissed. 'Please remember yourself, Mrs Pritchett.'

He's about to blow his stack, Sam thought, and she liked him more for it. She put her teacup down next to her uneaten bread – it was mouldy.

'When can I see Lady Cooper?' she asked.

Mrs Pritchett dabbed at her nose and stared into the fire sorrowfully, as if she were sad to lose Sam's company. 'I expect she's asleep. Perhaps before dinner.'

'Does she know I'm here?'

'Yes. She'll be greatly cheered to see you.' The housekeeper's woeful tone suggested otherwise.

*

'What is wrong with her?' Sam asked as she followed Alec back through the dim servants' passage to the great hall.

'She's had the care of the place too long,' he fumed. 'She's confused.'

'But that doesn't explain why she talked about my mother that way.'

'I'll sort it,' Alec said through gritted teeth. 'Gladly.' A grandfather clock chimed three, but the hall was dark; the storm had obliterated any remaining daylight. Sam left the subject for now, only to turn to another unpleasant one. So she was to stay in Vera's old room. Would she be able to sleep in there? Or would the anger keep her awake? Vera hadn't told Sam she was sick until it was too late. She had cheated Sam of time. And now this; it felt like she'd been cheated out of a whole other world. Why? For a small moment – infinitesimally small – she had an insight into Mrs Pritchett's behaviour. The housekeeper was angry at Vera, too.

She shook these thoughts from her head; they weren't helpful. She tried to imagine Vera here as a young girl. Had it always been this quiet? That would explain why her mother's favourite spot was by the kitchen window, where she could hear the gossip fly across the alley. In the summer, Vera would sit on the fire escape and sew – she was good with her hands and took in some tailoring work – while listening to the other mothers talk and the echoes of kids building go-carts out of crates or blowing pea-shooters at each other. She and Sam even slept on the fire escape if it was hot enough. *What did Vera listen to here?* she wondered as she looked around. *Beetles eating through all this wood.* Maybe that's why she left. She was dying of boredom.

Sam knew she was being petulant. Trying to find reasons to reject the house and the family she'd never known. Mrs Pritchett had said Lady Cooper would be 'greatly cheered' to see Sam, so why had she not demanded to see her granddaughter the minute she arrived? Oh that's right. Because she wasn't supposed to be here till Tuesday. Baloney.

Alec picked up her suitcase in the front hall and they climbed the stairs in silence, Sam trailing her fingers over the dull nicks in the old banister. The square staircase spiralled up three floors altogether and through a small open well in the centre she could see an opaque skylight in the house's vaulted roof. Alec walked ahead of her, attacking a new cigarette.

He took a right at the top of the first flight of stairs and they passed through what Alec called a gallery. It was narrow, with the interior panelled wall hung with large faded tapestries; the upper storey of the great hall must be on the other side of it, Sam reasoned. She slowed down to look through the stretch of windows that made up the gallery's outer wall. Unlike the front of the house, save for the protruding stone enclosure of the porch, the back of the house had extensions of various sizes growing off it. Beyond them, she could see nothing but the white static of the storm.

In truth, it was a lovely house; she felt as if she were walking through the Met's European rooms – with a bonus ticket, she got to sleep here. And yet Vera had preferred their tenement in Bensonhurst. Why?

They went through an arch at the end of the gallery and up another short flight of steps, then Sam found herself in a deep, dark corner set with several doors; the corridor made a sharp right at this point and sloped downward again into one of the extensions off the back of the house. Underneath that passage, she reckoned, would be Mrs Pritchett's sitting room and the kitchens. Alec dropped Sam's suitcase outside a door that, if her navigation held up, would open onto a room overlooking the front drive.

'I'll come back in a bit, but I need to get back downstairs. That woman knows more than she's telling and I'll scrape it out of her if I have to.'

'About what?'

'Her conversations with Roger. I don't believe her. This business about a Tuesday arrival. It's not the kind of mistake Roger would make.'

'Are you worried about him?'

'Frankly, yes.' Alec went down the steps and back towards the gallery, where he scanned the obscured sky. 'That he's in his car in a ditch somewhere. He lives outside of York. It can't have been the storm, it hadn't started yet. Did he take a turn too quickly, or did someone else?' He cranked the casement window open and flicked out his cigarette. 'There may be a simple explanation waiting for me back at the office. But I'm stuck here in a house I loathe, with a woman I loathe.'

'I hope you don't mean my grandmother,' Sam said icily.

Alec cracked a half-smile. 'By all accounts, Lady Cooper was' – he caught himself – '*is* a good woman.'

The dull throb of a headache behind Sam's eyes became a piercing pain. She'd had little more than a few drops of tea that day, on top of a sleepless, nerve-wracked night on the ship. Donna would roll right through the house and find Lady Cooper and stop all this double talk. But Sam could barely think of anything other than rolling into bed.

She put a hand to her head to stave off the weariness, and managed to say, 'I saw a phone in the hallway. Can't you call your office?'

'The line is down, with everything else.' Alec nodded towards the bedroom door. 'Go on now. Get some rest. I'll find something decent for you to eat and send it up.' He cracked another half-smile. 'Does one need any more evidence than that bread that things aren't right here?'

He abruptly turned and with fast, long strides hurried back

towards the stairs; he had no interest in sticking around for the thanks she was about to give him. *Things aren't right here*, Alec had said. So it wasn't Sam or her sense of dislocation. Before this trip, she had never been further from home than the subway to Manhattan. The only boat she'd ever taken was the ferry to Staten Island. Yet in one week, she had crossed the ocean in a ship so glamorous Katharine Hepburn was rumoured to be on board – Sam had hovered around the powder rooms hoping to catch a glimpse – and then driven to a grand home presided over by a Lady.

But the society-party atmosphere of the ship had crashed head-on into the unnerving quietness of the house, the stifling reluctance of Roger, Alec or Mrs Pritchett to explain much of anything. Their manner was so strange, yet familiar. Vera had never explained anything, either.

9

Sam stood at the door to her mother's childhood bedroom. The oak was aged to a delicious caramel and panelled into nine squares. She placed her palm on it, finding it silky smooth and unexpectedly warm in a house that was colder inside than out. She lifted the black iron latch, then let out a cry as the door flew open from the inside. A girl stood before her, with a startled look on her face that must've matched Sam's own. But the girl recovered quickly and she clapped her hands together and laughed in delight at their mutual shock. Then the girl drew back, lowered her eyes and curtsied in apology.

'Sorry, miss. I'll be on my way, miss.'

Sam held up a hand. 'Please don't go.' There was something refreshingly pleasant about the girl; her laugh had been full and rich, and her brown eyes were open and guileless, not suspicious like Alec's. The apron she was wearing over a grey dress and a small white ruffled cap were the giveaway. *The maid sent to prepare my room.* The girl kept sneaking glances at Sam, trying to study her too, and Sam laughed.

'Don't be such a dope; go on, let me see the place.'

The maid flashed Sam a smile then twirled around on her toes to lead her into the room. Sam picked up her suitcase and as she walked in, the floor seemed to shift beneath her. This had been Vera's room? Sam couldn't see it. It was unbelievably formal, like that of an old lady. From 900 years ago. Like most of the other rooms Sam had seen in the house, the bedroom was panelled in wood and the ceiling was an ivory plaster, but sectioned into decorative squares by carved beams. The floorboards were wide with ample cracks between them and a patchy, crimson rug was thrown down by the bed. The pale stone face of the fireplace lightened the room somewhat, but above it ran a series of mahogany panels etched with elaborate and tragic biblical scenes. Vera couldn't have grown up in this room. It was just so... heavy. Vera may have been a minimalist in some ways – sparing with her words, her emotions, her possessions – but she liked to flop down on a sofa or slouch in a chair. Sam thought about her mother's old chenille robe, worn but comforting. This room... Sam felt her back straighten. This was not a room to relax in. If it hadn't been for the maid and the fire in the grate, she would have gone to find Alec, convinced he had the wrong room.

'Well...' was all Sam could say. Two squat and cushionless chairs sat near the fire, and the giant bed looked more like a tomb; she half expected to see a marble queen laid atop it. Thick, turned oak posts held up the ornately carved tester, and dark orange velvet curtains hung from it. Sam touched one and recoiled at its damp, grimy feel. She couldn't tell if the dark tint was original or the result of years of dust. This had to be a joke. But what was the punchline? In some ways, it was a marvellous room. A place to explore, to pretend in, to imagine different worlds and different times. In other circumstances, she would have been thrilled to stay here and think about all the others who had slept here before her. But that was the thing. This was a museum, a room only an adult could appreciate. Not a child.

Sam caught herself – at how quickly her standards of what was acceptable were changing. She'd never had anything remotely like a child's bedroom. No teddy bears on the bed, no doll house in the corner or curtains the colour of daffodils. *Well, that's it, isn't it then?* As she and Donna had always suspected, Vera had never been a child. She'd been born a grown-up.

Sam put her suitcase on top of an old chest at the foot of the bed and a thin ribbon of rising steam caught her eye. It was coming from a cup of tea on the nightstand, and next to it stood a beautiful china jar painted in vivid colours – a brilliant blue kingfisher perched among lime stalks of grass and magenta flowers. Sam walked over to get a better look and on a whim, she lifted the lid of the jar and looked in.

Now that's more like home, she thought. There was a dead mouse inside. She quickly replaced the lid, but said nothing; she didn't want the maid to feel bad for overlooking it. Sam would toss it once the girl left. The maid couldn't have been much older than sixteen. She was much shorter than Sam and had a good shape to her – meat on her bones, as the grannies back home would say. Sam felt a stick figure in comparison. *Well, aren't you, Sam?* Peanut butter and soup had made up most of her diet the past few months.

She held out her hand for the girl to shake. 'I'm Sam.'

The girl didn't take it, only curtsied again.

'Yes, miss.'

'What's your name?'

'Ivy, miss.'

It suited her. As much as the girl tried to hide it behind her servant's uniform, it was clear she was full of life. Sam thought back to the nicer parts of Brooklyn, where some of the houses were lush with the vibrant green vines. She liked it especially when the ivy patches rippled in the breeze; the vines gave the houses a sense of movement, a break from the stagnant stone and brick. Then there was the ivy in Sam's neighbourhood. It was insatiable, unstoppable, its rootlets boring into the bricks and scarring the apartment buildings where the landlords were too cheap to keep it pruned back.

But whether it was the charming glow of the fire or the girl's natural complexion, this Ivy was radiant. There was no blight here. If Ivy had known trouble in her life, it was like water to a duck and she let it wash right off her back.

'Are you from around here?'

'Kirkbymoorside, miss,' Ivy said, still not meeting Sam's eye.

'Is that far from here?'

'Yes, miss.'

'It's okay, Ivy. You can talk. I want to know. How long have you been here?'

'This is my first position, miss. I'm eager to make a go of it.' She looked at Sam for a moment, then added shyly, 'I want to be a lady's maid.'

'Aren't you that already?' Sam knew nothing of this business. Only that Ivy was a maid and that her grandmother was a Lady.

'Goodness no, miss! You have to know how to do hair and keep the jewellery and tend to the clothes. I am rather good at getting stains out – that's something. Am I talking too much, miss? Mrs Pritchett says I'm not to talk. Or I'm to stop talking. All of it. Oh, and I'm too rough. And I don't know which dress should be worn at which time but I am learning and I'm a quick learner and I have been practising any chance I get, miss. Sorry, miss. I'll stop talking, miss.' She quickly looked down again and curtsied reflexively. 'I mean after I've finished all my other work. I'm a good worker. I don't need much sleep, miss.' The girl put a hand to her hair as if suddenly embarrassed. 'I don't like it much.'

Sam laughed. 'What, sleep?'

'No. My hair, miss. Mrs Pritchett says we have to wear it like this and only with a plain clip.'

Sam thought back to the servant she'd seen on the stairs earlier. Her hair was cut blunt to the shoulders like Ivy's. Why did Mrs Pritchett insist on that style?

'It's pretty, Ivy.' Sam felt protective of the girl; she seemed so unguarded, so trusting. And Sam wasn't lying; she did think Ivy's hair pretty and the cut attractive on her. Her hair was thick and brown like Sam's, but there was a nice wave to it. If nothing else, before she left, she'd find Ivy some nicer barrettes. *A house like this must have all sorts of fancy crap like that*, she thought ruefully.

'May I, miss?' Ivy had picked up a silver and ivory comb from the dressing table and walked behind Sam and began to comb through her ponytail, which had become knotted from the wind. She gently held Sam's hair, teasing out the ends first so as not to pull on her scalp, much like Vera had done when Sam was a little girl. Combined with the scent of wood smoke and the crackle of the fire, the low light, the soft tugs began to make Sam drowsy, as if she could fall asleep standing right there. But she hadn't quite forgotten who she was; her unease in her own skin. She pulled away, thanking Ivy. She wondered how to get the girl to leave. Playtime was over. Sam put her suitcase up on the bed, snapped open the clasps and lifted the lid to get out her spare sweater and skirt; her clothes were damp from the sleet and snow and she wanted to change out of them. Ivy watched over her shoulder then ran to a large wardrobe against the wall.

'Oh, miss, you have such a gorgeous colouring! Like you were born under a harvest moon! I know just the dress for this evening. Emerald silk. It's cut high across the front, but it dips right down to here.' She giggled as she turned to point to her lower back. 'Do let me help you!'

Is she for real? Sam wondered. *Is this place for real? Wear a gown that's open down to my ass?* 'This evening?' Sam asked. 'What's this evening? Oh, Ivy. I don't think I'm up for that.' She laughed as she pulled off her sweater, she couldn't help it. They wanted her to dress up *in that* to meet her grandmother? The situation seemed so silly and Ivy was so sweet – and perhaps, yes, misguided. She went back to her suitcase and grabbed a blouse. 'I think this is good enough. You can practise on me another time, perhaps.'

Startled, Sam jumped as the girl clapped her hands loudly in excitement and gushed, 'Thank you, thank you, miss! You won't regret it!'

Wait, what had Sam just promised? She started to ask, then watched in puzzlement as the girl gave another little curtsy, picked up the teacup and raced out. Did Vera have someone waiting on her like this? And she gave it up to spend her life in the company of cockroaches? *And why'd she take the tea?* Sam thought as she unbuttoned her blouse and stripped off her skirt. *Never mind.* She didn't want it anyway.

She peeled off her snagged nylons and frowned. Sam only had one extra pair; maybe she could ask Ivy to find her some more. She draped the rest of her damp clothes over the chairs and stood for a moment in her slip before the fire, letting it warm her. She thought about Ivy, then Mrs Pritchett and Alec – they were probably still arguing downstairs. *It's a nuthouse, all right. But exactly what kind of nuthouse?*

She put on a yellow flowered blouse with a Peter Pan collar, and her other sweater, which was dark green. Ivy had been right about that colour suiting her. But born under a harvest moon? What did that even mean? Both of the skirts she had brought were brown, but that was because the colour went with everything and hid wear and tear. A hardy brown skirt for a hardy Brooklyn girl. Not some paper-thin dress that probably ripped at any sudden movement. 'Stop it, Sam,' she said to herself. *Knock off the attitude. Get down to business.* She took two Heath bars out of a lining pocket in her suitcase – she'd bought a bunch of them for emergencies at the ship terminal in Manhattan – ate them both and waited for the sugar rush to kick in.

'Where are they?' she asked, turning to survey the room. 'Where did you hide them, Vera?' She pushed her sweater sleeves up, then pulled back the crimson rug and tapped around with her foot for a loose floorboard. Not one budged, so she walked over to the dressing table and its delicate bottles.

'Your goddamn secrets, Vera. I've come for them. All of them,' she huffed as she pulled the table away from the wall and felt along its back for anything taped to it. Then she twisted and pushed on the wood carvings over the fireplace, hoping for a secret lever – old houses like this were supposed to be full of hidden entrances and secret passages. Still nothing. She sat down on the chest at the foot of the bed and chewed at her thumbnail for a few minutes while she considered taking down a portrait of a shepherdess from the the wall. Instead, she stood up and examined the chest more closely. She lifted the lid and rifled through the old blankets inside. Then, she shut the clasp and turned the chest on its side and examined the bottom. It was plywood, which was strange because the rest of it looked to be hundreds of years old. Sam pushed at a corner and the plywood easily gave way; a surge of giddiness passed through her. The board was resting on a series of small, slight nails studded around the base of the chest. She needed pliers, *or*, she thought, looking at the dressing table, *a good pair of tweezers.*

Inside a drawer, she found a silver button hook and the prettiest little tweezers and between the two of them she was able to prise out or bend back some of the nails. She wiggled the thin board away from the chest, and there taped to the real bottom was a thin book; it wasn't much bigger than her hand and its red cloth cover was discoloured with age. A quick tug freed it from the rotting tape.

Sam sat back on her heels and opened it.

10

26th May 1924

*Today at breakfast Mummy said I was turning into quite
the barbarian and so I'm to be sent away. I replied that I
didn't understand for only the day before she had called
me dumpish. How could one be both dumpish and a
barbarian? I asked.*

The little red book was a diary. It started in May 1924
and ended in December, a little over a month after Vera's
sixteenth birthday. Some weeks she had written every day,
but the entries were often short notes about what she had
eaten or little pencil sketches; the back half of the diary was
blank. On the whole the book revealed a girl with a lot of
time on her hands and who, it seemed, rejected all the ways
in which she was asked to spend it. This particular entry was
one of the longer ones.

*I said, I suppose so, if all you really mean is that one is
stupid, but that I wasn't stupid at all because I knew a
great deal about what was going on in the house. Then
Daddy – from behind his paper – said that I wasn't stupid,
I was a bore, and I was to go to a school in Germany*

or Switzerland. *Then Mummy said no, it hadn't been settled. She preferred a convent school in Italy. I said I would compromise, that I preferred to be educated at Oxford. St Hilda's would do.*

Mummy froze mid-sip of her coffee; her eyes turned dreamy, her nunnified mind so taken at the mention of that great abbess who presided over beast and fowl at Whitby; I had hooked her. But Daddy said absolutely not, it would only make me worse. At which point I excused myself to go upstairs to pack. I said I would run off, to wherever all those other girls had run off. Mummy then spilled her coffee in a most indelicate manner and Daddy didn't say anything. He simply folded his paper and poured her a fresh cup like the galling knight he is.

Pritchett was standing outside the door when I left and hissed that I was a heathen and I told her that her breath smelled of dirty knickers and oh my, if that dear woman didn't look fit to cry!

Poor Mrs Pritchett, Sam thought. Then again, her attack on Vera was certainly out of place – and from the conversation as Vera told it, unwarranted. Her mother didn't want to be sent away to school and wasn't taking it well. But who was *this* Vera? She seemed, by Brooklyn standards, spoiled. The girls that Sam knew would have leapt at the chance to go to some fancy private school in another country. Even a convent in Italy. *Well*, she smirked, *not Donna*. This mouthy, argumentative girl was not the Vera Sam had known, not by a long shot.

Sam thumbed through more of the pages. Vera lost the

battle and a week after that entry she wrote that she was leaving for Kent for the summer and then on to some school in Switzerland. *Dear god*, thought Sam. Vera got to live in Switzerland? And complained about it? Her mother must have forgotten to take the diary with her, for there were no entries for several months, but then came this in November:

13th November 1924

I found it. Dear Mama – as I call her now to remind her that Switzerland was not entirely a waste – was at one of her committee meetings and Pritchett was stuck upstairs supervising our wretched maids. I had smeared some chocolate cake onto one of the tapestries in the gallery – rubbed it right into the Wounds of Jesus. They would be at it all morning.

I got into the horror chamber and picked the lock on Mama's desk – I learned an awful lot in Lausanne – and what did I find? A pistol. Loaded. Mama! Who is she planning to use that on? Me? Because I'd been sent home from school? I took the bullets out. One never knows with Mama.

I was running out of time and a bit frustrated – it was nearly noon and the maids would be coming down for their lunch – so I picked up one of Mama's musty old horror books and was going to draw a moustache on the Virgin's face when I heard a most miraculous sound – metal hitting the floorboards. There at my feet was the blessed key, a velvety red ribbon tied to it. Mama had been using it as a bookmark. How perfectly perverse.

So Vera had been sent home from school, but she hadn't said why. Was she sent home for just a few weeks? Or kicked out for good? What on earth could Vera have done? Her mother was no rebel. Or so Sam had thought. The Vera in this diary had smeared chocolate cake into a presumably valuable tapestry and knew how to pick locks. The entry was written a week after Vera's sixteenth birthday, a fact that was head spinning in and of itself. In less than two years, Vera would give birth to a daughter in America and all traces of this mischievous, headstrong girl would be gone. What the hell could've happened to change Vera's life so much? Sam felt her stomach turn. An illegitimate pregnancy at the age of seventeen could do that. But... a pregnancy alone didn't explain the decades of secrecy that followed; it didn't explain why Sam was told nothing about the family, about Begars.

She thought more about that last entry. Vera had wanted a key her mother had, wanted it so much that she came up with a subterfuge to search Lady Cooper's desk. What was the key to? And why was it perverse to stick it inside a book? What was a horror chamber? A horror book? And a gun? Did she really think Lady Cooper capable of using it? Vera had seemed surprised by the gun and scared enough to take the bullets out. Or was she just being mischievous again?

Sam heard someone call her name from the corridor outside the bedroom. Alec. She turned the chest upright and kicked the plywood board under the bed, slid the book between the bed covers. *Why am I hiding this?* she wondered. *There's nothing in it but silliness.* But Vera had a reason for keeping it secret, and for the time being, Sam would follow her lead until she knew more.

She opened the door and saw Alec holding a plate and a candle.

'No luck with the electricity?'

He sighed in resignation, then nodded at the plate. 'I've brought you this. Apples and cheese. When you're ready, would you like to come down for a drink before dinner?'

Sam wasn't much of a drinker, just a few sips of beer or red wine with dinner at Donna's. At the moment, though, alcohol of any kind sounded good. 'Yes, that would be nice,' she said, taking the plate. 'How about Mrs Pritchett? Did you get anywhere with her?'

'A more infuriating person I've never met. You will be pleased to hear that I did rescue dinner. The woman was planning on cooking some old rabbit that had been hanging up since the previous century.'

Sam laughed and picked up an apple slice, stepped back into the room to let Alec come in. 'Can we see my grandmother before dinner?'

He took a deep breath.

'Is it that bad? The way she's talked about – or not talked about – I'm expecting to meet a preserved corpse, dressed in lace and covered in lilies.'

'We put chrysanthemums on the dead.'

'I wish you'd stop it. These jokes about my grandmother aren't funny. What's going on?'

He paused, took out a cigarette and tapped it on his case.

'Not in my room,' she said, taking the case from him and slipping it in her skirt pocket.

'I'm sorry. Your mother. It's how she died, isn't it? Cancer.'

'You know, you're the only one who's asked.'

'Roger didn't?'

'No.'

'I see. Finish that up, then I'll introduce you to Lady Cooper.'

*

They passed the main stairs and crossed into the south wing of the house, then Alec stopped.

'Lady Cooper is not what she once was. A series of strokes. The first one was the worst – left her without speech and confined to a wheelchair, a good deal of her body paralysed. She's had several others since then, each leaving her significantly worse. Not much of a life for her, at this point. I haven't seen her myself for some time, this is all from Roger. We don't talk much about the family, we both prefer it that way. It's been like that for years, and nothing much goes on out here these days. But' – he drew in his breath, then met her eyes – 'he did say to me once that he wondered if Lady Cooper even knew she was still alive. Her room is this way.'

Sam looked around. That was why the house was so quiet. Why there were so few words in Roger's letters to Vera. There was nothing to say, other than that Lady Cooper still breathed. But surely he must have written to Vera at some point, told her of the decline. Was that why Vera hadn't come back? Because there was nothing to come back to? But Vera wasn't hard-hearted. She must have known her presence might have helped in some small way. Vera had always helped their sick neighbours in Brooklyn; she'd watch the children or make a supper. Even sit by the bedside of the dying. She wasn't sentimental but she wasn't callous, either.

88

Sam thought about the poor, old, lonely woman on the other side of one of these walls, the agony of her misery.

'Is there anyone else left in the family? Did my mother have a brother or sister? Does anyone come to visit?'

'Not anymore.' Alec lit the candles set about on tables in the short corridor, grumbling that someone had bothered to put them out but not light them.

'And Vera never came back to visit? Not even once?' Sam reached far back into her memory, tried to recall a time when her mother hadn't been at home. Maybe when she was a baby? Other than that, Vera had always been around. The last face Sam saw at night and the first she saw in the morning, whether she liked it or not.

'Not that I know of.' They had turned left into what seemed to be a later addition to the house, stretching off the back of the southern wing. The walls were no longer squares of wood panel but papered in a delicate yellow silk.

'Here we are. Lady Cooper's rooms overlook the gardens. Sir Thomas's old rooms are there' – he motioned behind them towards the front of the house – 'overlooking the drive.' Without ceremony, Alec knocked on the door and called out, 'Visitor for Lady Cooper.' Hearing no answer, he gave an impatient huff, knocked harder, then called more loudly. After a few more moments he tried the door handle, then gave her his candle so he could use both hands.

'It's locked,' he said, jiggling the latch. 'Have they locked her in? There should be someone with her at all times.' He walked to the next door over. 'Her dressing room – they're adjoining.' He tried the handle but it was locked also.

Sam could tell that Alec was furious. 'This won't do. Not at all,' he said, more to himself than her. He turned and snapped out his hand, looked her hard in the eye.

She knew what he wanted, but she had a candle in each hand, so she pushed her hip towards him. 'It's in there.' She nodded to the wide skirt pocket. He shook his head in mild annoyance at the familiarity of what she was suggesting but reached in for his cigarette case anyway. 'Roger has wanted to make changes around here for years, but there was no real impetus,' he said as he lit a cigarette and took one of the candles back. 'But with your arrival, he knew the time had come. He had decided to move Lady Cooper to York where she'd get better care, not be left to rot out here. Remove Mrs Pritchett, too. Her retirement's long been overdue. It's clear from the state of this place and this' – he nodded back towards Lady Cooper's rooms – 'that Roger waited too long.'

Alec's old urgent stride was back and they weren't even down the stairs before he started yelling: 'Pritchett! Mrs Pritchett!' He coughed in between shouts and Sam wanted to take the cigarette right out of his mouth. Instead, she braced herself; she could tell he was looking forward to this fight.

*

The kitchen was the size of Sam's whole apartment back in Brooklyn. Several large dressers were set against the green walls, each open shelf stacked with dishes and copper pots and pans. Mrs Pritchett was humming away in front of an old black range that was fitted into what had once been a hearth.

'That little gas ring over there is all you need these days, but it's an electric light!' she said, looking up briefly and pointing to a small modern stove in the corner. 'So I'm stuck cooking with this fussy devil. Once upon a time, I enjoyed the challenge – keeping the heat going nice and steady, its belly fed just right. Not these days, mind you, not with these joints.' She sighed and wiped a hand on the apron she'd put on over her blue dress. 'Haven't had to cook for years, have I? But we can't let Miss Samantha starve, can we?' The housekeeper turned to Sam and gave her a kindly smile, but when she saw the angry set of Alec's eyes, his jaw, she merely shrugged and resumed stirring the contents of a pot.

Alec took a seat at the table and crossed his legs – Sam almost thought he'd changed his mind. He reached inside his coat for his cigarette case and put it on the table.

I see, thought Sam. *He wants to toy with the poor old woman, bat her around between his paws a bit.* Those piercing black eyes, the sharp edges of his cheekbones and long nose – his features were rendered all the more cutting in the flickering shadows of the candles. A lock of oiled hair had sprung loose and hung over his eye. He looked more like a gangster than a nice country lawyer. *Screw that*, she thought. 'Mrs Pritchett. My grandmother. Is she in her room? We were just there; we knocked but no one answered.'

'In fact,' Alec said quietly, 'her door was locked.'

The housekeeper turned back to them, wooden spoon held up and dripping some sort of thick substance onto the range. 'No one answered?' She looked from Sam to Alec. 'Locked? Lady Cooper's room?' She held out the spoon to Alec. 'Stir this. Silly empty-headed girl! What's she gone and done now? Another one of her flippity adventures?'

'Who?' Sam asked.

'The night nurse!' Mrs Pritchett took off her apron and handed that to Alec, too. 'A few peas short of a casserole, that one. And it's all your brother's fault! She's only been here a few months and she's the most brainless one yet!'

'But it's not yet night,' Sam said, confused.

Mrs Pritchett scoffed and looked at Sam like she'd gone silly, too. 'The storm, Miss Samantha! The storm! The day girl's not here, is she? Didn't want to step out of her comfy bed and get her toes cold. We end up with the worst of the lot, don't we? The ones that can't keep a post anywhere else. They won't scrub a pot or empty one. Nor apparently take proper care of an old lady as sweet and gentle as a lamb. Mr Bell, this is on your head!'

Arms thrown up in outrage and keys jangling wildly, the housekeeper limped towards the doorway. As she passed Sam, she paused and grasped at her sweater sleeve, said in a dropped voice, 'Miss Samantha, homespun is not the same as bespoke.' She was looking off to the side as she said this, as if her mind was at war with which problem to focus on. 'I'll find you some nicer things. You're the lady of the house now, aren't you?' Her mood shifted, as if she had just realised her problems were solved; she smiled at Sam, squeezed her elbow affectionately and left.

Lady of the house? No way, Sam thought. She looked down at her green sweater, the yellow flowered blouse underneath. Were her clothes that bad? She looked at Alec to see what he thought, but he was in front of the bread box, his back to her.

'Lady of the house?' she repeated.

'Yes.' He pulled out two stale-looking muffins. 'But it's a trick.'

'What's the purpose?'

'To make you think she's on your side.'

'I have a side?'

'Yes. A very good one.'

Sam glared at him. 'Aren't you going to go with her? Make sure everything's okay?'

'In a bit.'

'You're as hot and cold as she is.'

'No. I'm hungry.'

'How can you eat?' The whole situation turned Sam's stomach. 'What if something's wrong?'

'Leave her. She'll take care of it.' He left the kitchen, snatching a plate from a shelf as he went and a butter dish, and Sam followed him into the housekeeper's sitting room. He took a toasting fork from beside the hearth, speared the muffins and held them near the flames.

'You're making me dizzy. I'm going upstairs to see if everything's all right.'

'It's fine. Let her tick the girl off.'

There were several minutes of silence as they both watched the flames brown the muffins, Alec carefully rotating them to stop them from catching. Finally he pulled them from the toasting fork and put them on the plate. 'She can't stay on, not after this.'

'Who? The night nurse?'

'Well, she'll have to go, too. I meant Mrs Pritchett.' He sliced both muffins open, buttered them, then handed one to Sam. 'Now eat. I'll put a chicken in that pot she was stirring, but it won't be ready for a while. From the smell of it, I think she added the rabbit anyway. It's clear she's not all there anymore.'

'That would explain a lot.'

'Yes. For instance, I think that's a lovely green jumper. Perfectly befitting a lady of the house.'

Sam gave Alec a sideways look. 'Knock it—' she began. But then she noticed his eyes were fixed on his muffin, he wasn't even looking at her. *No*, she thought, *you're being an idiot*. Sam was more than used to boys, men, cretins – whatever – making passes at her. It was an hourly occurrence on the streets and stairwells of Brooklyn and had been since she'd turned ten. The subway was the worst; her stomach cramped at the memory of those encounters. It had nothing to do with her looks. The come-ons were brash, crude, dirty. But what Alec had said – there was no spike to it. He didn't sound like he was making fun of her. He almost sounded… sweet. *No*, she thought. He'd only known her for, what, a few hours? Not possible. She shook her head.

'You stay here if you want. I'm going to see my grandmother. If I can get into her damn room.'

11

A plush ruby-red carpet covered the stairs and the passage into the south wing, but it changed to an elaborate and no doubt very old Persian carpet in the corridor outside her grandmother's room. It was pale green and bordered in vines and flowers, but the interior was woven through with once-golden creatures engaged in a hunt. A cheetah sinking its teeth into a gazelle; a lion clawing after a buck. Combined with the muted yellow silk wallpaper, the effect was one of elegance – a deliberately faded elegance. Sam didn't see the signs of a family that had truly lost its wealth; the wallpaper wasn't peeling and the ceilings didn't bulge from water damage; the house was in good repair.

But as evening came and the temperature dropped even more, it brought with it such a dryness to the air, a brittleness, that the house seemed to shrink around her. She could glimpse the truth in what Mrs Pritchett said, that Begars was not what it once was. The passage seemed to darken before her eyes as she reached her grandmother's room; Alec had only just lit the candles, but they were already out, the draughts having their say.

Outside Lady Cooper's door, she could hear the murmur of a soothing voice and instantly felt better. It was going to be okay. *It really will be, Sam.* She was finally going to meet her grandmother.

'Hello?' She tapped lightly on the door. 'Mrs Pritchett? Can I come in?' She heard more murmurings but no reply. As she put her hand on the latch, anger flared through her; she'd kick it off the hinges if it was still locked. But the door opened easily, and her anger subsided as quickly as it came and she stepped in.

She braced herself for the smell of stale urine and sickness – she knew the odour of invalids all too well – and was surprised that the room smelled pleasantly of lavender and talc with a hint of jasmine. It was the polar opposite of Vera's bedroom in the north wing. This room was larger but also soothing. A comforting sanctuary, not a place of stiff-backed chairs. Curtains were drawn across the windows, but there was light enough from the fire and a few candles; the silk of sky-blue wallpaper seemed to glitter.

The frame of the tester bed was much more delicate than Vera's; the teal satin bed curtains and thick blankets were newer, and there were cream pillows trimmed in gold piled delightfully high on the bed. It took her breath away.

A few feet away from a dressing table, a woman sat in an old-fashioned wheelchair facing the windows. All Sam could see over the wicker back was the elaborate sweep of paper-white hair into a beautiful chignon and the trailing end of a cream silk shawl hanging off the chair's arm.

The woman moved in her chair – a small, hasty jerk, as if she'd been sitting there quietly sewing, got lost in a dream and accidentally pricked her finger. Sam closed her eyes, then willed herself forward, afraid to break the illusion and see a face that might tell too sad a tale.

'Lady Cooper?' She slowly walked towards the figure. 'It's

Sam. Samantha. Vera's daughter.' She put a hand on the woman's slightly slumped shoulder and stepped around to see her. Sam felt a catch in her throat. Despite the years of ill health Lady Cooper had endured, her face was still that of a commanding and handsome woman. Her grandmother's eyes were closed – she was asleep – but Sam could see a proudness in her face, a strength still visible in her high cheekbones and square jawline. Sam didn't see disease or weakness. She saw family. She knew this face, knew it very well. Lady Cooper had the same long, distinctive nose, the same hooded eyes as Sam and Vera.

And with this thought, her knees buckled. Sam was looking at the woman Vera would never live to be. She took a step back, knocking against the dressing table, and her grandmother stirred. The old woman's heavy lids fluttered open but her eyes were clouded over. *Cataracts*, thought Sam. Lady Cooper fidgeted in her chair and moaned, then reached out as if she were trying to grab something, as if she knew someone was there. Sam took her hand but the old woman didn't settle on it, she only kept grabbing, her agitation mounting. Sam looked at the dressing table behind her. There wasn't much there: an embroidered jewellery box, a silver brush and comb, scissors, some small vials and a glass of red wine. *She drinks wine?* Well she'd seen stranger things in Brooklyn.

Sam picked up the glass. The woman seized Sam's wrist; her grip was surprisingly strong. But as soon as she felt the wineglass touch her lips, Lady Cooper let out a sob and thrashed in her chair. Her arm flailed in front of her – it was purposeful – an attempt to knock the glass away. Sam put the glass back on the dressing table and knelt down, shushing her grandmother, restraining the woman's arm. It's what they had done to calm old Mrs Catania during her fits.

At that moment, Mrs Pritchett came hobbling through the door. She stopped when she saw Sam, then limped quickly over to Lady Cooper's chair. 'It's all right, m'lady, shhh, it's all right, shhh.' The housekeeper began stroking Lady Cooper's hair, whispering to her. The sick woman dropped her head, allowing it to be cradled in Mrs Pritchett's arm. The housekeeper looked up at Sam. 'What happened?'

'I don't know,' said Sam. 'She was reaching for something. I thought she wanted the wine, but then she got really upset.'

'It's all right, Miss Samantha. I think she wanted the brush; it's getting towards her bedtime and she does like her hair brushed. Go on now, I'll take care of her.' She turned back to Lady Cooper and started to undo her chignon. 'Just like old times, isn't it, m'lady? We don't get to see too much of each other these days do we? What with our old bones. We're a sorry sight, you and I.'

Sam backed towards the door, unable to sort through what she was feeling. She should stay; this was her grandmother and she knew how to care for people like Lady Cooper. She stood for a moment, still deciding whether to leave, when she felt a wave of cold overtake her, as if she'd fallen through ice. There, in the far corner of the room, someone was lurking in the shadows. A woman. She was so still, she could've been mistaken for a dressmaker's dummy. She must have been there the whole time. Sam recognised the black dress, the blunt-cut hair, the round glasses. It was the woman she'd seen on the stairs and earlier on the porch. The night nurse. Sam felt her anger returning. The woman had stood there, quietly watching Sam trying to calm Lady Cooper. Practically spying on her.

'Creep,' she said fiercely. Then she turned on her heel and left.

12

Christ, Sam thought, as she walked back to her room. *That's it. I'm done for the day.* She would skip dinner. She'd get into her pyjamas, get under the covers, and read Vera's diary until she fell asleep. Get up tomorrow, and take a page out of Donna's book: clean house on this madness.

She found Ivy in her bedroom. Even though Sam was pretty beat, she was happy to see the girl. There was a freshly blazing fire and the girl had laid a nightgown over the chair near the hearth.

Ivy saw Sam's questioning eyes. 'To take the chill off. That's what they do, isn't it?'

'Who?'

'Proper ladies' maids.'

'I wouldn't know,' Sam said distractedly.

'Do you like them, miss?' Ivy gestured at two dresses hanging on the wardrobe door.

Huh, Sam thought. 'I do, Ivy... but I'm not going anywhere.'

'I think the green, miss, it really will brighten up the table on such a gloomy night.'

You could knock me over with a feather, Sam thought. Mrs Pritchett was serious. She really did want Sam to change clothes, and into something fancier than Sam had ever worn in her life, or probably ever *would* wear. And for dinner in a house without heat or electricity. With only one other person, Alec. *Oh boy*. Sam reached out to touch one of the dresses; she couldn't help it, it was so delicate, so dazzling. It was an ethereal metallic emerald-green silk sheath – it must have been the dress Ivy mentioned earlier. Sam had only ever seen such a dress in the movies and it was completely at odds with the heavy room around her. The style wasn't exactly recent, more like something flappers would've worn, but it was in remarkably good condition. Had it been Vera's dress? *Impossible*, thought Sam. Her mother despised glamour. Lady Cooper's, when she was younger? Sam didn't know any mothers back home who would've dressed like that.

Ivy walked over to the dressing table and picked up two cut-glass bottles with black fringed atomisers.

'Which scent do you prefer, miss? Jasmine or irises?'

Sam didn't know how to answer; her eyes kept returning to the dresses. The other was black silk and chiffon threaded with metallic gold geometric patterns. Sam, the temple goddess?

'The jasmine, then,' said Ivy. 'It'll hold its own a bit more in the cold.'

The girl put the bottles down and held up two long necklaces – one gold, the other jet. 'The gold would go with either dress.' She bit her lip as she thought about it. 'But perhaps not the jet with the emerald dress.'

Sam didn't want to hurt her feelings. Not yet, anyway, so she changed the subject.

'Ivy. Do you know much about my mother?'

Ivy looked away shyly. 'No, miss.'

Sam hated herself for a moment; she realised she'd put the

girl on the spot. Too soon. Servants aren't supposed to talk about their employers, even Sam knew that. But she also knew that servants heard a lot of gossip.

'Do you live here then? Do you miss your mother, so far away from home?'

'Yes, miss. She died when I were little.'

Sam's heart melted even more for the girl. 'It's a rotten thing. Not having a mom. I'm sorry, Ivy.' She wasn't about to ask her about a dad, afraid of the answer. She didn't have room for it.

'I lived on my uncle's farm. There were lots of cousins. I liked that part. Lot of pigs. I didn't like that as much.'

'Lots of mud.' It was the only thing Sam's mind let through. She was well aware that her own vocabulary for grief was stunted. But it worked. Ivy giggled, breaking the tension.

'Yes, miss.' Ivy's smile returned and as she picked up a kettle warming by the fire, she prattled on about how she only ever had the one good dress and it wasn't so good, it was never her own and how she never could get the smell of muck out of her hair or her clothes, and how happy she'd been when a cousin told her about the position here.

'So many fine things, miss, I never did see such things in all my life. Oh, I'm talking too much.' She poured hot water from the kettle into a washbasin. Sam realised that she was expected to wash before dinner, and grew even wearier at the reminder. She looked at the bed, thought about how she'd like to lie down in it, even for just a bit. Otherwise she might fall asleep at dinner, her face in Mrs Pritchett's rancid rabbit stew.

'May I suggest a dress for the ball, miss?'

Sam's heavy eyelids snapped back open. Then she reminded herself that she shouldn't be so surprised. She'd seen enough movies. The voyage over had been an education itself. Clothes. Parties. Dancing. It was the fodder of this world.

She cleared her throat a little to try to hide her ignorance. 'I don't know, Ivy. When is the ball again?'

Ivy blushed and looked down at the corner of the rug. The act of thinking was transparent with the girl. Sam could tell she was deciding how much she should say. 'They haven't said yet, miss. If they're to have it or not. It's the Twelfth Night Ball, miss. The servants' ball.' Then Ivy couldn't hold back any longer, her excitement taking over. 'I've never been to one but one of the girls – Nesta, she's ever so nice – she said I might borrow one of her dresses. She showed me just the one.' Ivy sketched out the dress in the air with her hands. 'I'd have to take a few things apart to make it work. There's just enough time.'

'Twelfth Night?'

'Yes... but what with the mistress so poorly...' She wrapped a section of hair around her finger like it was a curling iron. Sam felt sorry for her, though Ivy seemed happy enough, seemed to enjoy these little fantasies of her.

But Sam didn't think Ivy could be right about the ball. The storm had thrown Mrs Pritchett back on her heels, sure enough, but the housekeeper talked as if she were beleaguered at the best of times. Sam couldn't see Mrs Pritchett arranging a servants' ball, especially one that was only days away. Twelfth Night wasn't something Sam was very familiar with, beyond that song about the twelve days of Christmas, but she knew it was soon. On the ship over, there had been talk of Twelfth Night celebrations, and she had gathered it marked the end of the Christmas season.

She looked at Ivy, thought about the big empty house. Yes, something was lost in translation here. More than likely, what Ivy was expecting to be a grand ball would be a small party in the kitchen with some punch. She hoped so. Sam didn't think she could stomach a ball. It had taken all her energy just to make it to England. In a few days it would be exactly one year since Vera's death. She had stupidly hoped her arrival at Begars would push it to the back of her mind, but it hadn't. Sam let out a long, sad sigh and she saw Ivy cast her eyes down again. The girl had interpreted her silence as a rebuke.

'Your dress sounds marvellous,' Sam tried to sound cheery, to make amends, 'I can't wait to see it.'

The girl smiled but turned away. She had clammed up. Sam sighed again. Thought about what Mrs Pritchett had said about the staff; they were indeed odd creatures. Sam wouldn't have survived if she'd been a naive kid like Ivy. She wanted to sit her down and screw her head on tighter. If Ivy behaved like this in Brooklyn she'd be kept under lock and key. Otherwise she'd be knocked up in a minute. Yet the girl's sunny nature and her innocence were so infectious that Sam was utterly charmed.

Looking at the girl, Sam regretted what she was going to say next. 'Ivy. You are going to make a terrific lady's maid. But I don't think you're going to get very far with me. I need to skip dinner; it's been a long day and I've a bad headache. Can you tell Mrs Pritchett?'

The girl didn't look at her, only gave a quick, nervous curtsey and left.

'Oh geez,' Sam groaned. She'd upset the nicest person in the house. She stared into the fire, her eyes tracing a burst of sparks as a log broke apart, then she dragged herself over to the bed to retrieve Vera's teenage diary. She decided against putting on her pyjamas – they were too thin – or the flimsy nightgown Ivy had put out, and climbed into bed fully dressed. She made a face as soon as she got in. The bedclothes were damp – the fire couldn't penetrate far into the room on a night like this – and smelled of mould and mothballs. For the hell of it, she opened the china jar on the nightstand. The mouse was still in it. The mattress had probably been its home. She thought about Ivy. The girl's head was all silk and satin, balls and perfume. Mouse removal didn't figure in. She got out of bed, levered open the window and dumped the mouse out. *It was the cold, the damp. That's why Vera fled*, Sam thought drowsily. *It had nothing to do with me.* Brooklyn was the opposite of this place. Thick with heat even in the winter from all the bodies crammed around you. There was a lot more energy there, a lot more people Ivy's age. Would she like it there? *The girl must be lonely*, she thought. She'd probably been lonely for a long time.

Sam opened Vera's diary, meant to read more of it, but her final thought before falling asleep was to laugh at herself. To think that she was somehow better off than Ivy. Sam was just as lonely, just as lost.

*

The house rattled around her – an angry fit of wind had hit it hard enough to shake Sam awake. When she opened her eyes, she expected to see someone standing over her, such was the vividness of the nightmare she'd been shaken from. She had been dreaming that she was at a great ball and searching desperately for someone. But she couldn't find them and ran to her bedroom to hide. Then from under the covers, she watched as her door opened and someone came in, carrying an old-fashioned lantern, its black metal dented with age. Sam recognised the mottled, dry skin and the round glasses of the woman standing over her: it was the night nurse. The black cloth of her dress was faded from too much wear, too many washings. It seemed as if the woman wanted something from Sam, was about to say something, but she turned at the sound of a wail and then the wind had struck the house, Sam was awake and the nightmare over.

Sam burrowed back down into the wet, cold covers. *Get up*, she thought. *Make the fire.* But she was starting to drift off again when she heard a creak, like that of a rusty hinge. The creak was insistent, rhythmic. She was sure it was coming from the south wing on the other side of the gallery and stairs. She listened as the sound seemed to move closer but then died away. Then came a wail – exactly like the one in her nightmare – the cry of someone in distress.

Sam threw the covers back and swung her feet around to the floor. Who was it? Her grandmother? Mrs Pritchett? She stumbled to the door and opened it, just in time to see another door shut across the corridor. She thought about waking up Alec, but she didn't know which room he was in. She fetched a candle from the nightstand then crossed the corridor and opened the door she'd seen shut.

As she did so an icy torrent of air swept by and snuffed out her light. She stepped through the door anyway and as her eyes adjusted to the dark, she realised she was actually in a stairwell that housed a set of spiralling wooden stairs. Directly above her she heard the sound of another door closing. She headed up the stairs, thought for a moment about turning back; likely it was one of the servants and she should mind her own business. But that cry – and wasn't Begars her business now? Hadn't Mrs Pritchett called her the lady of the house?

At the top of the stairs, the door opened onto a narrow corridor that seemed to travel down the long spine of the house. In the distance, she could see another landing, lit from overhead by a pasty square of light. *The main staircase with its skylight*, she thought. There were doors on either side of the corridor, and as she tiptoed down it, she checked the transoms for light. She was about to give up – she'd be damned if she'd lose another pair of nylons to the rough floorboards – when she heard the sound of laughter coming from behind one of the doors. She put her hand on the latch and opened it.

The room beyond was coloured only in shades of grey. Light trickled out of an old black metal lantern on a little table under a dormer window. Two small brass beds stood on either side of the table. Ivy was sitting on one bed, a pale shawl wrapped around her shoulders, her eyes red from crying. There was someone else in the room too. The night nurse stood by the younger woman, and turned to look at Sam with accusing eyes, an unwanted intruder.

'Oh my god, I am so sorry!' Sam backed out of the room and rushed downstairs, cringing with embarrassment.

13

3rd January 1954

Hooks scraped across wood, followed by the rustling of soft but heavy fabric, and Sam saw a glow of light appear around the edges of her bed hangings. It was morning. Ivy's face appeared as she peeled back the curtains at the foot of the bed and then Sam remembered. She had barged in on the maid in the middle of the night.

'Oh, Ivy, I don't know what I was thinking.' Sam bolted up, Vera's diary falling to the floor. After her misadventure in what she now realised was the attic – Mrs Pritchett had told her that's where the servants slept – Sam had come back to her room, eaten the sandwich someone had left for her on a tray along with a cup of tea, and read more of her mother's diary long into the night. 'Ivy, I'm so sorry. I didn't mean to come into your room like that.'

'Miss?' the girl said with a curtsey, lowering her eyes.

'Last night. I came into your room. You were sitting on the bed. I'd heard a noise – someone crying – I wasn't thinking straight. I thought perhaps someone needed help.' The girl didn't respond, but resumed her work tying back the bed curtains.

'I'm sorry if I scared you. That was really rude of me. I was half asleep myself, otherwise I don't think I would've done something so stupid.'

'It's nothing, miss. I didn't see anything.' Ivy's eyes said otherwise. Sam could see a flash of panic. Ivy darted over to the nightstand and picked up the sandwich plate, returned it to the tray with the untouched cup of tea. Then she went over to the wardrobe and buried her head inside, no doubt searching for an outfit that Sam would refuse to wear.

Chilled and grumpy, Sam got up and stood in front of the roaring fire that Ivy must have started. It made her feel worse. She'd been sleeping while Ivy had been working. Even if it had been in a soggy tomb of a bed.

Sam felt a cheat, a cuckoo. She had no right to someone pulling back her curtains or cleaning up sandwich crumbs or making tea for her that she had blithely left untouched. Ivy reappeared holding a white blouse and a pleated camel-coloured skirt. She grinned and raised an eyebrow at Sam, then shrugged and put it back when Sam shook her head.

'How do you do it, Ivy?' Sam marvelled that the girl had recovered so quickly from the earlier awkwardness. 'You're chirping around like a bird at dawn.'

'I'd never!' Ivy shook her head and laughed, like Sam was the silly one. She dived back into the wardrobe. *Are we allowed to be friends?* Sam wondered as she listened to Ivy talking to herself. 'Oh yes, this one! No. Wait, that's better for tea. Maybe this? I should've asked Nesta...'

The girl was so sweet. Could Sam somehow be her fairy godmother? Sam laughed to herself. More like the other way around.

'This one!' Ivy pulled out a dark blue dress. 'Smart but warm! Or would you prefer a softer shade for the morning?'

For the morning? These people weren't going to give up. It was a smart dress, Sam had to agree. A navy-blue wool with a sailor's neck and a straight, column silhouette but she was sure it was from another decade. Likely one of the last dresses Vera had worn here. It was a good, practical dress – why hadn't Vera taken it with her?

Then it hit Sam like a slingshot to the head. *Oh god*. She knew what her mother had taken. The box of jewellery Vera was always moving around the apartment; each time Sam found it, there was one less ring, one less necklace. Vera had told her they were fake. But the jewels were real. Last night, on her grandmother's dressing table, that little embroidered box. So similar to the one they had back in Brooklyn. Part of a set. Vera had stolen the family jewels. Mother of Christ. That was what had kept them alive all these years. What an idiot Sam was! What must they think of her? Calling up the family lawyers – the lawyers! – and the first thing she says is, 'I want to see my grandmother.' The daughter of the family jewel thief, making demands. She looked at Ivy – the girl was back in the wardrobe, pulling out shoes. Sam had thought these people were crazy, and now she understood. They thought she was the crazy one.

That's why no one is saying anything. Why they're not asking me any questions. Why they're not asking about Vera. Did they think Sam had come to make amends? Or to get more loot? She thought back to Roger Bell's first telegram. *'Will wire funds but a visit is not advisable.'* She sat there helpless, poisoned by memories. She watched dumbly as

Ivy mulled over two pairs of black leather pumps. The girl said something – Sam couldn't hear through the tornado in her head – and put a pair with a lattice design back into the wardrobe. She had deemed them too blowy for Texas. No, no, she said too showy for breakfast. Sam shook her head. The girl had no idea.

Ivy went over to the dressing table and picked up a gold-coloured watch with a thin metal band prettily cut with holes. She presented it to Sam. 'This one, miss?'

Brass, Sam thought glumly. Otherwise Vera would've taken it. Sam's head was pounding again. Who had originally picked out these dresses, the shoes, the watch? Vera? Or Lady Cooper? She'd always thought her mother on some level had been colour blind or just immune to aesthetics. Vera's clashing outfits, the hodgepodge of furniture – Vera went for whatever was free or too cheap to pass up. *Except she never dressed me like that.* She never made Sam look a fool. Her mother had been a chameleon, her true nature completely hidden from her daughter. What an awful thought. One that Sam had never really dwelt on until Vera died. Until she found the letters. Until she got to Begars Abbey and saw this strange room that had not a single trace of the Vera she had known. How much worse was it going to get?

'Ivy, could I get a cup of coffee?' She wanted her out of the room, she needed to get back to work. She needed to see if there were more diaries.

The girl frowned. 'I better go, miss. Mrs Pritchett...'

'Of course,' said Sam, feeling embarrassed that she didn't know the rules. Ivy could help her with her clothes and her hair, but she shouldn't ask the girl to get things; that was some sort of breach. But why? If Sam were Donna, she would straight out ask.

Ivy curtsied and turned to leave, but not before Sam saw a trace of disappointment in her face. The costume party was over and once again no curls had been set or lipstick applied.

I don't care, she thought. She took the blue dress off the wardrobe door and reached in for the lattice pumps. 'Take these. For yourself. A gift.'

Ivy looked over her shoulder. Sam recognised the furtive gesture.

'Don't worry. I'll tell Mrs Pritchett I gave them to you.'

'Oh don't, miss!'

'Take the watch, too.'

'I couldn't, miss!' But nevertheless Ivy grabbed the dress, the shoes, the watch and scurried out.

I've done it now, Sam thought as she closed the door. *Cemented our reputation as thieves.* But what she'd just done, that was more like Robin Hood. She combed her fingers through her hair and pulled it back into a ponytail. Then shook her head in disgust. What bullshit. This place was getting to her. She was forgetting herself. She wasn't Robin Hood. She was the beggar.

*

There was a key in the lock of the bedroom door. She turned it, then pulled the nightstand in front of the door for good measure. Once upon a time, there would have been a steady stream of people in this room. Maids changing the bed, beating the curtains, taking up the rugs, polishing the furniture, organising Vera's clothes. It would have been hard to keep a secret in a room like this – a secret with a physical presence. That explained the diary hidden under the chest, a thin piece of plywood creating a false bottom. Things that Vera could prise open but others were unlikely to notice.

Sam opened the wardrobe. On the right was a series of drawers. She opened one, then closed it right away. Vera's underthings. Another drawer had silk scarves. The one below it was stuck. Glued shut by Vera? The maids would've thought it broken and ignored it. Vera would've reached up under from the drawer below and pushed out the bottom to hide something in there. Maybe. Sam would come back to it. She wasn't ready to touch these clothes, these beautiful things that had belonged to a Vera she never knew.

She surveyed the room again. Not the mattress – she was sure mice were a constant presence and they would chew up any paper hidden in it or use it for a nest. Behind the headboard? Possibly, but the bed was massive – how would she move it? Atop the tester? The maids would dust up there. What about a trick compartment in the skirting boards? She gave one a kick. Which part of the room was most in shadow, and therefore most likely to be ignored? There. Yes. The corner on the far side of the bed. She pulled a table away from the wall and knelt down. The dust was thick on the floor, and a sooty grime had built up in the corners and crevices. The joints where the wood met were soft and dotted with black mould from years of damp and neglect.

Sam ran her fingers along the top of the skirting board and pulled, but it didn't give. She sat back on her heels and examined her hands in disgust – her fingers were black with sticky dust. *In for a penny*, she thought and continued along the walls, tugging at the skirting boards as she went, tapping on the nearby floorboards too, the squares of wood panel above. When she reached the bathroom door – it was on the same wall as the fireplace – she sat down on the floor and took a break. *The tiles*, she thought as she looked in the bathroom. She could check those too, look for loose ones in the corner, or behind the fixtures. Under the claw-foot tub. Her eyes itched from the dust and her stomach growled. She needed food and soon.

She was about to haul herself up when she noticed it. A dark corner, easily overlooked because the dressing table was angled in front of it, where the floor had sunk or settled over the years, revealing a thin gap between it and the skirting board. She stuck her fingers into the gap. She didn't care what horrors she might touch; she'd met them all in Brooklyn by the time she was five. She hit against something hard – but it skittered away. She grabbed a comb from the dressing table and slid it in, hooking the object with its teeth, and pulled it out.

Another diary. It was a thin, plain book like the other one, and the first entry was dated 6th December, 1923; a month after Vera turned fifteen. Sam flipped through the pages, skimming the text. This Vera spent a lot of time writing about dead nuns, the ghosts of dead nuns and ghosts in general. *Alec's sisters must have gotten to her*, Sam thought. Vera also wrote about her birthday, and the 'awful' clothes forced upon her. About Christmas and giving a 'nun-besotted' Lady Cooper a copy of an Anne Boleyn portrait, wrapped in Martin Luther's *Ninety-five Theses*, and falsely bemoaning her mother's reaction and that Lady Cooper hadn't appreciated the effort and thought required to fashion such a gift, especially for a girl as trapped in the country as Vera was. Another entry mentioned a Twelfth Night servants' ball – how everyone, particularly Lady Cooper, had drunk too much. Then on 9th February 1924:

At the end of lessons my governess gave me the worst news: on the morrow she shall quit Begars. Miss Harold said she had not yet told Mummy. She wanted to speak with me first because she couldn't be sure of Mummy's reaction and wanted me to know the truth of it.

She said she could no longer remain in the employ of my father. That it was her decision solely and one that she came to after much agony. She said she could not continue to work in a house such as Begars; her conscience would not allow it. She then said, 'I want you to know, Miss Vera, that nothing untoward has happened to me. Nothing at all.'

Through my tears I begged her to tell me what she meant and what horrid thing had happened to take her away from me. But she would not. I fell into her arms sobbing and implored her not to leave me, to take me with her. She met my pleas with her own bitter tears and we stayed like that for quite some time. She truly was lovely. I shall never forget her.

Sam paused in her reading and gently brushed a fingertip across the page; the ink was smeared in parts – Vera's tears.

This must be something, she thought. And unlike the other entries she had read, there seemed to be some sense, some logic to this story. Vera had a governess, and the governess had left Begars and a young girl she seemed to care for because she found something extremely objectionable about the place, something to do with Sir Thomas, not Lady Cooper. Sam turned to the next entry:

10th February 1924

As soon as I awoke this morning I ran straight to Miss Harold's room and all was bare. I fell upon her bed crying. Then ran down to the kitchens to find the hall boy. He was outside filling the coal scuttles. I pushed him up against a wall and asked him why Miss Harold left.

'Dunno, miss,' he said, but I knew he was lying. I told him I would beat him black and blue if he didn't tell me, and I pinched him to show that I was good for it. He still said nothing and so I pinched him again, hard enough to make his little badger eyes well up.

'Tell me,' I said, twisting the skin on his arm and baring my teeth. The poor boy really started crying then, the tears leaving white trails down his dirty face. I told him if he didn't tell me, I'd bury him in the coal heap.

'Miss Harold didn't like what was going on. But them's just stories, miss! They say she shoves people in a hole when they're bad, but they ain't been bad, miss.'

'Who is "she"?' I demanded.

'I don't like to say, miss.'

I grabbed his bony forearm and told him that I would rub him a rather nice burn if he didn't spit it out.

'M'lady, miss, m'lady.'

I was so shocked by his admission I threatened to whip him for his cheek.

'Please don't, miss. Them's only stories. They ain't true.'

'There, there,' I said, the seriousness of his words settling upon me. I dried his eyes with my handkerchief and put an arm around his shoulders and took him into the kitchen. I ordered Cook to give him a good meal, all he could eat, and the nicer food, not the slops as I knew she was wont to give. I told her that he was a very good boy and had helped me enormously and that I should return later to see that she had done as I said. I then went to breakfast and Mummy told me that Miss Harold had been dismissed. I rather calmly enquired why, and Mummy said that Miss Harold had irreparably stained her character and it would not be appropriate to have her continue as my governess. I will not let this stand.

'Sam!' Alec shouted from outside her bedroom door. 'Which would you rather have? Porridge burned by Mrs Pritchett? Or scrambled eggs burned by me?' He knocked gently. 'Come on out. I promise to tell you wicked tales of your family over breakfast.'

Sam looked down at her hands in mild panic. She had been biting her nails, her grime-coated nails, and her lips were probably black with it. *God.* She ran into the bathroom and spat into the sink and wiped at her mouth, then hurried back into the room, realised she was still wearing yesterday's clothes. She put the diary on the dressing table. 'I need a minute to get dressed. I'll be right down.'

'All right, but no more of this hiding. We're in this together and I'll drag you out myself if I have to. Oh, and I've brought you a coffee.'

Sam pushed the nightstand away from the door and opened it a crack, took the coffee from Alec. He smiled at her, then confusion clouded his face as he took in her dishevelled hair, her eyes red and puffy from the dust. She cut him off before he could say anything more. 'I'm not a baby,' she said and shut the door.

'What's going on?' He genuinely sounded worried. Sam was almost touched. *We're in this together.* That's what he said. What did he mean?

'I'll come down when I'm ready.'

She took her coffee and sat down at the dressing table, turned to the next entry. Vera was questioning more servants, but it seemed most of them were older and wiser than the hall boy and she wasn't learning much. Sam flipped ahead, then found in a later entry a mention of the horror chamber:

15th May 1924

I'm getting closer, my dear Mummy. I was in the great hall. It was quite late, and I had come down for no other reason than to discover your secrets. At that hour, even the butler would be face down in his cups.

Yet the ghouls were up and about after all. I could hear their fiendish voices from inside the horror chamber. And I was quite pleased to hear that one of the fiends was you, dear Mummy. I couldn't make out the words; you were speaking in a hushed tone. Yes hush hush, Mummy, hush hush! And there was that sting in your voice, the one you save for behind closed doors. But I felt no threat from it anymore; I'd been freed of it. As I listened to you, I wondered, who would you whip this time? Who would you take into your hidden cell, with its braids of copper wire and corroded chastity belts?

I crept right to the door and heard your poor, poor victim. Was this what Miss Harold had heard? What drove her away? The tones of a plea, a beg for mercy. I was steaming up to shove right in when I heard a whine of heavy hinges. The sounds of shuffling, of protest, then silence. You had opened the cell, I was positive. I knelt down to the keyhole to see where the door was, but there was no sign of you or your worm hole. Where had you gone? I stayed there, waiting, and then I saw you. Walking through the wall. The door to your cell was the wall beam! It had been hidden behind the tapestry! I saw it as the bottom of the beam swung out and you emerged and retrieved something from your desk before returning to your sulphurous lair. Oh, Mummy, you have turned a priest hide into a hell hole. What would the old prioress think?

I ran across the hall and hid behind a table and its urn of corpse flowers. I parted the dried-up baby's breath and watched. But God forgive me, I fell asleep. I woke up under that table with the light of dawn. Angry at myself, I went straight into the horror chamber – but all was normal. The curtains prettily tied back to reveal the garden; papers and books neatly arranged on your desk. Not a rug or pillow out of place. The false beam hidden once again behind the tapestry. I was about to get down on my knees and prise it open when I heard buckets clanging and the poisonous warbling of Pritchett. I retreated. Tonight I will go back. I will enter the devil's maw.

A shadow dropped across the page and Sam yelped and slammed the book shut. Alec stood over her.

'What the hell happened here?' He looked around the room, bewildered at the disarray, at Sam's appearance. 'I know I shouldn't barge in like this, but I did knock again and you didn't answer. I was concerned. That glimpse I had of you was rather alarming.'

'You don't look so great yourself,' Sam said, angry that he had sneaked up on her. He was in the same clothes as yesterday, too, and his chin was dotted with stubble.

He grimaced and smoothed back his dark hair. 'Yes, one does not rest easy at Begars. I had them bring you a sandwich last night.' He looked around for the tray. 'Did you eat it? I see now I should've brought it up myself. Now please, tell me, what are you doing?'

Part of Sam was touched. But still. She had been right in the middle of some very bizarre reading.

'Well, then. I see we're not getting anywhere.' He pointed towards the bathroom. 'You'd better go and clean up and make an appearance downstairs before Mrs Pritchett has a heart attack. She probably thinks you've died in your sleep, and I'm to blame of course; it's my fault there's no heat, she says. What's that in your hand?'

Sam looked down at the thin book, but she wasn't sure how much to tell him.

'It's a diary. Vera wrote it, when she lived here. '

'Really?' Alec sounded surprised. 'Where did you find it? Oh

I see.' He put his hands on his hips and looked around. 'That's why you did this. Very well then.' He went to her open suitcase and pulled out a red flowered blouse and her orange sweater. 'These will go nicely together.'

Sam looked at the sweater he was holding up, astonished. The bed curtains behind it. Her stomach heaved. Her mother had made that sweater. Knitted it from yarn the same burnt-orange colour as the bed hangings. Sam thought back to her childhood. Every year Vera had knitted her a thick winter sweater, always in the same dark orange wool. Until one day at school they were reading *The Legend of Sleepy Hollow* and the other kids had started calling Sam Ichabod Crane and Pumpkin Head. She'd told her mother she wanted a new colour, that she was sick of it. Vera looked at her and said, 'Quite right. I'm sick of it too.' Vera knitted her forest-green sweaters after that, until as an adult, Sam had shaken off the taunts of those stupid kids and decided that she did like orange after all. Why had Vera dressed Sam in the colour of her childhood bedroom, of a home she'd hated? Sam felt her temper rise. What else had been hiding in plain sight?

She decided to share some of this with Alec. 'I found two diaries. They don't go much past her sixteenth birthday. And they're so strange. It's almost as if they're written by a completely different person. I can't see my mother in them at all.'

'May I?' Alec asked, holding out his hand.

'You'll see,' she said, passing the book to him. 'She's kind of a brat. Gets into things she shouldn't. I think they sent her away to school because of it, and then she was expelled not long after.'

'Really? Why?'

'She doesn't say. I think she's mad. Her governess left suddenly, or was fired, and Vera goes and tortures some little boy – a hall boy, she called him – to find out why. She has him in tears, she's so mean to him. I think he was younger than her, much younger. But he tells her some story... a rumour... that Lady Cooper is shoving people into a hole somewhere as some kind of crazy punishment and that's why the governess left. She calls it a priest hide. What's that?'

'It's where Catholic families hid priests during Elizabeth's time. They were one of the queen's favourite sweet meats. But this wasn't a Catholic house after the priory was dissolved; they wouldn't have been hiding priests here. And the governess got shoved into one as a punishment? That makes absolutely no sense, either.'

'No, I don't think the governess was. I think she thought it was happening to others and left in protest.' Sam started biting a nail. 'But after that, Vera becomes obsessed with spying on Lady Cooper. And talks about some room she calls her mother's horror chamber. It sounds...'

'Bonkers?'

Sam suddenly felt angry. She might think that, but it was another thing for a stranger to say it. She got up, thought for a brief moment about wiping her dirty hands on his white shirt. 'You don't have to worry,' she sniped. 'I'm not crazy like my mother. And I'm not here to steal more jewels.'

'What? What jewels?'

'The ones Vera stole.'

'I don't know anything about that but if she did, good on her.' Alec was marching about the room, putting the furniture back in place, shaking his head as he went. 'And I didn't mean Vera was bonkers. I don't think she was. Begars, however, is and always has been bonkers. I'm sorry for not being clear. I don't want to offend you. Not at all. Quite the opposite.'

'But it's true, isn't it? They all think I've come back for money?'

'I don't know who you mean by "they".' Alec pushed his hair out of his eyes again then made a face when he realised his hands were dirty. 'You need food. More coffee. *I* need more coffee. You have five minutes.' He nodded again towards the bathroom door. 'I know very little about why you're here, but I should like to hear more. And hopefully' – he gave an exasperated shrug – 'it might help explain where Roger is.'

14

'So what is the horror chamber?' Sam asked as they made their way through the gallery to the main stairs.

Alec laughed. 'Yes… I hadn't heard that in a while. It's what your mother and my sisters called Lady Cooper's study. It was once the prioress's chamber – her main place of business – when this was a nunnery.'

'Why did they call it that?'

'No idea. I assumed at the time it was just to frighten me.'

'What's the difference between a prioress and an abbess?'

'A prioress led a priory. They were smaller houses – fewer nuns, less wealth – inferior to the abbeys. The priory churches around here were small – a village church type of thing – whereas the abbeys might have a very grand cathedral. Someday, if you like, I could take you to Whitby on the coast. There was a great abbey there, though it's just ruins now. Have you heard of Whitby?'

'Not really,' Sam said vaguely. 'Vera mentioned it in her diary; she knew Lady Cooper liked the place. Vera tried to use it to her advantage.' She had stopped to look through the last gallery window before the stairs. The storm had subsided and now there was only a gentle flurry of snow; she could see in the back garden the branches of small trees and bushes sheathed in ice and drooping under the frozen weight. And there, about 150 feet north of the garden, stood the old medieval church and its bell tower.

'Well, consider yourself warned. Dracula went to Whitby, then came here for a good rest in the crypt.'

'What?' She turned to look at him.

He laughed wryly. 'According to my sisters and Vera. They could be quite wicked, really.'

'Wicked how?' He had her full attention now. 'Evil or just pranks?'

'I certainly thought they were evil at the time; they were great big girls to me. Quite ferocious. But no, they were just clever. Liked a good story, liked to get into things.'

Well that certainly fits with the Vera in the diary, Sam thought.

Alec started for the stairs but Sam lingered a moment over the scene before her. Snow drifts lapped high up the tawny-hued walls of the church; they were made with the same stone as the house. Some of its window arches remained eerily intact, as if the builders might return any day to install their panes. On the other side of the church, she could see a vast, snow-covered courtyard, enclosed by the ruins of the buildings that once surrounded it. Alec – his huff of annoyance very audible – came back up the stairs and followed her gaze. 'That was the cloister, and over on that side of the quadrangle' – he pointed to the western block of stones – 'was the dorter, where the nuns slept.'

The northern ruins were barely visible, overtaken as they were by the nearby woods. Sam thought about what it would've been like to live here as a nun hundreds of years ago, and shivered. With a storm like this, they might have been cut off for weeks.

Alec had left her again, so she ran to catch up to him. 'So which room is it? The prioress's chamber?'

'It's through there.' He gestured towards the squat door at the rear corner of the entry hall, the one Mrs Pritchett had come through to greet them the day before.

'Can we go in?'

Alec continued on his path into the great hall, only stopping on the other side of it at the arched doorway that led to the kitchens. He then pointed to another squat door, this one to their right and angled into a corner. 'That's the main door to the prioress's chamber. If she liked you, she'd let you wait for your appointment by the fire in the great hall. If she didn't, you'd wait in the cold front hall.'

It was a plain door, its great age evident in its warped and furred planks. Its texture was almost like a rough suede, as if something were slowly dissolving it. The latch was a simple bolt and lock with a wide keyhole in it – no doubt where young Vera had knelt to spy on Lady Cooper.

'That's where she said the hole was, the one Lady Cooper shoved people into. Vera also talked about horror books; she said her mother collected them. Do you know what those were?'

'No idea,' Alec said, turning around and heading into a connecting room at the northern end of the great hall, one she hadn't spotted before. It was a small parlour with a roaring fire and a table set for breakfast.

'I thought we'd eat here.' Alec held out a chair for her. 'Easier to keep an eye on Mrs Pritchett.'

'Why do you want to do that?'

He frowned. 'Isn't it obvious, after all you saw yesterday?'

He continued with his oral history of the house before she could argue. 'The great hall used to be the main dining room but I'm told it was only used for parties in Sir Thomas's day; he preferred the renovated south side of the house and spent most of his time there. That's where his study was and a far less draughty dining room.'

'Which side did Lady Cooper prefer?' Sam asked, looking around. The parlour was certainly comfortable enough, almost cheery with its fire, and its small round table was far more intimate than the tree-length slab in the great hall. But it was very different from Lady Cooper's silken and cushioned bedroom; it was more in keeping with Vera's old room. The walls were a simple cream plaster, the furniture heavy and dark. There were two unmatched windows, one a small square, the other a narrow rectangle, and she could see a fringe of dripping icicles on both.

'Neither, I think she'd say.' Alec poured a cup of coffee from a tarnished silver pot on a sideboard and handed it to her. 'Lady Cooper was quite enthralled with the nuns' lives, according to my sisters, and probably would've claimed to have preferred the old dorter.'

'But her room upstairs,' Sam said. 'It's so elegant.' *Extravagant* was really the word she wanted to use, certainly extravagant by her standards.

'Yes,' Alec agreed. 'Notice that I said "claimed".' He threw her a devilish smile. 'I don't think she would've lasted a night.'

'You don't sound like you've ever liked anyone here.'

'Not true. I like you.'

She gave him a blunt stare. 'It can't be true,' she said.

'What?'

'Oh my god, it's just like *The Heiress*!' Sam feigned a head slap. 'You're Morris Townsend. You're a fortune hunter!' She peered more closely at Alec. 'Well your features are a little sharper than Montgomery Clift's. There's not a hint of lost lamb to you.'

'I haven't the faintest idea what you're talking about,' he replied as he began to fiddle with the dishes at the sideboard.

Sam tossed a sugar cube into her mouth like an aspirin and chased it with the coffee. 'That makes me shy, naive Catherine.' She suppressed a laugh. *Donna would agree with that.*

'Are these neighbours of yours in Brooklyn? This Morris and Monty?' Alec said, presenting her with a plate of eggs.

'And look at these eggs,' she went on in mock horror. 'They aren't burned. They're so raw you could hatch a chick out of them. I knew I couldn't trust you.'

Alec smiled and handed her a bowl filled with a congealed yet half-burned mass. 'Yes. Well. I was spot on about the porridge.' They were laughing when the housekeeper came in, carrying a platter of thin slices of what looked like boiled meat.

'A question, Mrs Pritchett,' Alec said. '"Horror books" in Lady Cooper's study, the prioress's chamber. Does that mean anything to you?'

'Horror books? What?' The housekeeper put the platter down, and pushed up the sleeves of her dress – she was wearing violet today. 'Afraid I don't know what you're talking about. I can't imagine Lady Cooper having any such thing.'

'A legitimate question.' Alec threw his hands up. 'Miss Vera's words, and she had no reason to lie. So what are they?'

'That girl.' The housekeeper scowled. 'Still causing tr—'

She caught herself, tried to smooth it over with a warm smile at Sam. 'Nothing but fun and games, I imagine.'

'Yes. But not Vera's from the sound of it. And we have reason to believe that she called the room itself the horror chamber. Any idea why? No? Well then, let's look now, shall we?'

'Suit yourself,' the housekeeper said, checking the coffee pot. 'You know where it is. I'm much too busy. Though I thought I heard the telephone ring just a bit ago. Do you think that means it's working again?'

Alec stared at her for a second. 'You didn't think to mention that earlier?'

'Oh!' Mrs Pritchett blinked rapidly, as if trying to remember something. 'Were you waiting for a call?'

Alec drained his cup and excused himself.

Mrs Pritchett put a hand to her cheek and pursed her lips. 'Or was it the bell at the back door I heard?' She shook her head and sighed. 'Hard to tell one ring from another; my hearing's not what it was. Oh never mind.' She smiled and walked over to put a hand on Sam's shoulder. 'Now, Miss Samantha, did you sleep well? Were you warm enough? I thought about checking on you, but I then said to myself, she's a smart lass, if she needs help, she won't be shy.'

She's lying about the phone, Sam thought. She was as sure of that as the Dodgers choking against the Yankees. 'What if that call was about his brother?'

Mrs Pritchett only shrugged and clasped her hands in front of her, rocking slightly on her heels. There was an air of expectation about her and Sam realised the woman was waiting for her to invite her to sit down.

'Mrs Pritchett, can I get you a cup of coffee?' Sam got up

and held out a chair for the housekeeper. It would be a good opportunity to get the woman talking.

'Oh that would be lovely. Thank you, Miss Samantha,' Mrs Pritchett said, clearly pleased.

Sam poured out a cup of coffee and put it in front of the housekeeper, along with the silver sugar dish and milk jug.

'Oh I really shouldn't,' the woman said, smiling. 'But I suppose it's unusual times, what with the storm and you here, and there's so much for you to catch up on. I am sure Lady Cooper would understand if we suspended the formalities just a bit?'

'Of course she would,' Sam agreed, understanding the hidden meaning of the housekeeper's remarks: the housekeeper was not to sit with the family unless invited.

Sam sat back down and started to eat her porridge; she was positively starving. 'It does seem strange,' she said after a bite. 'Do you think Roger got caught in the storm?'

Mrs Pritchett clucked. 'I wouldn't worry about those boys. They know a shovel from a spade, all right. Why if I were Roger Bell, I'd have made sure I got myself trapped somewhere nice with my sweetheart. That's what one should do in a storm like this.'

There was a note of disappointment in her voice and she pulled out her handkerchief and unfolded it.

'Oh, where's Mr Pritchett? Where does he work?' She regretted asking as soon as she'd said it; the woman had mentioned that her bedroom was downstairs in what had been the butler's parlour. It seemed an odd location for a married couple, and now Sam realised the woman might be widowed.

Mrs Pritchett sniffed, dabbed at her nose. 'Never had time for a husband.'

'Oh,' said Sam, slightly relieved. 'But I thought you were *Mrs* Pritchett.'

The housekeeper waved her handkerchief and laughed a little. 'Aye, the *Mrs* goes with the title of housekeeper, not with a husband. A bit old-fashioned I suppose; the masters thought it more dignified than to say some old spinster was ordering the staff about. Fewer questions, too, I expect.'

She sipped at her coffee, went on. 'Might have got a husband once things got quieter here, sad as it were – after your grandfather died and Lady Cooper had that big stroke. I still had some beauty about me then. But no, those solicitors kept us too busy. Henry Bell – Alec's father, you know – came in and cut the staff, the wages, the expenses.' She stirred her coffee in an aimless sort of way. 'Then there was the war, and what capable servants we had left. They went off to fight or work in the factories. These days we only get the ones dropped on their heads as babies.'

'It can't be that bad, can it?'

'Oh aye.' The housekeeper folded her arms across her chest. 'Those boys do expect me to do it all myself. It's not that I mind the work. But it's not fair to Lady Cooper. It used to be such a fine house. Everyone wanted to come here to visit, to dine with the family. It's all gone now. I can't think of a Christmas worse than this one. Not a single visitor. Only that Roger Bell came by, and I wouldn't call his visit friendly. All I asked was that he raise the wages a little, so I could get some proper help. But he wouldn't hear of it! Said things had to change! What does he know about "things"?'

'Well, it's nice that he came to see you, isn't it?' Sam wasn't sure what to say. 'Maybe you misunderstood him. Maybe he didn't want to mix business with pleasure.'

'Bah!' said the housekeeper. 'He wouldn't know pleasure if it was wrapped up in Princess Margaret's brassiere!' Sam laughed, but Mrs Pritchett's eyes had taken on a red, watery tinge. Sam got up and threw some more wood on the fire. She picked up the coffee pot and poured the last of it into the housekeeper's cup. 'I'll go make some more.'

Mrs Pritchett suddenly grabbed Sam's wrist, fear in her eyes. 'He only comes when he has bad news. But now you're here! You can change things, can't you, Miss Samantha? You can talk to them. Get those boys to see the sense of it.'

'They wouldn't listen to me, and they shouldn't – what do I know? Besides…' Sam thought back to yesterday. How they'd found her grandmother's door locked, with Lady Cooper presumably inside alone. Then later, once the door was unlocked, the night nurse standing there, doing nothing, while Lady Cooper had a fit. Something wasn't right here. *Something* needed to change. It was one thing to lock your demented granny inside the apartment for a few hours so you could go to the store. Another thing when the family was rich and had no excuse.

'Maybe things *should* change,' Sam said. 'It might be for the better. Better for you too.' She put her hand on top of Mrs Pritchett's, trying to calm her.

'That's not what they have in mind at all,' the woman whispered, her lower lip trembling. 'They used to come here when they were children, when their father had business with Sir Thomas. Sometimes they'd get lost out in the ruins and we'd have to go and find 'em and dry their tears. Now they come here and issue orders! Telling me this and telling me what I should do!'

133

'What's this about tears?' Alec had come back into the room.

'Is the phone working?' Sam asked.

'No. And there's a good two feet of snow on that drive. I don't know what I'm going to do.' He pushed his fingers through his hair, spiking it up in frustration.

He looks like a cooped-up Dobermann, Sam thought. *He needs something to do before he starts biting.*

Mrs Pritchett was thinking the same thing, apparently. She said: 'Well, there's more than enough work for you here.' The housekeeper rose from the breakfast table. 'The coal scuttles need filling if we're to get through this storm. Might give you a proper sense of what it takes to run this place.' She strode out with her nose in the air.

Sam sat back down and cut into a slice of the cold boiled meat, then stopped. It wasn't boiled meat but barely cooked bacon. She went back to work on the porridge. 'I'm sure your brother is fine,' she said between spoonfuls.

'We've no idea.' Alec was tapping a cigarette on the top of his case and Sam frowned at him; she particularly hated the smell of cigarette smoke when she was eating. Her mother had always opened the window, but it never helped.

'What about his wife? Is she gone, too?' She thought back to what Mrs Pritchett had said, that Roger might be off with his sweetheart somewhere. A wife, or a lady friend? 'Maybe he took her on a surprise trip to celebrate the new year, and they got snowed in somewhere.'

'Roger isn't married. My sisters used to tease him…' He laughed nervously, then stopped and gave her a funny look.

'Tease him about what?'

'Oh that was all nonsense, really. Roger is married to his

work. But' – his tone became serious again, adamant – 'Roger isn't impulsive. He's punctual, reliable. Never missed a day of work in his life. Never knew him to miss an appointment either. Certainly not one as important as this.'

He lit his cigarette and took a seat next to Sam. *Does he have to sit so close?* she thought and then suppressed her irritation. 'Mrs Pritchett said that when she saw him around Christmas, she didn't notice anything unusual.' That he hadn't been any more unpleasant than usual was what Mrs Pritchett had implied, but passing that along wouldn't help.

'She didn't tell me that. She never said Roger had been by.' Anger flashed across Alec's face and he fixed his eyes on the doorway Mrs Pritchett had just gone through. 'When did she tell you this?'

'Just now, when you were checking the phone. She said he came here, sometime between Christmas and New Year's.'

Alec took a deep drag on his cigarette. 'Of course. I bet she knows exactly where he is.'

'Why would you say that?' Sam didn't understand. It was obvious how concerned Alec was; if Mrs Pritchett had any information, of course she would tell him.

'From the moment we arrived, she's been lying. That business about expecting you on Tuesday instead of Saturday. Mrs Pritchett is a resourceful woman, and as I've said, my brother doesn't make mistakes like that. Then she claims she heard the telephone, but doesn't bother to answer it – how often do you think they get a phone call here? Not bloody often. She doesn't think it urgent to tell me that the phone is working, or think that I might very much be interested in a call? She made it up to distract me.'

'But why?' This certainly was an earful; at least Alec was finally divulging something. But this business with the housekeeper wasn't Sam's priority. Vera was.

'For one' – he looked around the table in distaste, at the uncooked bacon, the burned porridge, the tarnished silver milk jug – 'I'm not Roger. She's afraid that I'll see too much and push Roger to make a move. And she's right. The daffiness is an act.' He pulled an ashtray towards him and tapped his cigarette against it. 'Putting a rancid rabbit in a stew. What nonsense.'

'I don't know,' Sam said. 'Isn't she digging her own grave with that one?'

'No, not in her mind. It's not her job to cook, it's beneath her; she thinks we'd not expect her to do a good job. She's trying to make the point that the house needs more live-in staff, better trained, better paid. Can't you just hear her? "Those Bell brothers, do you know what they expect me to serve Lady Cooper? And who am I to tell them otherwise? I've only been the housekeeper here thirty years!"' He threw up his hands and fluttered them in imitation, then jabbed his cigarette towards Sam, 'But she greatly underestimates me.'

Sam took the cigarette from between his fingers and put it out in the ashtray; he was getting too worked up.

'If Roger truly thought her incompetent,' Alec went on, ignoring her, 'and Lady Cooper was in harm's way by Mrs P's neglect, he would have done something sooner. As it was, he merely saw her as eccentric, a housekeeper who in absence of a strong master or mistress had taken on too much a sense of ownership of the house. I hate to use the phrase, it's such a nasty one, but it's the easiest way to say it. He seemed to be of the opinion that she was only "getting above her station".'

Alec saw Sam wince at that, and apologised. 'The fact remains, Begars has long needed a change. A very big change.'

*

'Off to get that coal in? Good on you,' the housekeeper said to Alec when he and Sam walked into the kitchen. She was standing at the large oak table, a paring knife held awkwardly in her misshapen hand as she slowly peeled a potato.

'When was Roger here?'

'Hmmm?' She dunked the potato in a bowl of water to rinse it, and picked up another.

'When was he here?'

'Oh I can't be expected to remember!' Mrs Pritchett waved the knife in the air, eyes looking off to the side; Sam noticed she did that when agitated. 'He showed up sometime last week; he didn't even bother to let me know he was coming. Would have had a nice tea ready for him. But I told you all this.'

Alec narrowed his eyes; he thought she was lying. 'Would you mind telling me again?'

'Not much to tell. It was a short visit.' She cocked her head, as if it were an irksome memory. 'You boys are much too important for a chat by the fire these days.'

Alec took the knife out of her hand and began to peel a potato. 'Here, let me help you,' he said sweetly. 'My sisters would never let me hear the end of it if I didn't, letting you do all this work by yourself.'

Mrs Pritchett smiled at Alec, pleased with the offer of help.

137

'Thought I'd make corned beef and dumplings, with some cabbage and potato. A good dish for a cold winter's day. Would you fancy that?'

'I think that sounds lovely. Did he tell you anything in particular?' Alec wasn't letting the matter go.

'The usual... more things to economise. Cut this, cut that.'

Sam could tell his good-boy routine was an act. What was the saying? You can catch more flies with honey?

'When exactly was he here? Three days ago? Six days ago?'

'Yes, yes, somewhere around there.'

Alec nodded. 'Roger likes talking about the old days at Begars. He is quite fond of the place. We both have happy memories of it, our father, too.'

'Oh he did want to talk about the old days! But none of the happy memories! He only wanted to dredge up the bad ones. "Now why do you want to ask about that, Mr Bell?" That's what I said to him! "Vera's dead. Lady Cooper has suffered enough. It can't matter!"'

'*Miss* Vera,' Alec seethed.

Game over, thought Sam.

'What happened back then must matter,' she interrupted. 'Or else Roger wouldn't have asked about it. And we all would've known about each other long before this.' She saw why Alec had an aversion to the woman. She was dotty for sure, but there was an edge to her words. The way she said Vera's name, as if it were bitter in her mouth.

Mrs Pritchett shrugged her shoulders, then disappeared for a moment into a storeroom off the kitchen. She came back carrying a cabbage and an onion. 'I told him, I'm sorry, Mr Bell,' she continued, 'but I don't have any answers, and I don't appreciate these questions. That was such a hard time! So hard on Lady Cooper.'

'The questions, then. Remind me what they were?' Alec walked over to a jug and poured a glass of water, handed it to Sam, murmured, 'It's good, from the well. I suspect you have a headache, listening to this. This will clear it right up.' She gave him a half-smile as he poured another glass for himself. His back to the housekeeper, he muttered, 'I know I do.'

'Why he said he wanted to tidy everything up for Miss Samantha.' Her reedy voice was starting to shake. 'Said he wanted to look through the family papers. I told him he had all the family papers, didn't he, back at his office! Your father took them all years ago.'

'That doesn't make any sense,' Alec said, looking at Sam.

'That's your family, isn't it!' The old woman rubbed her swollen knuckles. 'He asked all sorts of questions about Vera. *Miss* Vera,' she quickly corrected herself. 'Did I remember this and did I remember that! Why did she leave, that sort of thing. I told him, I didn't remember anything and I don't want to! So he said he would go to London. Vera – *Miss* Vera – went there right after she left. Roger said he had the address of where she had stayed.'

Sam saw Alec visibly relax. He took a breath, gave Sam a nearly imperceptible nod. They were getting somewhere. 'I don't know where she went in London or why,' Mrs Pritchett went on. She took her handkerchief out of her pocket, dabbed at her nose, then pointed to the kettle, her hand shaking. The woman was clearly rattled. 'Tea? Would anyone like a cup of tea? Whatever her reason, I'm sure it was not a good one. Any more than that you'll have to ask your brother! Why was he asking me after so long? He had years and years to ask Vera these things! Is it my fault he didn't?' Mrs Pritchett was quite emotional now, wringing her hands. 'Why did he expect me to have the answers? He and Vera did have that in common, didn't they! Always late to the party!'

15

Sam stood up, her chair scraping hard against the floor, and left the room without a word. She'd had enough of listening to Mrs Pritchett dodging questions, her snide comments about Vera, and didn't pity her one bit the tongue-thrashing she would now get from Alec.

She was unsure of what to do. What was she *supposed* to do? She headed towards her room but as she climbed the stairs, she heard a rumbling in the distance. As if a great engine were nearing the house. She reached the gallery and peered through its windows, the air changing around her. It was brittle, charged, almost as if it were biting into her. Just then, a bolt of lightning ripped through the sky and struck a tree near the back of the ruins. The crack of its trunk and the thunder that followed were almost deafening. Moments later, another flash lit the sky, eerily illuminating the ruins and falling snow.

Thundersnow, she thought, marvelling at the scene. She'd seen it once when she was little. A devil of a cold front had come down from Canada and smashed apart a warm front off the Atlantic, and damn if it hadn't sounded like the building was coming down on their heads. Vera hadn't been much bothered by it, but Sam had jumped into her mother's bed and begged Vera to hide under the covers with her. Vera had only smiled softly then nestled Sam's head against her chest, and eventually the sound of her mother's warm, steady heartbeat had lulled her to sleep.

Sam jumped at another crack of thunder – this time joined by a prolonged screech from Mrs Pritchett – and imagined Donna saying, 'That's your cue, dope.' She reversed course and headed back down through the great hall, stopping at the squat planked door that led to Lady Cooper's study. Vera's horror chamber. Was any of it true, that's what Sam wanted to know. Vera had written that somewhere beyond this door was a hidden cell, one that Lady Cooper imprisoned people in. She drew back the bolt.

The first thing Sam noticed was that the ceiling seemed to sag and the walls bowed out in places; something was amiss with the foundations here. The floor sloped down towards the outer wall, and then, across the room, her gaze locked on a set of beguilingly wide eyes outlined in thick black. She stood frozen for a second, until she realised it was a crude, larger-than-life fresco of the Virgin Mary holding the baby Jesus and encircled by angels. Sam walked over to get a better view, then slowly traced the faded brown outline of an angel's wing, its rippling edge. A few hints of the fresco's original colouring remained – a dirty cream for what had once been the gold of Mary's halo, a dark grey for a gown that might have been a vibrant blue. *A ghost of a fresco, but in its day it would've been stunning*, she thought. A door was to the right of the fresco; the front hall and stairs would be on the other side of it.

The wall opposite the fresco – the one near the door she'd come through – was covered with a large tapestry. According to Vera's diary, behind it would be a false beam that opened onto the hidden cell. She crossed the room and paused at a desk in front of the tapestry. Its wood was nearly black with age, and there was a grimy glass display case in the centre of it. Next to it, there was a bust of a woman – a netting of cracks ran through the ivory paint of her face and the gold of her hair. Sam shuddered and looked away. She noticed a wide shallow drawer tucked underneath the desktop – perhaps this was where the pistol had been kept? Sam gave it a tug, but it was locked.

The desk was not the focus of her search, so she got on with it and turned to pull back the tapestry, coughing at the dust it released. The wall itself was plaster and just as Vera had written, there was a beam set into it. In fact, there were two beams, each no more than a foot wide. *Way too small to be an entrance*, Sam thought. *Who could fit through there?* Only a very thin person; certainly not anyone stout, like Mrs Pritchett or Donna. She laughed darkly at the image of Donna stuck sideways in the entrance.

Sam pinned the tapestry back with a chair that had been behind the desk and squatted down to examine the beams, looking for anything that might suggest a lever. There was a small gouged section in the wood at the base of one, but it looked like nothing more than a mouse hole. She cupped her fingers around its edges and pulled. To her astonishment, the beam shifted slightly away from the wall and she heard the dusty sound of bits of old plaster falling to the floor. This was it. She got down on her knees and pulled harder, and when the beam refused to give any further, she pushed her fingers deeper into the hole. She brushed against something metal and blindly pushed and pressed around it, searching for a latch that might give.

Finally she heard a click and then the bottom edge of the beam swung out violently and knocked against her knees. She fell back swearing, staring at the beam that now stood ajar from the wall at its base. *Goddamn, Vera was at least telling the truth about this.* There *was* a hidden door. She felt a catch in her throat – what else was Vera right about? She got up into a squat and with great effort – it was a solid piece of wood, seven or so feet long and a good five inches thick – swung the beam up a little higher, revealing an empty space beyond, the entrance covered with cobwebs. *This is just crazy.* It couldn't all be true. It had to be some sort of game of Vera's, like Mrs Pritchett had said. Lady Cooper couldn't have stuffed people in here.

Sam slipped out into the great hall, stopping only for a moment to watch as another flash of light filled the sky. The thunder was not as quick to follow – the storm was moving off. *Good riddance*, she thought, as she grabbed an old oil lamp and matches, went back to the study and quietly closed the door behind her. She took the chair, and with some manoeuvring used its back to lever the beam up higher, all the while using her body to hold the dusty tapestry at bay. She then swivelled the chair so the beam rested across its arms, and resecured the tapestry behind it. She pulled at the sticky tangle of cobwebs from the entrance, grimacing as she did so, then wiped her hands on her skirt and bent under the beam. She shone the oil lamp into the space behind it.

She gasped – there was a small vestibule on the other side, not much bigger than the wardrobe upstairs in Vera's bedroom. But it wasn't a cell. It was an entrance to a spiral staircase heading one way. Down. Every bone in her body screamed *turn back*. *Get Alec*. She didn't listen.

The steps were narrow and steep, descending about eight feet. There was another vestibule at the bottom, with an iron gate opposite the foot of the stairs. She held up the lamp and peered through its bars – a tunnel stretched out behind it. *Holy moly*, she thought. *What is this?* She half-heartedly pulled on the gate; she wasn't sure she was up for this adventure, but the gate squeaked open in response. She willed herself forward into the darkness.

A swell of wind came towards her from down the tunnel; as it passed by she felt a shock, similar to what she'd felt upstairs in the gallery, right before the lightning strike, and then, the day before, when a gust of wind had blown open the front door and seemed to tangle around her. The wind was icy, yes, but it carried something with it – the feeling of desperation, of panic. She shivered, then looked ahead into the pure black of the tunnel. *There's nothing down here*, she reminded herself. *There's nothing in the house. It's all empty.* Did Vera really think Lady Cooper came down here? She thought of that elegant woman two floors above, sitting in her wheelchair in her immaculate room, that beautiful cream silk shawl over her shoulders, her proud profile. Sam couldn't see a younger Lady Cooper traipsing about down here, getting her satins and silks all dirty. And for what purpose? Vera had said her mother was punishing people, imprisoning them in a cell, but didn't say who or why. Looking down this dreary passage, it didn't make sense. 'Christ almighty, too much work!' she imagined Donna saying. 'All this dirt? Who does that? If you wanna teach someone a lesson, all you need is a belt!'

Nonsense, pure nonsense, she thought, but decided to keep exploring – the flame in the lamp seemed confident enough. The ceiling was low and rounded, the walls were made out of pale stones once plastered over but now spotted and cracked with age; broken bits of stone crunched under her feet as she walked. There were rusted sconces set periodically along the tunnel walls, and wispy waves of cobwebs reached down from the ceiling, brushing her face and arms as she went. The souls of dead nuns, she imagined, released at last from purgatory by the singe of her lamp's flame. *Knock it off*, she told herself. *That's not gonna help.*

The tunnel seemed to go on forever, though for all she knew she might have only walked thirty feet. She was shaking a little – it was a strange and threatening feeling to walk underground all alone in the dark, destination unknown. She stifled a nervous laugh; every horror movie she'd ever seen told her not to do this. Some scabbed, slimy hand was sure to reach out to drag her down down down, never to be seen again.

'Cool it, Sam,' she said out loud. She was too giddy, too lightheaded. Was it a lack of oxygen? She took several deep breaths, blew out hard. Then she heard a long, low whistle – the wind was building again. She imagined more dead nuns sweeping towards her, their mouths open in a full discordant chorus, the notes snagging on their broken teeth. The wind rose to a piercing, pleading howl. It swept right through her, the ice of it so cold it hurt her chest as she breathed it in.

That's enough, she thought. *I need a coat, a knife, a wooden stake. A map. A bigger light.* She was just about to turn around when the sound of her footsteps changed, the floor no longer littered with broken stones. She had come out into a large octagonal chamber and as she held up her lamp, she could see a vaulted brick ceiling. Several other arched passages veered off the chamber, and she thought she saw a faint light in one, but then breathed a sigh of relief. As soon as she had shifted, it disappeared; it was nothing more than a reflection from her lamp.

On the walls in between the passages, there were three large stone blocks. Tombs. Sam realised what this place was: the crypt. She must be under the ruins of the convent church.

The lid was cracked on the tomb closest to her; half of it lay smashed on the floor. She braced herself and looked in – empty. She walked towards the next one, but her light caught on something white on the floor and her heart stopped. Laid out along a nearby wall were six skeletons, each arranged in a different position. Sam felt the hair on the back of her neck rise; she had never seen such a ghoulish sight. She took more deep breaths to steady herself, then took a step closer to the bones.

One skeleton was set slightly apart from the others. It still had hair attached to its skull: thick and black, startlingly neat and shiny, as if the skeleton combed it every morning. Its bones glistened in the lamplight; they were coated in a thin layer of some yellow substance. *Grave wax?* She'd heard a lecture on ancient burial practices and tomb raiders at the Met but never thought she'd see something like this first-hand. This couldn't be normal, leaving skeletons lying about?

Then she felt as if someone had run a finger right down her spine; behind her, there was a skittering sound, like something was stumbling across small stones or debris. Something large. Then she heard a low, hoarse plea: 'Stay. Please stay.'

Sam turned and ran. She was back at the tunnel gate before she knew it, trying not to pant from the exertion and give her location away. But the damn thing had swung shut – the wretched wind – and only now did she notice there was a lock on it. She pushed at it and put her shoulder against it, cursing herself for not propping it open. She put the lamp down on the floor and tried lifting up on the gate, thinking the bolt was slightly unaligned and just needed a good shove, but there was nothing doing. *Son of a...* She rattled the bars, hoping to shake loose whatever rusted crap was trapping her in. The wind swelled down the passage again, buzzing in her ears as if she was stuck inside some diabolical radio. She was shivering now from the wind, the cold; her fingers were numb but she had no doubt they were bloody from trying to prise open the gate. She reached down to get the lamp, thinking to use its light to inspect the lock mechanism, but she misjudged where she'd put it and knocked it over. The globe shattered and the light flickered out. *Son of a...* she thought again. She knelt down to relight the flame... then paused. The wind had stopped blowing and the air had become heavy, intolerably heavy – as if she was suddenly in a sealed submarine sinking to the very bottom of the ocean. A fetid smell surrounded her and her stomach heaved; she knew that smell. Donna's grandmother. In her Sunday best, laid out flat on the parlour table. All the relatives and neighbours coming by to pay their respects. For days. The kids daring each other to go up and touch her. The sweet, putrid smell of death.

She heard a crunch in the tunnel behind her. Then another.

A step. Steps. It had followed her. Of course it had. Her back was to it, but she could sense its eyes on her, its anger palpable. It was willing her to turn around, to look at it. She was frozen in a crouch, unable to move. She heard another crunch, a phlegmy inhalation. It was almost on her, close enough to feel its breath. She heard a howl of wind sweep up from behind, and she wished for it to carry her away... but goddamn if its iciness didn't jumpstart her this time and, channeling Donna, she rammed through the gate like a wrecking ball. But not before she felt the scrape of fingernails against her neck.

16

Sam leapt up the spiral steps, scrambled under the beam, burst out into the prioress's chamber and nearly bowled Alec over. Mrs Pritchett was there too, and Sam could've sworn the woman looked as scared as she did. Alec just looked mad.

'How did you manage this?' he asked. 'I only left you for a minute.'

Mrs Pritchett pushed Alec out of the way and pulled the chair out from under the beam, letting it slam shut and the tapestry fall back over it. 'Don't go down there again! People get lost down there!' She waved her gnarled hand and handkerchief at Sam. 'Your mother got lost down there once! We didn't find her for days!' The housekeeper turned on Alec. 'It's your fault. You don't listen to me! I told your brother to seal this up! It's dangerous! You don't listen! What will it take?' She hobbled towards the door. 'I'll get cement, I will. Seal it up myself! I blame you! You've tied my hands. Always have! What will it take to make you boys see sense?'

Alec didn't respond, just kept his eyes fixed on Sam. She knew what he saw. Another pair of ruined nylons. Her face red with cold, her fingers bloody. He pulled a cobweb from her hair, then brushed the sticky strands from his hands and started to say something but Sam cut him off. She wasn't going to let him lecture her.

'There's a tunnel,' she said. 'It leads to the crypt. There were skeletons lying around on the floor. And god…' She hesitated; she knew how crazy this was going to sound. 'There was… *something* down there. Walking. Talking. It chased me down the tunnel. It asked me to stay.'

'Yes. I told you, didn't I? Dracula,' he said, unmoved.

'Shut up.' She was still shaking from whatever had happened in the tunnel. 'If you don't believe me, let's go back down, right now.'

He arched an eyebrow and said, 'Ah Christ, not you too? And here I thought you a sensible sort of person.' He walked over to the tapestry and pulled it back to examine the beam. 'It's not that I don't believe you. Something scared you down in that tunnel. I can see that.'

Sam pointed to the fake mouse hole. 'The latch is down there.'

'How did you find this?' Alec knelt down and whistled, ran his hand along the beam.

'Vera wrote about it in her diary; she was spying on her mother and saw Lady Cooper come out from under it.'

'What? Are you sure?'

Sam nodded. He looked at her for a moment, then reached his fingers into the cavity at the bottom of the beam.

'You'd better move out of the way,' she warned. 'It packs a punch.'

Alec inched over to the side of the beam, then she heard the latch click and the beam swung open.

Impressed, Alec whistled again. 'I didn't know about the

trick door. But I've seen the bones myself. Old dead nuns.' He stood up and pressed the beam closed. 'We used to play down there with kids from the village, from the estate. Vera, too. Easy way to soil your trousers. Though we went in through the door down by the church ruins. But I have to agree with Mrs Pritchett. It's not safe and my brother should have had it filled in years ago.'

Sam felt hot, flushed. She wasn't going to let him dismiss what she'd seen. She was fed up with that kind of treatment. She'd had too many years of it with Vera.

'I'm serious.' Her voice was shaking. 'There is someone – something – down there.' She felt her legs start to shake too; was it shock setting in? Or was it merely this confrontation? For most of her life she'd given in to those with stronger temperaments. They had always left her feeling that they must be right, because their convictions were so much stronger than hers; they were so much more willing to hold the line. Even Donna was like that. Especially Donna.

Alec's expression changed from his usual one of annoyance and disbelief to something softer. He was looking at her the same way he had after the car crash. He was worried about her again.

'I'm sorry, Sam; I hadn't realised how upset you were. I can't imagine what it's like for you, coming to this strange place. The thing is, you are right. There probably *is* something down there.'

She clenched her fists, waited for the punchline.

'This house is filled with ghosts. I have no doubt of that. Ghosts are a dime a dozen in Yorkshire. But I've always been far more concerned about the living than the dead. I think they do the worst damage. It's possible you saw a ghost. But really, I think it's some vagrant sheltering from the storm, or come to think of it, someone could've been living down there undetected for quite some time, the way this place is run. There's another entrance to the crypt from the woods.'

Sam felt the tension drain out of her body. She felt better and worse at the same time. Yes, that made far more sense. A bum, that was all. A stinking bum.

'That would explain the smell,' she admitted. The scrape of fingernails against her neck... it had been trying to grab her; there was a real physical presence to the thing. Sam didn't believe in ghosts; she had never been the fanciful type, and neither had Vera. Well, not the Vera she had known.

'Now come on, let's get you something warm to drink.'

Sam hung back, glancing around at the room as if it might reveal more secrets. She looked down at the old black desk and her eye stopped on the glass case. Its frame was an ornate, gilded wood, but the glass was cloudy with years of dust. She rubbed at it with the cuff of her blouse.

'My god, aren't you filthy enough?' she heard Alec groan.

Inside were three small books, carefully spaced. She checked the cuts on her fingers – they were minor, most of them had stopped bleeding, so she wiped her hands on her skirt and started to open the case. Alec groaned even more loudly at this and told her to stand back. 'I'll do it for you. Which one?' She pointed to the one in the centre. Its binding was leather, the corners frayed and the spine cracked with age. The stiff cover was bordered with gold leaf, and there were four miniature oval portraits framed in gold, each anchored to a corner and about the size of a doe eye. The subject was the same: the Madonna and Child. The book was secured with a fabulous silver clasp. Alec fumbled with its tiny lever, so Sam pulled her sleeves down over her hands to protect the book and took it from him. She used a dry nail to open the lever, her eyes lighting up at the gossamer-thin pages. She turned them carefully, stopping at a brilliant illumination of a woman on her knees praying to the Virgin Mary. This Mary's gown was still a vibrant blue, her gold halo bright as a comet. The woman kneeling before Mary was in a scarlet robe. The colours were as vivid as if they had been painted yesterday. Sam had seen books like this before, at the Met; it looked medieval or Renaissance. Not a Bible, but a prayer book of some sort. It had to be a replica though, surely it wouldn't be left out like this? She turned back to the cover page.

HORAE, in laudē beatiſs. virginis MARIAE

She could hear Alec lighting a cigarette, no doubt in irritation. She ignored him, focused on the words before her. She had never taken Latin, but she could guess some of it. *Horare.* Rare? Schedule? Time? *In laudē beatiſs.* In beautiful praise. Of the Virgin Mary. Or in praise of the blessed Virgin Mary? Maybe Alec would know. She looked at the text again. Not Horare. *Horae.* Hours?

She picked up one of the other two books from the case. It was beautiful, too, its cover set with semi-precious stones. There was an unusual texture to the pages in this book; she could see ripples – wavering lines in the material of the page itself, as if it were made from skin. The desiccation of the pages was in high contrast to the brilliant illuminations upon them, which looked so alive, so fresh. Sam shuddered and put it back. The third book was in French, and on the cover page above a delicately sketched skull she picked out the words *memento mori* and *heures*.

Memento mori, she repeated to herself. *Remember death*.

'Alec,' she said slowly. 'I think this might be it.'

He stood up from the behind the desk – he'd been examining the latch on the beam – and looked over her shoulder as she showed him the drawing of the skull, the words she had picked out. 'This might be where the name comes from, where Vera got the word horror from.' She leafed through the pages, showed him the various spellings. '*Hore intemerate virginis marie fecundū. Horae. Heures. Hore.* Horror. Maybe these are the books, Lady Cooper's horror books.' She felt somewhat deflated at the thought. 'But why? This is a little creepy' – she handed him the book with the pages the texture of dried skin – 'but not outright horrifying. What did they make this from? Just animal skin, right?' She looked around; the room was certainly on the dark side, with its heavy furnishings and only two thin narrow windows for light, and she tried to see it through the eyes of a child. 'Though I guess if I were a kid, I would find this place really creepy – but it can't be anything more than a play on words, can it?'

'I doubt it. There's nothing sinister here,' said Alec, who had already returned the book to its case. 'Just rot. Too much of it. I'd have come up with the same thing if I'd had to grow up locked away in here, in an ancient house full of secret passages, not to mention being next to the ruins of a church with a crypt full of dead nuns. Often women unwanted by their families, their lives wasted. Women like Mrs Pritchett.'

'Stop it. That's a disgusting thing to say. About her or anybody. You don't know that. The nuns, they might have had great lives here. At the very least, they had a good home and that's not nothing. That's a whole lot better than nothing.'

'You're absolutely right. I apologise. This place brings it out in me.'

'I doubt that.'

Alec's brow furrowed and his black eyes flared in anger. At himself, she could tell. 'The last thing I want to do is offend you. I didn't mean it. Except about Mrs P. I'm frustrated by this whole bloody situation. I need to find Roger. I don't like it at all, being stuck here and not knowing what's happened to him.'

Sam exhaled loudly; she was pretty exasperated too. 'I know, I'm sorry. It's just Vera was deeply disturbed by something at Begars, to the point that after she left, she never mentioned the place to anyone except your brother and father it seems. And then there's her diaries. She's fifteen and so worried about something here that she was spying on Lady Cooper. She thought her mother was whipping people.'

'A whip? Vera said that?' Alec looked shocked.

'Yes.' Sam paused. 'But I can't tell if she really meant it. But she definitely thought her mother was doing something she shouldn't.'

'Well, in a place as old as this, I'm sure there have been plenty of horrors. Lots of raids during the Middle Ages, the Viking invasions. Not to mention the nuns thrown out after the Dissolution of the Monasteries.' He looked around the room. 'There is plenty to be scared of here.' He nodded to the painted plaster bust on the corner of the desk. 'A forebear? A dead saint? Or a death mask of the last prioress? Sam?'

She had stopped listening. She was thinking about another face. The young woman walking towards them in the snow down the drive. Her thick unruly hair, her unflinching eyes. Could it have really been Vera? Was it her ghost? No, she refused to believe it.

'You're too pale,' she heard Alec say. 'You've had a shock. Let's get you in front of a fire, get some coffee – or brandy? – into you.'

'I'll be all right,' Sam said. 'You go ahead, I'll join you in a bit. I need to go clean up anyway.'

She saw him hesitate, so she forced a smile, an attempt to reassure him. 'Really. Go on. I promise. No more adventures without you.'

17

Sam thought about going straight to her grandmother's room; she had a strange need to see her, to look in the old woman's face and see living traces of Vera, not imaginary ones. But Sam knew she was a mess and so she headed instead for her own room – Vera's room – pausing once again at the gallery windows to look out on the church. Where was the door to the crypt Alec had mentioned? Directly below her, she suddenly realised, was the prioress's chamber – and the secret door and tunnel that led to the crypt. How many bodies were down there, stacked in those passages that had led off the main chamber? How many nuns exactly? Hundreds? And... she suddenly recalled Mrs Pritchett's face when she had crawled from under the beam, the woman's features rigid, waxen in real fear. What had she said to Sam? That Vera had been lost down there for days. Was it true? How old had she been? Was it that easy to get lost in the crypt? And why hadn't they sealed it off afterwards? If Sam had been trapped in some condemned old building for days – it wasn't unthinkable; rooting around abandoned buildings had been a decent enough way to pass the time as a kid in Brooklyn – she was sure the mothers would've bawled out the city council until it was torn down, and if the city took too long, the fathers would've done it with their own bare hands. A kid who always had a dirty face and dirty clothes, a kid who got the strap a little too often – people overlooked that. But not a missing kid. And if it was something more than an accident, if they caught whoever was responsible, they were never seen again. She thought about screwy Mr Thompson. They did find his billfold floating against a pier in the Hudson. His American Legion card still in it. Along with a finger.

She walked into her bedroom, the temperature rising an instant five degrees. The fire and the candles were lit, and Ivy was in the process of making her bed.

Ivy curtsied, and Sam felt embarrassed all over again. What must she think of her? Ivy obviously took a lot of pride in keeping things tidy, and here was Sam with her nylons ripped, hair a squirrel's nest, knees bruised and fingers covered in dried blood. But Ivy was too polite or well trained to show any disapproval. All she said was, 'I've your clothes laid out for luncheon, miss.'

Sam smiled. This was a rather clever way to avoid telling Sam she needed to change; she'd give Ivy credit for that.

'Two options, if you like, miss.' Ivy held up a dark green, drop waist dress in wool and the navy blue dress with the sailor's collar she'd seen that morning.

Sam looked at her, dismayed. 'But, Ivy, I said you could have that one.'

Ivy frowned. 'Mrs Pritchett wouldn't like it, miss.'

Sam was annoyed. What did Mrs Pritchett care about an old dress?

'Take it, Ivy. I'll make sure she doesn't make a stink about it. I'll wear the green one.' The thought turned her stomach slightly. She didn't want to wear Vera's clothes, at least not these clothes, the ones from Vera's other life. It didn't sit right with Sam, she wasn't sure why. But her own supply of clothes was running perilously low. 'What I really need is stockings.'

'Oh yes, miss! Of course. I'll get them right away. And I've drawn a bath for you. That'll cheer you right up. I won't be long.'

She made me a bath? Sam couldn't believe it, couldn't get over the girl's eagerness to help her. She thought about the kids back home who behaved this way, who trailed after you down the street, never taking the hint. They were usually kids who were growing up without anyone to love them. 'You don't need to do all this. Really. It makes me feel weird. I'm not used to it.'

Ivy's smile fell a little and she turned to put the blue dress back in the wardrobe. *You're such a wet blanket, Sam.* Ivy seemed to really enjoy playing lady's maid. Who knew what the poor girl had to do the rest of the day? It had been Sam's job to clean the bathroom at the grocer's. Never a pretty sight.

Sam took the dress out of the wardrobe and forced it into Ivy's hands. 'Not another word.' Ivy's face lit up and she curtsied nervously and flitted out of the door. *That girl has nothing but sunshine in her head*, she thought.

She walked into the bathroom and was floored to see that as Ivy had promised, the porcelain claw-foot bathtub was filled, with a lovely rose-scented steam rising off it. She stripped off her clothes and threw them over a small, hard-backed chair. She dipped her foot into the warm water and it was as if she'd died and gone to heaven. They only had cold water in

Brooklyn – if you wanted hot water, you had to heat it up on the stove. When Sam was a little girl, her mother had done that once a week only in the winter – heating up pot after pot of water and pouring it into a tin hip tub. It took a surprising number of spaghetti pots to get even a few inches of hot water in the tub; she didn't know any different so she didn't mind at the time. But now... *This proves it*, she thought as she settled into the bath. *None of this is real.*

*

Sam didn't let herself soak for more than twenty minutes. She couldn't. She was still filled with the same nervous energy she'd had all morning; she was also sure that at any minute someone would come bursting through the door and ruin it anyway. Ivy. Mrs Pritchett. Alec. But it was long enough for her to dismiss what had happened in the crypt. The stuck gate. The skeletons. The clutching nails against her neck. Of course there were bones down there. Of course it stank. It was a crypt for god's sake.

The bathroom was narrow and behind the tub faucet was a rack with a thin white towel and a quilted dressing gown folded across it. She stood up and reached for the towel and was surprised to find that it was warm as she wrapped it around herself. She touched one of the satin spirals on the wine-coloured gown and almost drew her hand away in shock. It, too, was warm – Ivy must have heated both the gown and towel in front of the fire. And like everything else in these rooms, the gown must have belonged to Vera. She'd seen its cousin, knew it like an old friend – Vera's faded red chenille bathrobe.

Something suddenly occurred to her. There was no electricity and Mrs Pritchett had said that the boiler had gone out the day before the storm. She looked at the bathtub. How had Ivy gotten all that hot water? What army had she used to fill up the bath? *Dump Mrs P and put Ivy in charge.* That's what she would tell Alec.

Back in the bedroom, she looked at the green dress. It still struck her as wrong to put it on. It wasn't the same as wearing Vera's clothes back in Brooklyn. She knew that Vera; there was comfort in those clothes for Sam. But these? Her mother had fled this life. She thought back to those crazy get-ups Vera used to wear back home – all those duck prints and prancing ponies and mismatched clothes. Vera had not wanted to look elegant; she had not wanted to look 'put together'. Sam had thought it had all been an act so Vera could keep her distance from people. But it was more than that, she was starting to realise. And Sam knew for sure that Vera would not have wanted her to come back here and step into these clothes. And that's not why Sam was here.

She thought about the stolen jewellery. The voice in the crypt. The woman they'd nearly hit out in the storm. What was real? What wasn't? She tore at her thumbnail, got out the first diary she had found, the one written when Vera was older. Towel still wrapped around her, she sat down on the bed and flipped to the back. The last entry was dated December 1924. Vera was sixteen.

17th December 1924
Where is it? Where is that damn cell? It can't be the crypt.
There are lots of ways to get in and out of there. You

can't lock someone in down there. And the tomb lids are all broken. The blasted key is to a rusty old gate; you can kick the bloody thing open.

Sam paused. Vera must have meant the gate beneath the prioress's chamber.

Roger was down from Cambridge and I tried to get him to help me search but he's gone soft. Takes himself quite seriously these days. I told him that his father had his balls so tightly twisted they were in danger of snapping off. He still said no. I told him that if he didn't come with me, I'd invite his little brother along and forget to bring him back out. Roger did get angry at that, threatened to tell Mama. I do not think we shall marry after all...

Whoa. Whoa. Whoa. Vera had wanted to marry someone? She had wanted to marry *Roger*? Sam's head was spinning. That her mother had once had romantic thoughts. And that they were about Alec's brother. Roger Bell of the single-line yearly letter fame? The Roger who had told Sam not to come to Begars Abbey? *No way.* Vera had to have been teasing; it was as unlikely as everything else Vera wrote in her diaries. Who was this passionate, emotional, inventive, *suspicious* creature? Sam was starting to think there had been two Vera Coopers. She tore into the nail on another finger. This morning, at breakfast in the little parlour. They had been talking about Roger, where he could be, and Alec had said that his brother had never married, that their sisters used to tease Roger about it. *That jerk*, she thought. *He knows.* Roger and Vera had been an item. 'When I find him, I'm gonna wring his neck,' she hissed.

She flung off the damp towel and put the diary on the nightstand, then stared at the green wool dress hanging on the wardrobe door. *Fine, I'll wear it.* Sam quickly put on her undergarments, pulled the dress over her head, zipped it up then examined herself in the mirror. It was a good dress, but it still felt all wrong.

There was a timid knock on the door and Ivy came into the room, a silk bundle in her hands. The girl squealed with delight when she saw Sam. 'Miss, you look so beautiful! All it wants is this.' She laid the bundle on the bed and ran over to the dressing table. She took a brush to Sam's long, straight hair, then in a few flips had pinned it up into what Sam had to admit was a pretty good-looking chignon, much like Lady Cooper's. 'Such a lovely rich brown,' Ivy said, stepping back to admire her work. 'You might consider cutting it, miss. Could I try, miss? And a wave? With a curling iron?' With a last flick of the brush, Ivy artfully swept Sam's fringe to the side, then retrieved the silk bundle and opened it. Damn if the girl hadn't found some nylons. *No*, Sam shook her head in disbelief, they weren't nylons. They were silk, the real thing.

'And this, miss.' Ivy collected something from the dressing table, then came up to Sam and stood on her tiptoes. Before Sam could protest the girl had painted her lips red. 'Miss, with cheekbones like yours, you don't need anything more than that!'

She helped Sam slip into the black lattice pumps Sam had tried to give away – Sam scowled as Ivy did so – but then she caught her reflection in the mirror. Sam had never seen the woman looking back at her before. She looked nice. More than nice. Important. Mysterious. Sam sneezed. *That's more like it*, she thought. A touch of reality. The dress had been well looked after and was in good condition, but the dust had found a way in. She sneezed again and thought, *I'll put my slacks on, I don't care what Mrs Pritchett says. It's about time she joined the twentieth century.* But then she caught another glimpse of herself in the mirror. *Well, you've gone this far...*

18

'Do you know where Alec is?' Sam asked Mrs Pritchett. She had considered going to his bedroom, but she still didn't know where that was. She had looked in the rooms she knew downstairs, and then headed for the kitchen.

Mrs Pritchett, looking flustered and tired, hardly spared Sam a glance. She was at the old range, stirring a pot of something. Something oniony from the smell of it.

'You shouldn't be in here, Miss Samantha,' the housekeeper said, her reedy voice more querulous than usual.

'Have you seen him?' Sam repeated.

'No, and I prefer it that way.' Mrs Pritchett spooned up some of the soup and tasted it, then shook her head in frustration.

'Here, let me help.' It wasn't right to have this woman cooking for her, let alone cooking three meals a day, not at her age. 'What can I do?'

'Never you mind, Miss Samantha. I'm not ready for the glue factory yet.'

Sam saw an apron folded on the big oak table. *Ivy's*, she thought, and fetched it. There was a tray on the table with a single bowl and plate on it. Next to it, a rack of blackened toast. She grimaced. 'I think we should eat in here. Like you said, it's still the warmest room in the house.'

'Be that as it may, we still have some standards at Begars.' Then Mrs Pritchett let out a cry of pain and Sam turned to see her blowing on her finger – she'd touched the hot soup pot by accident. She turned on the tap to run cold water over it, tried to make light of it all. 'The dumplings didn't come out right. The suet had gone off. Bah, never cared for 'em much anyway,' she said in a tone of strained jovialness. The housekeeper wiped her hands dry on her apron and turned to face Sam fully for the first time since she'd entered the kitchen and her expression instantly changed; her eyes lit up, her smile widened into one of real joy. Sam could tell she approved of the green dress, her chignon. 'Ah, you're like your grandmother you are. She'd be so proud of you.' Sam blushed and felt immediately silly. 'Besides, I'm almost finished so there's nothing you can do. And that frock is far too fine for you to be in here. Go on with you.' She picked up her wooden spoon like she was threatening to chase Sam out with it. 'You're in the little parlour. Alec… Mr Bell… wanted me to serve lunch in the formal dining room, but I told him, the food won't be fit for dogs by the time I'd get these old bones over there.'

Sam reluctantly put the apron back on the table and had almost turned to go but paused when she took in what Mrs Pritchett had said. It was the exact opposite of what Alec had said earlier, that he didn't want them eating in the formal rooms in the south wing. That he preferred the little parlour because it would make it easier to keep an eye on Mrs Pritchett. She thought about saying something to the housekeeper, but she just didn't have time for their battles. She left the kitchen, hating to admit to herself that she was enthralled with the smart clack of her pumps on the tiles. She was a little disappointed once the sound was muffled by the carpet in the passage. *You are exactly like a four-year-old*, she thought. *Playing dress up in Mommy's clothes.*

She was making her way through the great hall towards the little parlour when she slowed her step. She felt a surge of motion around her, as if she were walking down the subway stairs at rush hour, going against the crowd. A slight brush of fabric against her, a hurried hand touching her arm; the smell of tea roses, gardenias, cheap perfume. She went to the nearest window, expecting to see that the storm had whipped back up and to feel the wind snaking in through the cracks and crevices, releasing the long-ago scent of flowers from the curtains. But all she saw was the same pewter sky and a soft fuzz of falling snow. There was little wind, no broken icicles to explain the tinkling sound in her ears, which sounded strangely like the clinking of glasses.

She heard the creak of floorboards coming from the front hall. *Ivy*, she thought. *She's probably dusting in there.*

'Hey, Ivy,' Sam called. 'I can smell your perfume from all the way in here. Mrs Pritchett won't like—' She walked across the great hall and out through its curtained arch, but there was no one there. She looked around, her eyes pausing on the large door beneath the staircase. It was a grander door – much taller and with an elaborately carved frame – than the one opposite, which led to the prioress's chamber. And it was ajar. *I bet that goes to the renovated wing*, she thought. Maybe Ivy had gone through there. Sam nearly had her hand on the door when she stopped.

In fact, everything seemed to stop – the dust motes appeared suspended in the air, she could no longer hear the tick of the grandfather clock just inside the great hall. Everything was muffled, it seemed, by a presence tightening itself around them. The scent of cheap perfume had been replaced by something ancient, unwashed. It was a familiar stench. It had been there, underneath the house when she was trapped at the tunnel gate.

Oh god, she thought. *The vagrant, he got inside.* She had shown him the way. Why hadn't Alec taken her more seriously? She knew without even looking that the source of the stench stood above her, on the stair landing. *Christ, he's going upstairs.* She couldn't let him get to her grandmother's room. She looked around for a weapon to scare him off with, spotted several antique swords hanging over the bench across from the stairs. She slipped along the back of the hall as quietly as she could, then grabbed the nearest sword, letting out a yell. As she swung around to the foot of the stairs the first thing she saw was a pair of scuffed women's boots, then dark grey homespun woollen stockings, followed by an old-fashioned black wool dress.

It was the goddamn night nurse.

Sam let the sword fall to her side. 'Jesus Christ, you scared the heck out of me.' The woman only stared back at Sam through her round, gold-rimmed glasses. Sam wanted to give her the finger. Instead, she cleared her throat, then said: 'You need a bath. Use mine if you want.' She left the sword on the bench and walked away as fast as she could.

*

The fire in the little parlour had gone out. Jittery and shaking, Sam tried to light it. She piled up some paper and logs, but she had no real idea what she was doing; the Brooklyn apartment had no fireplace. She lit as many matches as she could, willing the wood to ignite, then got down on her knees and started blowing. Eventually she sat back in satisfaction at the roar of the flames, until she looked down at her knees and realised she had ruined another pair of stockings. And silk ones, to boot.

She got up and looked at the table. There was still only one place set – where was Alec? Had he left without even telling her? She went to the windows, which overlooked the front drive, and to her relief saw that there were no tracks in the snow coming or going. But where was he? She pulled a chair close to the fire and sat down to warm herself. She thought back to the scene in the hall. *That smell*. She'd swear it was the same stench she'd smelled in the tunnel. The fetid odour that had flooded around her when she was trapped at the gate. She remembered the feel of the fingernails scraping against her neck. It wasn't a homeless vagrant. It was the night nurse. Why the hell was she screwing with Sam? *This is bad*, she thought. *Bad*. She did not want to be Mrs Pritchett when Alec found out.

Just then, the housekeeper backed into the room, a precarious grip on a large tray. Sam hurried over and took it from her and put it on the sideboard, while Mrs Pritchett leaned against a chair to catch her breath, then took a bowl from the tray and placed it on the table. 'French onion soup. Your grandmother's favourite.' Sam looked down at the bowl; one of the blackened pieces of toast was floating in the middle of the soup. She picked up a spoon and gave it a prod, trying to keep a straight face.

'Don't play with your food, Miss Samantha. Eat up before it gets cold and all my work goes for naught.'

Sam hesitated. She really didn't want this woman to lose her job. Not this way. 'Mrs Pritchett, do you want to sit down and join me?'

'Oh that's very kind of you. I will sit for a moment, but then it's on to Lady Cooper's lunch.'

Sam put her spoon down, wondering if her grandmother really was going to be given this. 'The night nurse,' she said finally. 'Is she all right? She's not… funny in the head, is she?'

Mrs Pritchett narrowed her eyes. 'What did she do now?'

'I think I saw her, down in the crypt,' Sam said with some reluctance.

Mrs Pritchett looked at Sam in astonishment. 'What? In the crypt?'

'Someone was down in the tunnel with me. Walking behind me. I'm sure it was her.'

'The night nurse?' Mrs Pritchett laughed, dismissing it all with a wave of her handkerchief. 'She's as dumb as a monkey in ribbons. Besides, no one's been down there in decades. Apart from you!' She tapped a finger against her cheek as if she were trying to recall something. 'It was probably rats,' she said finally, visibly shivering. 'Oh, I don't like to think about you down there with them. It's horrid, really. Promise me you won't go back down?'

'Mrs Pritchett, it was bigger than a rat,' Sam said in a tight voice.

'Well yes, there are a lot of them down there. You woke

them up, that's all.' Mrs Pritchett paused again. 'A fox then? Or badger? A ghost – we've got quite a lot of those here, too.' She laughed. 'Now, never you mind, Miss Samantha.' She patted Sam's hand reassuringly. 'It weren't the nurse, or she'd still be down there. I got a hammer and nailed that beam shut not long after you came out. And besides, I just spoke with her about the menu for Lady Cooper today. I told her we've got a nice fish for dinner. Lady Cooper always loved fish. Fried in the old days, but her belly can't handle that anymore.'

'I know what I heard.'

'Now, now.' Mrs Pritchett dabbed at her nose. *Like she can wipe the whole business away*, Sam thought. 'Whatever it was, I can see that it scared you. I'll have Mr Bell look around, make sure no one's got in from the woods. But I'm certain that no one's gone in from the house. No one but you. How did you find that door anyway?'

Should Sam lie? No. The truth might help. 'I found some of my mother's old diaries. Vera wrote about it.'

'Did she now?' said Mrs Pritchett, disturbed. 'What else did she have to say for herself?'

'Someone *was* down there.' Sam wouldn't be diverted. 'They spoke to me.'

'Ah. Now we're getting somewhere. What did they say?' She looked at Sam with a conspiratorial eye.

'"Stay. Please stay."'

'There you go then.' Mrs Pritchett patted Sam's hand again. 'That settles it. A ghost.'

There was a condescension in her voice that reminded Sam of Alec.

'I didn't imagine it.'

'Oh don't be so harsh on yourself, Miss Samantha. Of course you thought it real. Now listen to me. I've seen my share of ghosts here, and not a one has ever worried me. But you didn't hear her right. She was trying to say "stay out of the crypt". She was warning you!' She chuckled briefly at her joke, then said in all seriousness, 'What with all this snow on the ground, it'll come down on your head.'

'How do you know it's a she?'

'When has a man ever asked a woman to stay?' Mrs Pritchett laughed heartily at this, but Sam just stared down at her soup – a thin oily layer had formed around the bread.

'You said my mother got lost down in the tunnels. What happened?'

'I don't remember exactly. She was always down there, doing what I don't know. But she always came back and then one night she didn't. We searched the grounds – you never really knew where she was; she was fond of hiding, sneaking – and eventually they found her down there. She'd got trapped or lost or some such. They brought her up and she was hopping mad. As if she'd been done wrong by being found! Poor Lady Cooper took to her bed for a week after that. The shock of it all – she'd thought she'd lost her. She'd lost others, you know.'

'Children? She had other children?' Sam asked. Why hadn't Alec told her this?

'Yes. Three or four. Miscarriages. Those were terrible, terrible years. Lady Cooper had given up hope, and then along came Vera. She thought her a miracle…' The woman's voice trailed off, as if weighed down by the pain of the memories.

'I'm sorry, Mrs Pritchett. I know that must have been hard, on everyone.'

The housekeeper gave Sam a weak smile and shrugged her shoulders, as if to say, 'What can you do?'

But Sam could hear what Mrs Pritchett wasn't saying out loud. Vera, the bad seed. That Vera wasn't a miracle, but a curse. She held her temper. 'You said Vera was down in the crypt a lot. What was she looking for?'

'I don't know that she was looking for anything. Now, I've got to get back to the kitchen and get started on the washing-up.'

'I'll come with you.' Sam could tell that the woman was trying to escape.

'Stay, finish your lunch!' The housekeeper looked at the bowl of soup.

'I'll bring it with me. It's too cold in here.' Sam wasn't lying about that. The fire she had made had gone out; it never had a chance.

Sam put the bowl back on the tray and carried it to the kitchen. The walk was agonisingly slow; Mrs Pritchett couldn't do much more than shuffle. She said the cold, the damp, had stopped up her joints even more than usual. Sam, still holding the tray, stuck out an elbow and nodded for Mrs Pritchett to lean on it; the housekeeper smiled and did so.

Sam really wanted to know more about her mother, but Mrs Pritchett distinctly didn't like talking about Vera, or at least only had bad things to say about her. They reached the kitchen and Sam deposited the tray and Mrs Pritchett at the oak table. She would try a different tactic. 'Those beautiful books in the prioress's chamber, my grandmother's study. What are they?'

'Oh, you saw them did you?' Mrs Pritchett said, her face lighting up. 'They're books of hours. Do you know what a book of hours is?'

'No, they're in Latin. I couldn't tell.'

'You're not the only one!' She gestured for Sam to bring a chair over to the table then lowered herself into it, groaning slightly. 'They were made for wealthy ladies in medieval times and such. Half of them probably couldn't read them, either. Shows you, doesn't it?' She laughed. 'Always been a man's world. But they are lovely, aren't they? They're filled with prayers to be said at various times of the day and on the different days, like the saints' days. They've got a prayer for any kind of situation a lady needs one for.'

Sam spotted a teapot warming on the range and examined the stewed tea inside. Good enough. She poured Mrs Pritchett a cup and added enough sugar and milk to cover the bitterness.

The housekeeper gave a nod of thanks and Sam got a stool and sat by her, glad that the old woman was finally warming to her subject.

'They're that old then? Medieval? They must be worth a fortune. Shouldn't they be kept somewhere safe? Or in a museum?'

'I suppose you are right,' Mrs Pritchett said, folding her arms across her ample bosom. 'Lady Agnes Beaufort – she would have been your great-great-great grandmother – she collected them. Most of them are put away but Lady Cooper loved them so and kept a few out. Used some of them as her own book of hours. The difference is she learned Latin.' She tapped her teacup, as if to emphasise how clever she thought her mistress was. 'Wasn't going to go begging to some knock-kneed old priest to tell her what they said.'

'Oh,' said Sam, surprised. 'She was Catholic?'

'No. But Lady Cooper was a devout woman. And she loved

the abbey. She was writing a history of it before she took ill, biographies of the prioresses and the fine ladies that had run the house after the nuns left. Her mother had started the work and she was adding to it. It's a shame for all that to go to waste. But someone like you, Miss Samantha, perhaps you could pick up where she left off? Wouldn't that be just the thing?'

'I'd love to see her research,' Sam said. 'Perhaps you could show it to me sometime. But tell me more about the old days, what my grandmother was like then. I'd love to hear more...'

'Oh...' Mrs Pritchett's voice trembled. 'It were nothing like this. It was very much a house of joy. All of it down to Lady Cooper. She was stunning. Quite tall, but it suited her. She enjoyed the looks she got, knew how to carry it off. They would've modelled their statues on her if they could, those old Greeks – except she was always laughing. Lady Cooper loved to laugh! And she had this way of looking at you, like you were always in on it with her. You have her eyes you know – those French hoods – but there was nothing secretive about them; they drew you in.'

Sam bit her tongue. So whose were secretive? Vera's or Sam's? Both, probably.

'Her face was long and thin like yours too. You get that from the Beauforts. Did Vera ever talk about them?' The housekeeper's eyes were hopeful as she searched Sam's face. Then she shook her head. 'No, she wouldn't.' She looked away, disappointed. 'Lady Cooper wasn't a classic beauty; she was far better than that. She was striking.'

'Yes,' Sam agreed, thinking back to the woman she'd seen yesterday. 'She still is.'

Mrs Pritchett beamed at that; it was clear how fond she was

of her mistress. *And how much she misses her*, Sam thought sadly. The housekeeper fiddled for a moment with one of the clips holding back her dyed burgundy hair. 'Oh and this was the best time of year for a woman with her colouring. Hair like white honey. She insisted on candles at Christmas, candles everywhere. Candlelight made her look like silver and gold. She loved the dinners, the balls. We all did.

'That last Christmas her and Sir Thomas ordered a tree down from Scotland. The decorations were all made by the village children; paper chains and angels, salt-dough ornaments shaped like stars and dancing bears, hedgehogs even! And donkeys. Lady Cooper insisted on a donkey, you know, Mary's donkey. She always had a little tea for the children on Christmas Eve. She'd help them ice gingerbread men and we'd send them home with an orange each. Quite charming, really. Then that evening we had a ball, and the gentlemen and ladies from around the county came. Sir Edwin and Lady Westlake from Artis Hall. They came in a horse and sleigh, they liked to make a show. Even Lord and Lady Gresley came.' She pushed her sleeves up and took a sip of her tea.

'I remember every gown Lady Cooper ever wore to those balls. All the way back to the year she was married. 1900! Can you believe it? She wore pale gold silk, the whole thing embroidered with gold stars so delicate they disappeared if you tried to fix your eye on them. The bodice was trimmed with a darker gold lace and a touch of sequins. The skirt had more netting of gold thread and sequins along the bottom, and it trailed behind her, like she was dancing along on a cloud of gold dust.' She laughed, then coughed into her handkerchief as if overcome with the emotion of the memory. 'The hemlines got shorter each year. That last dress she wore, for a party out – it was New Year 1926 I think – it was no more than a gold slip! But she could carry it off, she always could.'

'What about my grandfather, Sir Thomas?'

Mrs Pritchett frowned. 'A busy man. He came. He went. Never said much. I think he was happy for her to be the centre of it all.'

'Did he and Vera get along?'

The housekeeper snorted. 'Get along? One wasn't expected to "get along" with one's parents in those days. You did what you were told and that were the end of it.'

Sam wanted to point out that Vera had not gotten along with her parents, and that was the real end of it, but she didn't want to provoke her. She got up to fetch the teapot – Mrs Pritchett had finished her cup and Sam was considering getting one of her own – and said over her shoulder, 'That girl Ivy, she talked about something called a servants' ball. She even asked if there'd be another one soon.'

Mrs Pritchett snorted again. 'Ivy? She told you her name was Ivy, did she? My my.' She shook her head. 'She does have her ideas, ideas that have little to do with what she was hired for. Talking to you, is she? She knows better.' She finished stirring the milk and sugar into the fresh cup of tea then let the spoon almost fall from her hand, like she was giving up. She looked at Sam. 'Do you see what I mean? They're untrainable.' Then more softly, 'I can't do it anymore. It'll be me down there soon enough. And there won't be anyone to notice, will there?' Suddenly there were tears in her eyes.

This had all gone wrong. All Sam had wanted was to find

out what had happened to Vera. Instead, she'd brought this woman to tears.

'Twelfth Night, right? That's when it usually is? The servants' ball? What is it exactly? We don't have that back home.'

'Well, you're better off for it.'

'For not celebrating Twelfth Night? Why?' Sam was surprised. It seemed a mean thing to say, given that Mrs Pritchett was the head servant. Why wouldn't she want a party for her staff?

'It ruined them, didn't it? The family. Good as killed them all.'

'I don't understand,' Sam said.

'Oh, Miss Samantha.' Mrs Pritchett pulled her handkerchief back out of her pocket and fussed with it. 'I begged her not to do it that year. Told her the staff wouldn't mind, they'd just as soon have the evening off to do as they wanted.'

Sam heard a sound at the kitchen doorway, dropped her hand; she'd been chewing on her nails again. It was Alec standing there, looking as if he'd caught a fox in the henhouse.

'What sort of story is she telling you now?'

Sam gave him a piercing stare. She wasn't finished with Mrs Pritchett yet and she wasn't going to get anywhere if he kept winding the poor woman up.

'Who? Lady Cooper?' she asked, turning back to the housekeeper.

'It had been a terrible year and only getting worse. Sir Thomas was poorly. His business wasn't going well and he was suffering for it, his face always the colour of brawn. It was his heart, anyone could see. We went ahead with the family party on Christmas Eve but Sir Thomas didn't stay long. He drank his fill – god knows he shouldn't have – and went up to bed; it was rude even for him, but we were worried. We were all worried.'

Alec came over and put a tray down on the table. It was piled high with cold meats, pickles and badly sliced bread; he had raided one of the larders. He took the onion soup away and whispered to Sam, 'Like the bottom of someone's shoe, isn't it?'

Sam rolled her eyes; Mrs Pritchett pretended not to hear. Alec buttered two slices of bread for Sam and nodded to the housekeeper. 'Go on.'

'I don't want to,' she sniffed. 'It's a black enough day without remembering all of that.'

'Please?' said Sam. 'For me?'

Mrs Pritchett smiled, and for all her backhanded verbal slaps, it was a warm, honest smile. The woman genuinely responded to affection; her vulnerability and her need were so apparent.

'Only if Mr Bell manages a kind word.'

Alec spooned a gherkin from a small bowl and forked a slice of ham onto his plate. 'I won't interrupt again. I promise.' Sam kicked him under the table; she knew he wouldn't hold to it.

'Please,' she repeated. 'I want to hear about the servants' ball. You wanted my grandmother to cancel it?'

'Yes! It was all taking a toll on her, too. Sir Thomas's health. He rarely spoke when he was here anyway. One had the sense he never really liked this place. He preferred their house in York. But once Vera was born, Lady Cooper insisted on being here more; said the country was where children belonged. She was right.' She looked pointedly at Alec.

Another dig. Sam assumed that meant Alec had been brought up in town. She threw Alec another warning look to stay quiet. He shrugged and lit a cigarette.

'But she wouldn't let go of it. That were her. She didn't want to let people down. Didn't want to let the staff down. Come what may, you had your duty, and to leave off – well, that was a sign of poor breeding.'

'Like Sir Thomas then,' said Alec.

Mrs Pritchett merely raised her eyebrows and looked away, a gesture that said she didn't disagree.

'What do you mean?' Sam asked.

'Lady Cooper's father was a baronet,' said Alec. 'Begars had been in the family for centuries. But he had no sons or brothers. So the land went to his daughter, Julia, your grandmother. It was heavily mortgaged and practically falling down. Tottering stones out in the ruins always ready to take someone's head off. Enter Thomas Cooper. He was much older than his future wife – a good twenty years older. By the time they met, he was already a prosperous sand and salt merchant who had gone into shipping and made a decent enough fortune. All he needed was a title to make the proud Julia Beaufort his, so he did some civic work for York – got himself appointed Lord Mayor for a bit – and a knighthood followed. That way his beloved wouldn't have to take a plain tradesman's name. She might be a Cooper, but at least she would be Lady Julia Cooper.'

'Don't listen to him,' Mrs Pritchett said. 'She loved him. It was a true love match.'

Alec scoffed and blew out a stream of smoke. 'My father said you could keep fish on him, he was so cold.'

Mrs Pritchett looked away again.

'So she went ahead with the servants' ball?' Sam asked, trying to steer the conversation back.

'Yes. There was music; she brought in the fiddlers. We still had to make the food but it was held in the great hall, a real treat. She spared no expense. Pheasant stuffed with chestnuts, dates, figs, mince pies, meat pies. Hams. Candied oranges. Jellies. A Christmas pudding of course. A cup of mulled wine each. The younger ones, those just come into service, or up from a less important house, they'd never seen the like. Eyes popping out of their heads, they were. Oh it were heavenly. We set oranges stuck with cloves all along the windows, put those draughts to good use for once and let them carry the scent through the hall. Then there was the aroma of the roast meats, the tang of the greenery. Oh nothing beats the scent of Christmas, does it? Holly and ivy everywhere you looked, mistletoe hung over the doors. Smartened up the red and gold bows tied on the tree; by Twelfth Night they were always tugged ragged by all the children who'd come in and out.

'She invited all the tradesmen – the butcher, the village grocer, the auctioneers from harvest time – plus the tenants from the estate, the bookkeepers; anyone the family relied on. The Bells usually deigned to show up. But not that year, eh? Abandoned us, didn't you? Only sent that Roger. Should've been your father. Might have changed everything.'

Alec gave her a hard look. 'You know why we weren't there.' He was suddenly as tense as she'd ever seen him.

'I'd say your father was upset. Fancied an invitation to the *family* party, didn't he?'

Alec looked directly at Sam. 'I'd rather tell you in different circumstances. But you came here for the truth, so I'll give you what I know. I spoke of it briefly to you, on the drive here. The year prior, Sir Thomas had committed an offence against my family. My father would have severed the account, but my mother convinced him otherwise.'

The housekeeper waved her handkerchief as if Alec were the melodramatic one. 'It was your family that was hurt, was it?'

Alec glared at her. 'Sir Thomas had been inappropriate with a member of my family. I won't say more out of decency.'

'One of his sisters,' Mrs Pritchett sniffed. 'One of the middle ones. She liked to tell tales. All those girls did.'

Sam expected Alec to throw the old woman out into the snow right there and then; that's how they would've handled the situation back home. But he merely looked around for something to flick his cigarette ash into. He was biding his time.

'I wish I hadn't been there that night, either,' Mrs Pritchett said at last, accompanying it with a long sigh. 'That I had tried harder, too. But I did have the first dance. A chance to wear something other than black. That's mostly what I wore back then,' she said as an aside to Sam. 'Lady Cooper let me borrow a stole. A sign of particular respect and my place in the family.'

She gazed down at her arms, as if she expected to see the stole wrapped around them. A look of disappointment crossed her face and she seemed at a loss for what to say next.

'It was about an hour after that first dance, wasn't it,' Alec said, 'that Sir Thomas was found dead in his study. A heart attack.'

'Oh,' said Sam. 'How terrible.' She reached out and laid a hand on Mrs Pritchett's arm; the housekeeper had begun to cry.

'My lady found him,' Mrs Pritchett said through her tears. 'She'd seen him leave the ball. She'd been so worried about him. But she was too late. He died in her arms.'

'I had no idea,' Sam said, getting up to pour the housekeeper a glass of water. That night was the beginning of the end for Mrs Pritchett, she could tell that's what the woman was thinking. When was the beginning of the end for Vera?

'Not quite,' Alec said callously. 'He was dead before she found him.'

'You don't know that,' Mrs Pritchett snapped. 'Why must you say such things?' She turned to Sam. 'Your grandmother fetched me right away. She could barely stand, her heart had been struck down too. If I'd only known... I should've put her to bed right then, kept her there. It was too much. But she stayed up the whole night, seeing to everything. When it were her who needed looking after. If only...' She drifted off into a haze of recrimination. What her fortunes might have been if she had taken a different path. Sam could tell. She'd been there many times herself. What she should have done, could have done. What might have kept Vera alive. She took a deep breath.

'Was my mother there?'

Mrs Pritchett turned her head away and started crying harder.

Alec continued. 'The next night Lady Cooper fell down the stairs. A stroke, brought on by stress and exhaustion, they said. Whether it was the stroke or the fall, possibly both, we don't know – but she never walked again after that. Never spoke again. It was lucky she didn't break her neck.'

'Lucky?' spat Mrs Pritchett. 'Was it luck? Look around you. Do you call this luck? Trapped as she is, and for more years than this one's lived?' She nodded towards Sam.

'Oh god,' said Sam, the grief of it sinking in. 'Both of them gone. In two days.' But not grief for Sir Thomas, or even Lady Cooper. Not yet anyway. For Vera. 'My poor mother. No wonder. How terrible. She was still a kid. What year was this? She couldn't have been any more than—'

'Seventeen,' said Mrs Pritchett in a flat voice. 'Yes. How horrible for Vera. So horrible. She left before the sun was up, before she even knew if her own mother would live or die. She sneaked out and never looked back. I'd had my doubts before—'

'Mrs Pritchett...' Alec warned.

'—but that confirmed them. Her leaving like that.'

Alec stood up. 'Mrs Pritchett, that's enough.'

'Her mother needed her then, more than ever. And what did Vera do? She left her. Cold, cruel girl. The more I think about it, the more I ask myself, what did she do down in those underground passages all the time? Who was with her? And was that why she left? Because she was—'

Alec pulled Mrs Pritchett up out of her chair and directed her towards the door. 'You're relieved of your duties for the rest of the day, Mrs Pritchett. If Roger didn't give you notice, I'm giving it to you now.'

'What? Why?' the woman cried as he took her by the elbow. 'What do you mean? She has a right to know, doesn't she? Isn't that why she's here?' The woman's voice grew fainter as she was marched away. 'Because she wants to know? All the village knows, all the village boys. Why shouldn't she? I don't want her to make the same mistake!'

Sam heard a door slam shut, and the sound of angry footsteps returning. With some effort, Sam lifted her eyes to see Alec; his outline was blurry, everything was grey around him.

She knew the answer, but she was going to ask it anyway.

'When is Twelfth Night? What day of the year is it exactly?'

'Fifth of January,' he said.

'Fifth of January,' she repeated.

Vera had died the same night as her father, only twenty-seven years later.

19

For some time after that, Sam sat in the kitchen, in a daze. Alec sat quietly beside her. The world around her wasn't making much sense. What she knew of her mother; what Mrs Pritchett had claimed. She was caught between these things, her mind stuck.

'Two days,' she said to Alec, 'Twelfth Night is in two days. That's when she died. Vera.'

He didn't reply, but she felt the warm weight of his hand as he took hers and held it.

'Roger and Vera. Were they in love? Did they want to get married?' she asked.

'What? No.' Alec shook his head. 'No. It wasn't anything like that. They were friends.'

'How do you know? Vera wrote…' she started to say, but then they heard a violent banging from what sounded like Mrs Pritchett's room and Alec rose. *There she goes again*, Sam thought drily as Alec left the kitchen. *Stealing the show.*

After a few minutes she rose too and left the empty kitchen, then turned down the servants' passage, but this time she headed in the direction away from the main house. At its end was a door to a courtyard. *A workers' entrance*, she thought. There were old coats and hats hung on hooks, and rubber boots lined up below them. The green paint was peeling around the door frame and there were cracks across some of its windowpanes. Sam looked out at the courtyard, the outbuildings, the hill rising behind the house.

Mrs Pritchett has no idea, she thought, chewing a nail. Village boys and dark places. Vera? Hardly. From what Sam had known of her mother, she was completely uninterested in sex.

It was time for a walk. Those tombs in the crypt with their lids pulled half off. She had an idea about one thing Vera might have done down there.

She took out Ivy's clips from her hair and roughly combed out the twist with her fingers, then tied her hair into a ponytail. She grabbed a ragged coat off a peg and kicked off her shoes, stuffing her feet into an old pair of galoshes. They were far too big, but she didn't care. Beside the door was an old sideboard, full of odds and ends – rolls of twine, wicker baskets, several rusty hammers and sets of pliers. After some rummaging Sam found some oversized leather work gloves and a torch. Its light was weak, but better than nothing. She put it in her coat pocket and set out.

*

The frosty air stung her cheeks. A blitz of snow fell into her boots with each step she took towards the church ruins. The cold felt good, it helped bring her out of the Pritchett-induced fog. She knew the woman was lying. Wasn't she? Right before Alec had cut her off, she'd been about to say that Vera left because she was knocked up. It seemed an obvious reason, and one of the possibilities she and Donna had considered back in Brooklyn. But the timing didn't fit. Mrs Pritchett had said that Vera left the day after Lady Cooper's stroke. That had been in January 1926. Sam hadn't been born until March 1927. There was no doubt about that; she'd seen her birth certificate recently when she had to get a copy for her passport. Sam didn't know exactly when Vera had left England for New York, but she couldn't have been pregnant with Sam when she left Begars.

Sam pulled a loose strand of hair away from her face. Mrs Pritchett. People weren't so sly back in Bensonhurst. If someone didn't like you, they spat as you walked by them. If a couple didn't get along, everyone in the whole building knew; heard every word of their fight through the thin walls. But with Mrs Pritchett, Sam couldn't tell if she was coming or going. She doubted whether the housekeeper herself knew.

She reached the ruins and looked up at the old medieval church tower that rose above what was once the main entrance. It was the tallest structure still standing; the belfry was intact, save the roof. She peered through the doorless arch at the base of the tower and into the church. The ground inside looked treacherous, with big mounds of snow hiding the wreckage underneath. In another time, another place, she might have thought it romantic. Might have liked to have walked here with Alec. 'God, this place,' she said out loud. 'I hate it.'

Sam continued east along the outside of the church – away from the house – to look for the entrance to the crypt. Alec hadn't said exactly where it was, but the church wasn't big.

It was slow going, however. The snow was at least two feet deep and with nothing on her legs but torn stockings, she was completely unprepared. Finally she saw a dip in the ground towards the back south-east corner of the church and headed for it.

A snow-covered set of stone stairs led down to a large boarded-up door. Sam funnelled all her pent-up anger into her arms and tugged with all her might on one of the boards, then felt her pulse quicken as the rotted wood broke off in her hands. She tore the other boards off and took a hold of the large iron ring in the door and pushed, but the hinges must have been rusted, or else something was blocking it on the other side, as it only opened slightly. She picked up one of the boards and slid it between the door and frame, then tried to monkey the door open. The board broke again when she pushed against it, so she tried with another one, a little more gingerly. At last she managed to get the door open wide enough to slip through.

She took another board and stuck it in the gap to keep the door propped open; she wasn't going to fall for that stuck-door business twice. She switched the torch on and stepped inside. There were more stairs leading down, and a rush of musty wind came up to meet her. The steps were slick to the touch; it was marginally warmer beyond the door and rivulets of snowmelt trickled down. There was no railing so Sam steadied herself with a hand on the cold stone wall. The ground levelled out about six stairs down. Well on her guard, she listened before going any further. She heard the forlorn cry of the wind chasing itself down the tunnels and then in a lull, she heard a jagged, sharp intake of breath, like a death rattle. It echoed around her, then receded into the tunnels. The sound was so eerie, so present, she thought about abandoning her mission right there. But what was there to go back to? She listened again, and in the absence of strange footsteps, declared it safe. *What an idiot*, she heard a voice say in her head. Thank god Donna was back.

She moved forward and into a wide, cavernous octagonal room with a vaulted brick ceiling. She recognised it immediately as the same crypt chamber she'd been in before. There were the three tombs, the skeletons laid out by a wall. She shone her light around, taking note of the dark passages splintering off. Which one led to the house? Which one had the creeping night nurse come out of? She couldn't tell, they all looked the same. She wondered how many other rooms there were, what else was down here. But for now, she went to the nearest tomb and angled her light into it. Lots of dirt. Grave dirt. She wasn't looking forward to this. *Okay, here goes nothing*, she thought. She plunged her hand in, sifting the dirt through her fingers. Another surge of wind rasped down the tunnels, and she could see why kids would find this place irresistible. Dark, spooky, faintly fetid – no grown-ups would be stupid enough to spend time down here. A good place to play hide and seek. Hold seances. Scare each other. All the things kids like to do. Would you meet a boy down here? Maybe. *Who are you kidding, Sam?* Of course she'd meet a boy down here. Like she had anything better to do as a teenager. Didn't sound like Vera had much going on, either.

Finding nothing in the grave dirt, Sam checked around the base of the tomb, the back, under the lid and around the smashed pieces on the floor. Then she moved onto the second tomb and repeated the procedure. There were holes in the fingertips of the old work gloves; she could feel the grit and gristle as she scratched through the dirt. It clung to her skin, compacted under her nails. Disintegrated coffin. Disintegrated nun. Who had been in these tombs? A prioress? Medieval lords and ladies? Whoever it was, she thanked them. She was damn sure she'd never chew her nails after this.

In the centre of the middle tomb, her fingers bumped against something sizeable. *Shazam.* She brushed the dirt away, pulled out an old tin box. It was black, with a picture of two chubby children on the lid. A Kewpie doll-like girl in a witch's hat sucking her thumb and a similarly eerie boy in a clown suit licking a lollipop. In between them, the words *Thorne's Assorted Toffee.*

Not bloody likely, she thought, mimicking Alec. Her teeth were chattering now, her toes numb – the snow in her boots to blame. She'd do a quick search of the third tomb – there might be another box – then come back another time to explore more. Wearing warmer clothes, better boots, and dragging a cart full of lanterns.

And then, *goddammit*, there it was again. She had lost all sense of direction down here, but from one of the passages she could hear a skittering of stones, the crunch of gravel. Whoever it was, they were back. Fingers itching and sluggish with cold, Sam fumbled to turn off her torch, and then came a sound so identifiable it stopped her breath: the rhythmic crunch of footsteps. She knew she should turn her torch back on, shine it towards the sound, but her first instinct was to hide. Quietly as she could, she backed up behind the tomb, crouched down and listened. The drip of water, the chattering of the crypt door against its doorstop in the wind, a ringing in her ears, and then something else. The crunch of footsteps was gone. In its place, a brushing against the floor. Whatever it was, it was no longer walking. It was creeping.

Sam wanted to shut her eyes tight and cover her ears, block it all out. The darkness of the chamber was almost complete, but she forced herself to look and saw a moving shape. It was short, not even the size of a child. *Yes*, she thought, *Mrs Pritchett was right*. An animal. A fox sniffing about its territory. She almost audibly sighed in relief. *Jesus, Sam*. It was moving down the centre of the chamber and her eyes stung from trying to follow its faint outlines. Did it really just look over at her? Or was she imagining it all? Did she really just see it triple in size? As if it had stood up? *No, my god, no.*

All of a sudden, Sam understood what it was doing. The creature kept shuffling forward, but not towards her. She was seized with panic. There was no way she could get there in time. It was going for the door. It was going to shut her in. She watched as the blur in the darkness moved up the stairs, away from her. Should she run now? Down the passage that might lead to the house? Goddammit, Mrs Pritchett had nailed that beam shut. How would she get out? An exit into the woods. Alec had mentioned that. But how would Sam find it? Her eyes were still on the shape. Did it really know she was here? It must. Was it leaving, or would it come back? Her heart dropped as she heard the slide across the stone of the broken plank she'd used as a doorstop; it was followed by the creak of hinges, then finally the dull thud of the crypt door closing. There was silence for a moment, save the sound of dripping water. Then the sound of something brushing along the floor returned, and Sam's throat constricted so tight she couldn't breathe.

The uncertainty of what was happening, the torment,

was suffocating. Should she run or fight? Which would be worse?

But then, she couldn't believe it, the creature was moving away, the sound diminishing. Going back to wherever it came from. Sam stayed in her crouch, her joints aching; even the inside of her cheek stung from biting down hard on it to keep her teeth from chattering. She counted to three hundred. *Give it enough distance. Then run for the door.*

...296, 297... She heard nothing, but she could smell it. The stench. The air choked with hatred; ugly, ravenous need. ...298, 299, 300. She had no choice; if she didn't run, it would come back and find her. And the easiest way out would be a lighted one. She clicked on her torch and screamed.

Two black, baleful eyes were staring at her. A pit for a nose; a gaping, hungry mouth. Stick-straight, glistening hair. It was kneeling down next to her, face to face. Sam screamed, cracked the hard steel of her torch against the monstrous thing and ran for the crypt door.

20

Sam didn't look behind her until she was inside the main house and didn't stop running till she reached the great hall. She was standing in front of its cold hearth when she realised: she'd left the toffee tin in the tomb. She banged her torch against the mantelpiece, chipping the stone, then threw it wildly behind her, hoping it would smash something expensive. She tore off the coat and boots. She needed to get out of these clothes, this stupid green dress. Then warm up and go back to the crypt. Where was everyone? Anyone. The house was quiet. Where was Alec?

She walked towards the main staircase at a fast pace to keep her anger, her courage up. At the landing, she changed her mind and walked towards her grandmother's room rather than her own. The night nurse. She needed to know where that woman was. She knocked and waited, then put her hand on the latch before she could talk herself out of it and went in.

Her grandmother was sitting exactly where she'd been the day before, in her wheelchair, facing the window. Her paper-white hair was in its elegant chignon, her head a little forward, as if she were sleeping. Standing in front of her – holding up her grandmother's beautiful cream silk shawl – was Ivy. She looked surprised to see Sam, and curtsied.

'Ivy. Where is everyone?'

'Miss?'

'Mrs Pritchett? Mr Bell? The night nurse?'

Ivy lowered her arms and looked at Sam with concern. 'Are you all right, miss? Can I help? Do you need a doctor?'

Sam suddenly felt foolish. She knew she looked like a wreck. Again. She glanced around the room. It was warm, well lit. The fire was roaring. A pot of tea, the steam rising from its spout, was on a standing tray near the dressing table. There was no one lurking in the corner. She walked around to see Lady Cooper. The woman had her eyes squeezed shut and her lower lip was quivering, but she made no movement to suggest she knew that Sam was there. *The poor woman*, she thought. *The poor, poor woman.*

'I miss her too,' Sam said to her grandmother. She nodded towards the teapot on the tray. 'Is there enough for two cups?'

Ivy curtsied. 'No, miss.'

She took a last look at her grandmother. Reached out and touched her soft hair. Without thinking, Sam leaned towards the old woman and breathed in. A trace of good strong soap, of warmth. The scent of Vera. Tears gathered at the corner of her eyes. She left before Ivy could notice.

*

Sam's room was cold, so cold she could see her breath; the morning's fire had been left to die. She took off her dress – her mother's dress – and threw it into the fireplace… then pulled it back out. It was a good dress; she shouldn't be so wasteful. Ivy could have it. She took off the silk stockings, and laid them across the dressing-table chair; she might be able to darn them later. She pulled on a blouse, cardigan and slacks, her old suede boots and got a glass of water from the bathroom and gulped it down. She came back into the room, surveyed it. Were there any more diaries in here that might give her some clues? How was she going to get back into the crypt and get that tin? She was as sure as day Vera had hidden another diary in it.

The shepherdess smiled at her from the painting on the wall. She pulled it down and tore off the backing. In the bottom corner – she knew it – there was another diary, the same style as the others. Had young Vera bought them all at once, a stack of thin red notebooks, bundled together, or did she keep going back to the same shop? Another thing Sam would never know. She flipped through it – the entries ran between April and October 1925. This was a later diary than the ones Sam had already found, but Vera was still no more than sixteen. In the back, a folded sheet of paper overhung the edges. She opened it. 'Thank you,' she said out loud. It was a hand-drawn map, a rough layout of Begars Abbey.

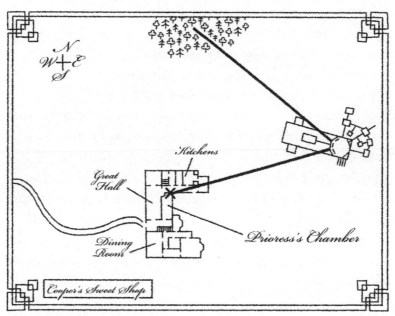

The map was brittle with age and there were small tears in the creases – it had been opened and refolded many times. It was drawn in pencil, the lines smudged and diffuse, a grey shading to the whole thing. It was an aerial view; there was a long rectangle representing the main house and a smaller rectangle for the medieval church. The ground-floor rooms of the house were drawn in and the prioress's chamber was labelled. An X on the wall marked its hidden door. There was the octagonal chamber with the three tombs; several lines shot off it, leading to smaller chambers. A thicker line led back to the main house, ending at the prioress's chamber: the tunnel Sam had almost become trapped in this morning. Another line – the longest – came out from the other side of the octagonal chamber; it crossed underneath the cloister grounds and ended at some distance beyond the walls, in the middle of some very neatly drawn trees. That made at least three entrances into the crypt: the prioress's chamber, the church stairs, and the woods.

Sam put the map down and went to the bathroom for more water. She thought about the face that had stared at her in the crypt. Now that the terror had abated, she knew what it had been: not an animated corpse, but rather the head from the skeleton with the dark hair. Someone had played a nasty joke on her. The night nurse was her best guess. But it was too demented. Why would she want to scare Sam? She took a sip of water, then looked in the mirror. Her hair was tangled and knotted, her face smeared with dirt. But she focused on her eyes, her nose. Vera's eyes and nose. Lady Cooper's. She thought back to what Alec had said – that Mrs Pritchett didn't like Alec; she was afraid he was going to fire her. That could be it. The servants were worried Sam would stay, and fire them all. Maybe they were all in on it.

Good grief, she tried to laugh at herself. Ivy part of a plot to scare off Sam? No way.

She came out of the bathroom and looked over the map some more. There in the bottom corner, Vera had written in another label: *Cooper's Sweet Shop*, as if it were the title of the map.

Cooper's Sweet Shop. Huh? Was it a reference to the toffee tin she'd found in the tomb? Had Vera buried more down there? And why Cooper? Why not Begars Sweet Shop? Or Beaufort's? Was it a direct reference to Vera herself, something Vera was doing – not the place? Making out with boys? No, Sam just didn't believe it. It had to be more than that.

'Sam?' She jumped at the sound of Alec's voice outside her door. She let him in, map still in her hand. 'What's this?' He took it from her and frowned as he looked it over. 'Where did you find this?'

'Where have you been?' Sam responded. Though to tell the truth, she was relieved now that he hadn't been around when she'd come crashing into the house like some silly schoolgirl.

'After I settled Mrs Pritchett back down, I came to look for you but you were gone. I assumed you had come up here to rest. So I tramped over to Bagshot's next door. The farmer's to come by with his tractor tomorrow and get me to the station. He thinks the trains should be running by late morning – he's heard them ploughing the tracks.'

Alec was leaving. Maybe she should too. Sam thought about Mrs Pritchett's foul words – her implication that Vera had been the village floozy. She wouldn't be able to find out anything from her grandmother, so the only other person who might know the truth about why Vera had left was Roger Bell. And he was not at Begars. He was off in London, hunting up more of her mother's allegedly dark, distasteful secrets.

She could take Roger up on his offer of money and go home. Start over. Leave her mother's secrets buried, the way Vera had wanted. She took the map back from Alec and slipped it into the diary, then put the book in her cardigan pocket. She thought about her mother, those last days. Vera's wan face. The eyes barely seeing. Her normally angular frame reduced even further to a collection of sharp points. It didn't have to end like that. Something had happened to her mother, something that made her give up.

Vera had never wanted Sam to know her secrets – about her childhood, about her cancer. Why? Did she think Sam wasn't strong enough to shoulder some of the burden? Well, Vera had been wrong. Sam was strong enough and she would do it for her now. She looked at Alec. 'Before you go, I need you to do something for me. I need to go back to the crypt. And I need you to come with me.'

21

'Absolutely not,' Alec said through a series of coughs. He had cleaned up some; shaved, had a fresh shirt on – he'd borrowed it from the farmer – but the expedition had kicked up some leftover inflammation in his lungs, he said. They were down in the little parlour, and he was repeating the same response he'd given her upstairs.

'You have to come with me. Otherwise I'll go alone, and how will you explain it to your brother when I get lost or hurt down there? How will that make you look?'

'Green wood,' Alec muttered as he drew two deep red velvet chairs back from the smoky, hissing fire; another lapse he blamed the housekeeper for. He took a tray with covered dishes from the table and placed it on the ottoman between them, offered her a seat.

Sam stood where she was, arms crossed.

'Sausages.' He nodded to the dishes. 'You hardly ate anything at lunch, and I'm starved after my march across the Yorkshire countryside. I already toasted the bread and I now declare this a feast.'

'Alec,' she said flatly. She wasn't going to humour him.

He sat down on the edge of a chair and uncovered the dishes, pointed with his knife to a decanter of red wine on the sideboard next to where she was standing. 'Would you mind? Your grandfather's finest. Château Latour. I thought it would go well with the toast.'

She still didn't laugh. Instead, she poured herself some wine then drank it down right in front of him, handed him the empty glass. Alec took it from her, bewildered, but then started on his dinner.

She waited till he had a good bite in his mouth, then said, 'I went back down to the crypt, but I left something in there. A box. In one of the tombs. You have to come with me to get it.'

Alec's fork and knife clanged down onto his plate, his eyes full of fury.

'You went down in the crypt? *Again?*'

'This afternoon. While you were planning your escape from the Stalag, I went in through the church. The door was wide open,' she lied.

'Was it?' His look of fury changed to astonishment.

'No. But the boards were rotten. Easy enough to pull off.'

'I see,' he said through another bout of coughing.

'You should have that checked out.'

'I have, since you ask, and the doctors gave me the all-clear.'

'That's how it starts you know. A cough that won't go away.'

'I'll get it checked again.'

He said this with so little resistance that she almost smiled, but she was still too worked up.

'Now, please,' he went on, 'come have a seat. This pacing won't do you any good.'

'Whoever chased me yesterday is still down there.'

'The vagrant? Never mind. Please.' He pushed the ottoman away with his foot, brought the other chair closer to him.

'Please, sit down. I promise you, I will listen.' Sam still didn't move, so he reached up and gently took hold of her hand. She kept her fingers rigid. 'But you must believe me, too. It's dangerous down there. That crypt, those tunnels, all of the ruins. They're ready to come crashing down at any minute. It's not a playground—'

Sam cut him off, withdrawing her hand. 'My mother left Begars, allegedly after she made out with every boy in the village if you believe half of what Mrs Pritchett says. Never to come back. Not even with her own mother in such a terrible condition. Not even when on a lot of nights there wasn't enough money for both of us to eat. Something happened here. Something so horrible that she never even mentioned this place to me. She was content to live the rest of her life just scraping by – for us to scrape by – and she never even…' Sam's voice started to falter, which just made her angrier. She hated to cry, so she swallowed hard, then spat the rest out like it was poison. 'She never even bothered to come up with a fairy tale about who my father might be. All she ever said was, "He was a nice boy." Can you believe it? That's it. No matter how much I asked. Isn't that enough to drive anyone insane, to hear that as the sum total of your father? But now, at least now, I can find out *something*. I can *know* something about Vera.' She took out the diary from her pocket and shoved it at him. 'You don't seem to know anything. Mrs Pritchett… well, I need full body armour around her. My grandmother is trapped in her own hell. All I have are these diaries. So if you're not going to help, stay out of my way.'

Alec took the diary, ran a hand over its red cloth cover. 'What does she say in this one?'

Sam sighed and finally sat down. 'I haven't had a chance to read it yet, I just found it. I hadn't got past the map.' She leaned forward and drew it out from the book, unfolded it. 'In one of the other diaries, she talks about finding a key. I think at first she thought it was to a cell, that hole I told you she was looking for. But then she realises the key only goes to the gate in the crypt tunnel, here.' She pointed to where it was marked on the map.

'So where is the cell?' Alec asked, his eyes running over the map.

'I don't know. She thought that's what was hidden in the wall of Lady Cooper's study, behind the beam.' Sam got up and poured him a glass of wine as a peace offering. 'When you found me there this morning, that's what I was doing. Checking it out, seeing if there was any truth to what Vera was writing. And that's all I really know at this point. Except that Vera asked Roger to go down in the crypt and help her search it, but he said no. And that's when she said she wasn't going to marry him. So you were wrong, there was something between them.'

'She said that to him?' Alec looked at her in pure disbelief. 'Vera said Roger actually *asked* her to marry him?'

'No, she didn't say that exactly.' Sam dragged the ottoman back between them, forcing Alec to move his feet out of the way. Toyed with the cover over her plate. 'Just that they were mad at each other and so that meant they couldn't marry. Why do you sound like you're shocked? You think he was too good for my mother?'

'God no! It's almost like you want to fight with me.' He took the cover out of her hand and pointed to the plate. 'Eat now. You'll still be stuck here, but a smidgeon less grumpy.'

She kept her eyes on him, waiting for an answer.

He sighed in exasperation. 'It's like I said, Roger preferred his work, his club.'

'You're only being polite,' she said despondently.

'*Yes*. About Roger. Not Vera.' He gave her a long look.

'Oh,' she said slowly. 'Oh. I see. *That's* what your sisters teased him about.'

'No. Not directly.' He seemed relieved that she understood, but rolled the stem of his wine glass back and forth between his fingers as he talked. 'They thought he was only shy and needed pushing. And by god if they didn't push him into the most embarrassing situations. They didn't know… don't know. It's not something we discuss.'

Sam thought about the dress and black lattice pumps she'd worn earlier. The other dresses upstairs. Thought about Vera wearing them. Sam pushed her knees together and angled her legs to the side, tucked one foot daintily behind the other so as to strike a more feminine line, like she'd seen in the movies. Wondered if her mother had ever done the same thing. Had she tried to catch Roger's attention with a pretty turn of an ankle? Had Vera loved him? Or was she only teasing him too?

She took a long agonised breath, then continued. 'I need to find more of her diaries. And I know where one might be. In a toffee box down in one of the tombs in the crypt. But I left it there. Like I said, there was someone else down there. They knew I was there, and they got between me and the crypt door. I had propped it open and they closed it. Then they came right up to me and…'

'And?' Alec's voice was hard.

'And well, it was dark, and they scared me.' Sam paused. Each turn of this story sounded crazier than the last.

'Do you mean to say they were deliberately trying to scare you?'

'I think so,' Sam said, drawing her hands along the worn velvet of the armrest. 'I thought they'd gone back down one of the passages...' She knew Alec was only holding on by a thread to this whole business, she didn't want to tell him about the floating skull. 'But they stopped right in front of the tomb where I was hiding, and at that point I just ran for it.'

Alec sat back in his chair. 'I see. I do believe you, it does seem like someone is living down there. I don't have the time to flush him out before I go, but I can board up that outside door properly, and I'll deal with the beam in Lady Cooper's study properly, too. Hopefully that will keep him away from the house for now. I'll ask the farmer to get some lads together as soon as he can, have them go in through the woods entrance and see what they find. Whoever it is, I can't think he means any real harm, or one of the staff would've caught sight of him by now.'

Sam shook her head. 'It's not a bum. It's the night nurse.'

Alec arched an eyebrow at that; she could see he wanted to laugh. 'What? Lady Cooper's nurse? I met her this morning, she's as harmless as a fly. About as bright as one too I gather, and she'll have to go with the rest of them, but, Sam, really? Why would she want to scare you? Why on earth would she be down in that crypt in the middle of a snowstorm? It makes no sense.'

The thread had snapped; she'd lost him. She wasn't going to tell him that she thought the woman might have been standing over her bed the other night, watching her. It was just too nutty.

'That's just it, you said it yourself. She knows she's about to lose her job. Maybe she thinks… oh it doesn't matter. I need to get that diary. Will you come with me or not?'

'Yes. Of course.'

'Okay. Meet you back down here in fifteen minutes?'

'No. First, I'm going to sit here and make sure you eat.'

*

They made their way out across the snowy ground between the house and church and then down the crypt stairs. Once inside, Alec shone his torch about, revealing long, vertical cracks in the walls. He looked grim. 'See? A death trap.'

Sam quickly walked over to the middle tomb, for half a second she was afraid that the puppet master behind the floating skull might have taken the box, but there it was inside, the rosy-cheeked girl and boy smiling up at her. She took the tin box, then looked at the floor around her, expecting to see the discarded phantom skull. She flicked her own torchlight across the floor and walked towards the skeletons.

'That wasn't there earlier. That skull, the one with the hair. It was over by the tomb when I left,' she said evasively. 'Someone's put it back.'

Alec stopped his inspection of the walls and came over.

'It's odd,' she said. 'Why would they bother putting it back?' The black hair was arranged decently enough and the skull was once again aligned with the body. 'Were these here when you were little? When you played down here?'

'No,' he said, shining his light slowly over each. 'They're

not very big are they? Half a foot shorter than you, I'd say. Women, most likely. I wonder if the bones match up, if the skeletons are intact or a composite. There are more chambers, with caskets stacked and set into the walls. Maybe someone was looking for treasure. Rings buried with the dead, that sort of thing. But why bring whole skeletons out here? And why does only one have—'

He stopped. Then looked around.

Sam had heard it too. A long, deep groan. Coming from one of the tunnels.

He quickly flashed his light back on the walls, the vaulted brick ceiling above. 'I did wonder. Yes, that's what you've been hearing,' he said at last. 'The stones shifting. We should leave.'

'Not yet,' Sam said. 'Back there... that's where I saw her come from. Let's take a look. Is that the way towards the exit in the woods?'

'It might be, I'd have to look at the map.'

They heard the groan again, the skittering of rocks.

Sam started to walk towards the sound and Alec yanked her back by the arm. 'No you don't.' Then they both froze as they heard the longest, deepest groan yet – like an ogre waking from a hundred-year sleep – followed by a tremor in the ground around them. Several bricks fell from the ceiling and before she could get another word out, Alec was hauling her up the stairs. Once they were in the open air he threw her clear of the church wall with such force that he lost his own balance in the wet snow and landed right on top of her, his elbow smashing into her nose.

'Idiot!' she hissed, pushing him off her and sitting up.

He rolled over and looked at her. 'Sorry about that. Hold

still.' In one swift movement, he held back her head then wiped around her nose with his gloved hand. 'Could've been worse,' he said, showing her the blood on his glove. He stood up and glanced behind them at the ruins. 'That was part of a wall coming down somewhere. It's exciting when you're six years old and you hear that. Not when you're six and thirty.'

Sam's eyes were watering from the sting of her bloody nose. 'You broke it?' she said, gingerly touching around it.

'I doubt it, just a good wallop. Now come on.' He pulled her up and they headed back towards the house.

22

In the kitchen, Alec dampened a cloth with cold water and tried to clean Sam up some more, but she grabbed it from him and did it herself. He handed her two aspirin and a glass of water. She chased it with a whisky.

They went back to the parlour, Alec stopping to put an ear to Mrs Pritchett's bedroom door as they passed. He nodded at Sam – the housekeeper was still asleep.

'When I'm gone, if she gets to be too much, mix a sleeping powder in her tea. They're in a cupboard in the kitchen, the one to the right of the large window.'

'Is that ethical?'

'Your choice,' he said offhandledly. 'Now let's open that box.'

As Sam had hoped, the battered toffee box contained a diary, starting in December 1925. Vera was seventeen by then and would soon leave Begars forever.

The diary was in terrible shape. A watermark stained half the cover, and the edges of the pages were yellowed and eaten away. Sam opened it as carefully as possible, but many of the pages were stuck together. Alec brought over a letter opener and she began to separate them. A section opened up but circles of a giant ink mould on each side had obliterated the text. Sam continued to separate more pages, finally stopping at one with some legible writing.

The date wasn't decipherable, nor the top paragraph; the ink was either too smeared or eaten by the mould. But there was a small section she could make out:

> *More names. I cr   ked Sekett with some gin   old cook over in Nether   ton wit   good gossip and a fat duck.*
> *Morr*
> *Smit*
> *That   kes six. Six girls. Sekett holding out   is clever. She wo   t come cheap.*

The list was repeated on other pages, and she finally came to one that was more intact than the rest:

> *James*
> *Callendwaller*
> *Sampson*
> *Taylor*
> *Edwards*
> *Morris*
> *Smith*
> *Sayers*
> *?*

'Who is Sekett?' Sam asked. 'And an old cook in something called Nether Ton?'

'Hmm, what?' Alec was sitting across from her, reading the other diary that had the map.

'Sekett? Don't know. Nether Silton is a nearby village. Listen to this.'

26th October 1925

That was a rather bad two nights. I had been careless and left my work out on my bed. I had only meant to be gone briefly, a trip down to Daddy's study to sharpen my pencil, but when I came back she – what shall I call her now? – was standing by my bed. And in her hand was the map I had been drawing. She threw it in the fire and left without a word. It was only a copy – I had been making some improvements – so it wasn't much of a loss. But I knew that wouldn't be the end of it.

Later she called me into her study. I remember wondering where she would send me this time. Another school for rude and unnatural daughters? Some dreadful convent in Bulgaria?

It shall always be a mystery to me, however, as I reflect upon that walk to her study, why I still trusted her, with all that I knew by then, why I went inside.

She was facing her faded Mary, head bowed as if in prayer. I couldn't help myself, I let out a little laugh, both at the sight before me but also because I had spied baby Jesus peeking around her arm, and remembered that as a child I had once drawn a biscuit in his fat little fist. I hadn't wanted him to go hungry. I stifled my laugh but she had heard me and turned and gave me a rather unnerving smile.

She swept towards me – as gracefully as if she were carried by angels too – and reached for my hand. 'Come, my darling,' she said. 'Let's stop all this nonsense. Let us be friends. I shall show you what you seek.'

I didn't want to take her hand, I so loathed the feel of its clammy snakeskin, but like a blind wretch I followed her. She pulled back the tapestry and opened the beam and down I went after her.

She had an oil lamp with her and when I heard the clang of keys as she glided down those stairs, my heart began to race. The key I had so often searched for was on her; I was to see the cell at last.

'What a silly thing you are,' she chided softly. Ever astute, she had sensed my excitement. 'These romantic notions of yours. I do regret that you haven't applied yourself to something more worthwhile, but I suppose I am to blame. I kept you too much in the country.'

I said nothing as we walked through those dreadful passages. Eventually we stopped and she lifted a long, languid finger and said, 'There,' and then she unhooked the keys from her belt and picked out the one that opened the cell.

'Go on,' she said to me in a weary voice. 'Have a look if you will, but do be quick. I won't catch a cold down here because of you.' And like the stupid little mouse I am, I went in.

A slight rush of air swept by me and then I heard the scrape and squeal of old metal, the turn of a key. Mummy, Mama, Mother. Witch. She had locked me in. I did not call after her as she slipped into the darkness, I would not give her that. I would never give her that.

She kept me down there for two days.

'No,' Sam said aghast, grabbing the diary from Alec. 'Lady Cooper locked Vera in the cell?'

Alec lit a cigarette as Sam read the entry for herself. 'Seems like it, and then let her out and sent her to some boarding school again.'

'Vera didn't tell anyone? She didn't tell Roger? Her father?'

'I don't know.' Alec rubbed at his temple.

'But Mrs Pritchett said Vera got lost down in the crypt.'

'Of course she did.'

'Do you think she knew?'

'No,' he sighed. 'I very much doubt it. Lady Cooper wouldn't tell a servant such a thing. She wouldn't tell *anyone* such a thing.'

Vera locked in a cell as punishment for two whole cold, rat-filled nights. She couldn't be making *that* up, could she?

'This one is pretty much destroyed, but I did find this.' Sam picked up the later diary and opened it to the list of names. 'What do you think?'

Alec frowned as he read it, flipped to the other pages she had managed to get open, but there was no confusion in his eyes.

'Alec?'

Finally he closed the diary and leaned forward, elbows on his knees as he worked away at his cigarette, his features growing tenser by the second.

'Alec? You know something.'

'I can't say with certainty, but Sekett was likely a servant. And Sekett and this old cook living in Nether Silton, they told her something, like that hall boy did. The thing is' – he took a long, hard drag on his cigarette – 'I've seen a list like this before. At the office. Handwritten like this one, with no context. At the time, I fancied myself a smart enough fellow and thought I knew what it was.'

'Go on.'

'You see, I thought it was a secret. No one dared talk about it. But if those names are what I think they are…' He looked away for a moment, then appeared to decide on his course of action. He turned back to Sam. 'It means Vera knew and perhaps that is what this is all about.'

'Spit it out.'

'It's… unfortunate.' Alec got the tongs and rearranged the logs in the fire, stirring it back to life. 'But – regretfully – not uncommon. Sir Thomas. He… he liked to wander.'

'Sir Thomas? What do you mean?' No one really talked about Sam's grandfather. She had half assumed there wasn't much to say. 'Wander where? Across the moors? Across the sea?'

'From his marital bed.'

'Oh.' Sam sat back, slightly deflated. It was a list of women her grandfather had had affairs with. Well, it was a long list, but she'd heard of worse. 'There has to be something more to it,' she said. 'Vera went to all this trouble over her father's affairs? I can see why it would be disturbing, and Jesus, the sheer number, but it can't be the reason she—'

'These weren't affairs, although I am sure he had those, too.' Alec hesitated, cleared his throat. 'These were different.'

'Prostitutes?'

'No. God.' He threw his unfinished cigarette into the fire and ran his hands through his hair. 'Damn it all. These names. They were servants at Begars. Or the daughters of local tradesmen. The tenant farmers. He took advantage of them.

My father knew. Roger knew... eventually.' He went over to the sideboard and poured a whisky, his back to her. 'I don't think it occurred to anyone that Vera knew.'

'What are you saying? These weren't affairs—'

'Sir Thomas was not the type of man to take his time.'

Sam's thoughts were clicking and sliding, spooling forward, reeling back. A young maid, the master falling in love with her, her fortunes forever changed.

'Not *Jane Eyre*.'

'I very much doubt it.'

'He raped them?'

Alec didn't answer right away. He took a sip of his whisky, his back still to her.

'Alec?'

He turned and met her eyes. 'No one ever said as much, but I would think so, yes. Some of them. They certainly had little choice if they were to keep their place, or get a recommendation to take them somewhere else.'

'Your father knew? He was Sir Thomas's solicitor and he covered it up?' Sam felt sick.

'It wasn't something that really needed covering up. At the time it wasn't considered unusual for a rich man to take advantage.'

Sam wanted to scream at him, at how calmly he said these words. 'No, not unusual,' she seethed. 'But disgusting. You know what my life was like back in New York, don't you? I didn't grow up much different from these girls.' They were working-class girls like Sam and her friends, but far from home and without protection.

Alec took a ragged breath and reached for her hand. Sam shook him off.

'God, Sam. I know it's horrible. You see, don't you? Why I feel the way I do about this place? My father felt the same. As does my brother.'

'That's not true. You still work for Sir Thomas's family.'

'Yes. But he is dead. No – that's not an excuse. I agree with you. I detest Begars. After the incident with my sister, I don't know why my father ever came back.'

'Oh Jesus.' Sam suddenly remembered. 'Are you saying that my grandfather raped your sister? And you and Roger still work for this family?'

'No, he didn't get anywhere near that far. Roger stopped it.'

'It's disgusting,' Sam repeated. 'The girls were poor. So he got away with it.'

'Yes,' Alec said faintly. 'He did. The girls were sent off and silenced with a negligible amount of money. Sir Thomas arranged that, not my father. The firm, it pains me to admit, turned a blind eye. No one made a fuss about it, not the girls, not their families. Sir Thomas chose his victims well. I didn't think that Lady Cooper knew, and I don't know how Vera knew. All we have is this list. It must have been very upsetting for her. Most of these girls were likely around her age.'

'*Upsetting* for Vera?' she repeated.

'Sam, I'm sorry. I am woefully lacking in my ability to talk about this. But I did tell you yesterday that the place should be burned to the ground. Now you understand why.'

Had that only been yesterday? Alec had said that, in the car on the drive up. She had just caught her first sight of Begars, and she'd been angry at him for saying it. Then another sordid thought emerged. 'Cooper's Sweet Shop,' she burst out. 'That's what it meant, the name on the map. Yes, Vera did know. All of it. She knew, knew it was revolting.'

Sam paced around the room, her body itching with agitation. 'Did it never occur to you, or Roger, that this is the reason why my mother left Begars? That she couldn't stand what her father was doing and that no one seemed to care?'

Alec nodded. 'Yes, I can see that now. But I was a child then, and have had very little to do with this place. I assume that Roger knows all of this and he should have told you. If he were here now, I would throttle him for not telling you. And for leaving this whole place to rot even further.'

'What about the girls?' she asked. 'Who thought about them? Other than Vera?' She didn't give him time to answer. 'The guy who managed our building back in Brooklyn – the super, the superintendent – we didn't call it "wandering". We called it what it was, we warned each other about him.' On hot summer nights, he'd stand in his doorway in his sweat-stained sleeveless undershirt, half untucked from his trousers. He'd yell out to Sam as she came home, biting into a chicken thigh, then lick the grease from his fingers and ask her if she wanted to come in for a soda. But he never got far with Sam; Vera had taught her plenty. It was starting to become clear why Vera had so much to teach. Sam felt her mind start to cloud over. 'Wait… tell me again… why did he get away with it?'

He sighed. 'I think… I don't think the families liked to get the police involved. Or perhaps the girls never even told their families. You know how it is… was… Listen, would you like a coffee?'

She looked at him like he was crazy.

'You've gone quite pale, understandably. I want to help, that's all.'

'Sure,' she said vaguely.

Before she had even realised he was gone, Alec was back in the room with two cups and a French press.

'When are you leaving?' she suddenly asked.

'Sometime tomorrow. I don't want to leave you here, not like this. But I have to find out what happened to Roger. Hopefully he's at home in front of the fire; it will make it easier for me to throw him in it.'

'Is there any real chance he's in London, like Mrs Pritchett said?'

'I have no reason to believe her.'

'Does Mrs Pritchett know you're leaving?'

He poured out the coffee, handed it black to Sam, with three sugar cubes on the saucer. 'I wouldn't give her the pleasure.'

A few more moments passed, then Sam asked, 'Should I go with you?'

'I'd rather you stayed.'

She looked at him incredulously. 'What? You and your brother have been trying to convince me not to come here since day one. And now all this...' She gestured to the diaries on the ottoman.

'Yes, well it's worse here than I thought.'

'So you want me to *stay*? For how long? And why?'

'Mrs Pritchett.' He poured milk into his coffee and added a sugar cube. 'I don't trust her. I don't think she's right in the head. I get the sense that even in the normal run of things, she never goes upstairs to check on Lady Cooper, check on her care. The locked door – that can't be the first time. The way she's treated you, the things she's said about your mother. The spoiled food. And then the electricity is still out and the phone line is down. I'd feel much better about it all if there was at least one sane person here watching over the place until I can make arrangements. I'll get back to York tomorrow and hire someone capable, send them back up here right away.'

Two more nights, Sam thought. *I suppose I can stick it out here for two more nights.*

'Okay,' she said. 'But I want to leave Tuesday morning. I don't want to be in this house on the day Vera died.'

23

4th January 1954

Christ. How do I do this? Sam's blankets were cold and clingy again, damp from her sweat and another fitful night of sleep. The wind had kicked back up, setting off all sorts of moans and wheezes in the house; she had been repeatedly woken by strange noises, including the same rhythmic creaking squeak she'd heard the first night. This time, though, she hadn't gotten up to check out any of it; her body had refused.

She looked at the cold cup of tea on the nightstand, and couldn't remember if it had been there the evening before. The room was still largely the same as last night: the curtains were open and stirring in the draughts, the fire was out. There had been no sign of Ivy then or now. Sam missed her. She needed a friend.

Only a weak light seeped into the room and she had no idea what time it was. She assumed early because otherwise Alec would have ordered her downstairs already. Her windows faced west and the clouds were still thick – she could see a light snow falling outside – but all she could really say was that it was dark and dismal o'clock. The usual time at Begars. She threw the covers off and made a dash for the bathroom, her bare feet slipping across the frosty floor. She'd slept in her slacks, had only taken off her socks; she didn't care how cold it was, she couldn't sleep with anything on her feet.

She splashed frigid water on her face and brushed her teeth, quickly combed her hair then threw it back into a ponytail. Her blouses badly needed a wash; she'd do it in the sink later. She thought about opening Vera's wardrobe and finding a fresh shirt, she even had her hand on its little walnut doorknob, but she couldn't do it. She put on the blouse she had been wearing when she arrived at Begars and a sweater over it, then a spritz of the jasmine perfume from the dressing table. Briefly wondered if Alec would like it.

*

She found the housekeeper sitting at the table in the kitchen. She was drinking a cup of tea, leafing through a tabloid newspaper.

'Good morning, Miss Samantha,' she said with a warm smile, as if the previous day hadn't happened. 'It's late, but I thought I'd let you have a lie-in; we could all use a bit of rest now and then, couldn't we? Now, I've got a good hearty breakfast for you. Your colour's off, more seaweed than sunshine. Would you like me to bring it to the parlour? Or would you prefer to try the dining room today?'

'How late is it?' Sam asked, confused. She'd been sure it was near daybreak. She looked out of the window above the sink, the sky withholding as ever.

'Near to noon.' Mrs Pritchett walked over to the range and picked up the kettle. 'I'll make you a coffee.'

'Noon?' Sam was shocked. 'Where's Alec? Why didn't you wake me?'

'He's gone. Soon as the sun was up, he walked over to Bagshot's farm for his ride back to "civilisation" as he calls it.' She laughed derisively. 'I told him, "It's all yours! I want no part of York and its stews and stinks!"' She laughed again as she spooned what looked like instant coffee into a cup for Sam. 'This'll hold you over till I get a fresh pot made.'

Already gone? Without a word? Well. It wasn't that surprising. Alec was abrupt about nearly everything.

Mrs Pritchett was sliding something onto a plate. 'Kippers, a bit of egg. Now where would you like it?'

'Here,' said Sam. 'Here is just fine.' She sat at the table, the hot cup of black coffee now before her. She looked at the smoked fish and fried egg and was surprised to see – after the housekeeper's previous offerings – that it looked edible. Mrs Pritchett sat down too, and poured herself another cup of tea. She seemed cheery, back to her old self – as if Alec hadn't fired her the afternoon before. As if she hadn't practically called Sam's mother a whore.

'Did Alec say when he would be back?'

'Yes, he said he'd call as soon as he got to town; hoped the lines might be up by then. Said he'd send word about Mr Roger as soon as he knew anything. And he gave strict orders for you to rest. I'll give you that tour later; there are so many wonderful things to see in the house. We can have a nice, easy time of it' – she patted Sam's hand, – 'now that the Sheriff of Nottingham is gone.'

*

After breakfast, Sam took a lamp from the great hall and went right back into the prioress's chamber.

Gusts of wind spat through cracks in the windows and the plaster; the room felt as exposed to the elements as a shed. Sam put her lamp on the desk and rubbed at her arms to take the chill off, and looked around. She noticed an old lectern by the windows. She walked over to it and ran her hands over its sloped writing surface; it was crossed with grooves and scratch marks, some of them deep and choked with what seemed to be centuries' worth of dust. The wood itself was soft, however; the untold layers of polish had given it a silken, sumptuous feel.

The desk faced in towards the room; the slant of its surface caught the light from the windows, a clever way to illuminate whatever was being worked on, she thought. Had this been the prioress's desk? She couldn't begin to tell how old it was. She lifted the lid of the lectern and discovered a narrow wooden box, about twelve inches long. Sam flicked open its brass clasp; a faint scent of mildew reached her nose and inside was a long dark braid of hair, with no explanation.

She put the box back, then knelt down to open the cabinet in the pedestal beneath the lectern. There were two shelves; the bottom one was empty but the top shelf held a petite ivory box. She picked it up and held it in her palm, groaned when she saw what was inside: three little teeth. Baby teeth, she guessed. Vera's? No… She put the box back and closed the cabinet, wiping her hands on her slacks as she walked over to the larger desk in front of the tapestry.

She examined the bust sitting on the corner, traced the golden strands of hair worked into the plaster. It looked like there was a little flap cut into the back of the bust's head, so she lifted it up and regretted it instantly. The flap opened onto a hard, curved surface. Sam tapped it. Bone. There was a real skull underneath the plaster; on a label on the underside of the flap she recognised two of the Latin words: saint and virgin. The skull of a virgin saint, the braid, the baby teeth; these were all old, Catholic relics. Leftover bits of ancient martyrs. She gladly let the little lid snap shut.

The desk drawer was still locked. She looked around and then into the lashless eyes of the virgin. Had Vera gotten her habit of hiding things from Lady Cooper? Sam picked up the bust and turned it over in her hands, pulled at the carved ears, pressed the half-open eyes, but nothing gave way. She shook the head, and was rewarded with a slight rattling sound. She turned the bust over, cringing as she slid her hand up inside the plaster neck and into the skull. Her fingers honed in on a cold little object between the teeth; Sam pulled it out – a key. Gruesome. She stuck it in the drawer's lock and turned; the rusted slides gave a stiff squeal but with some force she got it open.

And here is the gun, just like Vera said. But what she found more interesting were the two books next to it. One was a thin notebook, like the kind Vera had used, but larger with a blue mottled pattern on its cloth cover. Sam flipped it open. It was filled with handwritten dates and hand-drawn columns of notes and figures – a ledger of sorts. She laid it on the desktop, and turned to the other book.

It was smaller, the size of Sam's hand. Another book of hours? The cover was metal, but had become deeply tarnished with age. An elaborate pattern had been hammered into it and it had once been encrusted with jewels. Most of the settings were now empty; rusty little prongs reached out longingly for their lost treasure. Only a small sapphire and emerald were left. She carefully picked the book up by the edges – she wasn't going to risk tetanus – and put it on the desk with the ledger. Then she felt around the back of the drawer and flinched at the touch of something long and soft, like a tail. A dead animal? She knelt down and looked in. Not an animal. She pulled the object out. It was a heavy red velvet ribbon, its ends badly frayed. She smiled; attached to it was an old key, the one Vera had found, the one to the iron gate below.

24

Sam took the two books from the desk drawer and left; she wanted to examine them upstairs in her room. As she closed the door to the chamber, a breeze wafted by, carrying with it the scent of cinnamon, of warmed brandy; then of vanilla, like a cake rising in the oven. Sam lingered for a moment, letting the aromas surround her, then she heard the clash and clang of pans from the kitchen, excited shouts. What now? Had Alec come back?

She walked quietly towards the kitchen – she wasn't sure she wanted them to know she was there; she didn't want to be drawn into it. The closer she got, the more confused she became. She heard the clicking of shoes – not the rubber soles of the housekeeper but hard leather soles – and not just one person; rather it sounded like a dozen people rushing about. The closer she got to the kitchen, the hotter it grew, as if all the ovens were on full blast. The light scent of cinnamon changed to the headier, rich tang of roasting meat – pork, beef. She heard a peal of laughter, followed by a shout, then the sharp tones of someone losing their patience. Someone who sounded remarkably like Mrs P, but the high voice was clearer, firmer. Had the day servants come back? If Alec could get out, she supposed they could get in. The voices lowered to a whisper as she neared, then erupted in giggles.

Sam entered the main kitchen; she registered the tick and stretch of expanding metal under the heat of the great range's coals, the slow drip of water from the tap, the dull stream of light falling through a window onto the red tile floor. And that was it. The room was empty. There was no roast beef or chicken resting on the table; no cakes cooling on wire racks. No Ivy. No Mrs Pritchett.

From somewhere behind her, she heard a bow drag across strings, the tuning of a violin. She walked back and seeing the door to Mrs Pritchett's sitting room open, looked in. Empty.

With that, Sam picked up her pace and hurried back through the great hall and up to her bedroom, never raising her eyes from the floor in front of her. She nearly threw her arms around Ivy in relief when she found the girl there, putting a fresh log on the fire.

'Ivy, do you ever get lonely here? Do you ever... hear things?'

'Yes, miss.' Ivy picked up the old cup of tea and put it on a tray. 'I hate to go to sleep at night. I don't like sleep much anyway. There's so much to learn.'

'Like what?' Sam asked. 'What could be better than sleep?'

'The clothes, miss! There's always something to be seen to. A tear to mend, a stain to get out. There's always a bead to replace – oh the clothes here are so fine! A new stitch to learn. All made by hand, but not like my clothes, if you see what I mean.'

Sam thought about the skimpy evening gowns Ivy had put out for her. 'I don't know, Ivy. Sometimes the clothes here are...' She didn't want to offend her and say pointless, ridiculous, impractical. She settled for '...too fine.'

'Yes, miss.' Ivy curtsied in agreement, her servant deference back in place. But then she sneaked a glance at Sam. 'Miss. Tomorrow, miss?'

'Yeah?'

'It's Twelfth Night. Will they have it, miss?'

Sam's mood sunk even lower. This poor girl was so excited for a damn party. Why did Sam have to be the bearer of bad news? Perhaps because no one else spared Ivy the time of day.

'Ivy... did they have a servants' ball here last year?'

'I wasn't here, miss.'

'Do you know what happened to Sir Thomas, my grand-father?'

'No, miss.'

Of course she didn't. No one would bother to go into the details with someone like Ivy nearly thirty years later.

'He died during a servants' ball. Right here in the house.'

Ivy reached out for Sam but stopped shy of touching her. 'Oh no, I'm sorry, miss! Can I help, miss?'

'It's okay, Ivy.' Sam gave her a strange look. The girl really knew nothing. 'It was a long time ago. A heart attack. Still, just look out the window. Look at that snow. No one can get here. It's impossible.'

'Nesta could help.'

Nesta. Ivy had mentioned her before. 'Who's she again?'

'She's a servant, too, miss. We share a room.'

The night nurse. So that was her name. Nesta. Nesta the Nasty. Nesta the Grump.

'It'll get better, Ivy, I promise. Maybe next year.' When Sam was mistress.

'Yes, miss.' Ivy curtsied again, her head lowered.

*

Sam picked up her grandmother's accounts book first and opened its workaday cover. She scanned the columns of notes and figures, examined the receipts stuck in between the pages.

April 1925. A list of expenses for a spring garden party at the house. There were to be ices, salads and white damask table linens. Games and prizes for the children.

June 1925, expenses for a midsummer entertainment. A guest list, notations as to who would lead the games, and a note to order the fountains to be cleaned. A costume ball, at which Lady Cooper would dress as Dame Euphemia, the last prioress at Begars. A list of ideas for the menu – grouse, roast beef with horseradish sauce, olives stuffed with anchovies and capers – then Lady Cooper's mood appeared to take a turn. The next page was filled with what looked like a diary entry, rather than the business of running a household.

She had come here a widow. Her children grown and married, her husband sorrowfully buried. After his death, a vision came to her, that she should fulfil a longing from her childhood. Her earliest desire: to serve God. She would devote what remained of her life to Him. She took vows and became a Bride of Christ, and had never felt so much peace as that which filled her soul that day.

I have thought, too many times, God forgive me, that if my Thomas were to go before me, Dame Euphemia had shown me a path. I have devoted my heart to Thomas, but my soul is like that of Dame Euphemia's. As I pore through her papers, I see a way forward. I should give myself to

God and become a Bride of Christ too. But I could not
leave this house, so perhaps that is why I am here. To
restore Begars to its sacred life. To once again make it a
House of the Holy. A House of Contemplation. A House
of Charity. To help those in need. All its little lost souls.

It is the beauty of this thought that soothes and lifts
my soul from its bed of thorns.

As the midsummer costume ball neared, there was another
outpouring from Lady Cooper:

Moles have taken over the lawn. Wood rot has felled the
arbour. Sir Thomas is absolutely refusing a lantern walk
through the ruins for our guests. He says we couldn't
afford the lawsuit if there were an accident. I could not
hold my tongue; I told him, 'Such a thought would never
occur to those I consider our friends.'

It does make me wonder... What is the reward for
hosting such a ball, going to such expense? Certainly
not the sight of Mr and Mrs Scrope fondling the oysters.
Indecent. I shall think upon the day... perhaps sooner
rather than later... when our estate might sustain a quiet
community of sisters. Like-minded women. Mrs Pritchett
shall be my cellaress, despite her low birth; I cannot do
without her, that dear, good, faithful woman. We might
reasonably support twelve or fifteen ladies. We would rise
together in the purest darkness for matins, our walk to
the church deceptively quiet, for our hearts would riot
with the passion of our faith. The cold of winter's stone
as we kneel never a lament, but a desire.

*All thoughts would lead in one serene, uninterrupted
direction. Te Deum laudamus.*

Sam shuddered. Her grandmother had been given the
solitude she longed for and spent the second half of her life in
uninterrupted contemplation.

Had Lady Cooper seriously thought about turning Begars
back into a convent? Alec had painted her as a vain woman,
Vera hadn't trusted her, and Mrs Pritchett adored her. What
was the truth?

After the midsummer ball, there were entries for plans for
a harvest dinner, a Christmas ball, and then the servants' ball,
5th January, 1926. Sam felt a chill as she read the entry. There
was a note that many of the arrangements were in the capable
hands of Mrs Pritchett and Mr Flagge. Sam didn't know who
that was. The butler? A brief outline of the menu, a list of
expenditures. A worried note that Mrs Pritchett and Mr Flagge
would be too lenient, and allow the party to continue past ten,
as had happened the year before, *'much to the distress of all...'*

Those were the last words in the book. Possibly the last
words Lady Cooper ever wrote. Sam felt sick at the thought.

Did she know about her husband? Reading between the
lines, Sam could see there was some tension. But the conflict
appeared to be about Lady Cooper not getting her way. Not
that she found Sir Thomas revolting, as Vera clearly had.

Sam plucked out several more pieces of paper from between
the pages of the ledger. One was an advertisement for a new
type of pesticide. Another a cut-out from a magazine: a hair
style was circled and 'Vera?' written next to it. A drawing of an
arrangement of flowers. Transcriptions of prayers, of poetry.

In the back, a stack of receipts. Several from seamstresses in York and London. One for an abbess costume, presumably for the midsummer ball. Sam wondered if there were any photographs. Where *were* the family photographs? All she'd seen were the old portraits hanging in the entrance hall. There must be some...

A receipt for pills. Stationery. Perfume. Sam put them back in the ledger, picked up the book of hours. *Rust*, she decided as she examined it more carefully. Some other metal had been mixed in with the gold. As for the missing gems, had they fallen out? Or had Vera the jewel thief been the culprit?

The insides of the covers were lined with a dark velvet. Fire-engine red at one time, she imagined, now faded to a dull brown. Like the others, the book was written in Latin. She turned the pages looking for words she could recognise.

At the top of an early page, two cherubs danced among a bower of flowers. In the middle of them a medallion of royal blue and a gold creature with flowing hair. The title was *Ianuarius habet dies. xxxi*. And then beneath, a list:

> *Circuncifio domini*
> *Octaua fancti Stephani*
> *Octaua fancti Ioannis*
> *Octaua Innocentium*

Circuncifio domini, she thought. Circumcision of the Lord. *Sancti Stephani* – Saint Stephen. *Octaua*? Eight something? After that there was a black-edged hole in the page, as if someone had taken a flame to it. She turned ahead – saw similar burn marks, of varying sizes and shapes throughout the book; it was deeply damaged. By accident or deliberately, she couldn't know.

She skipped back to the page she'd been studying. At the bottom, there was a man in a red cap, sitting on a stool and warming his hands by the fire.

The next page, *Februarius habet dies. xxviii.*, also had a list of various saints' names, from what she could tell, and a cheerful drawing of a man with a pitchfork lifting hay into a cart. Then *Martius habet dies. xxxi., Aprilis habet dies. xxx.* The book appeared to be a calendar marking saints' days, just as Mrs Pritchett had said, but beyond that, there wasn't much she could understand.

She leafed through more pages, all arranged in a similar format, examining the images at the bottom. She stopped at September, and held the book up closer to the light. In the right margin just above the image of a woman crushing grapes with her feet, someone had written in a modern sloping hand: *Sayers £10 Lon.* The entry was in pencil and certainly not original to the book.

She turned the page back to August and saw in the margin *Edwards 12s 3d.* In July, across from *Octaua Petri et Pauli*, the words: *Callendwaller £1.*

She turned back to January, looking for other entries she might have missed. February had two – *Sampson £5 Lon.* and *Taylor £2* – while May had three: *James 6s 3d, Morris £2 Richmond, Smith £3 Manchester.*

She'd seen these names before. She took out one of the old receipts from the accounts book and copied onto the back:

Sampson	*£5 Lon.*
Taylor	*£2*

James	*6s 3d*
Morris	*£2 Richmond*
Smith	*£3 Manchester*
Callendwaller	*£1*
Edwards	*12s 3d*
Sayers	*£10 Lon.*

These were the same names Vera had written in her diary. Someone – Lady Cooper, it was her desk, wasn't it? – had recorded their names in this badly damaged book of hours. The names of the women her grandfather had attacked, and presumably the month they'd been attacked. It looked like Lady Cooper even knew how much each had been paid… £2, £3, £10… She knew. Her grandmother had known. And kept a record of it.

Manchester. Richmond. Lon. for London? The cities beside the names. Where some of the attacks occurred? Or where the girls had gone after? Why note that, and why only for some of the victims? And why the different amounts of money?

James, 6s 3d. Six shillings and three pence – Sam had picked up some of the monetary labelling waiting for the train to York. What had Sir Thomas done to a woman, with the last name of James she assumed, that he thought was worth only a few shillings, while Edwards was given twice that meagre amount? And what had he done to Sayers that he considered worth £10? How did Lady Cooper know how much each girl was given?

Dumbfounded, Sam closed the book. They all knew. Lady Cooper. Vera. Henry Bell. Roger Bell. And Mrs Pritchett? She had to have known. How could she not? The other servants knew some of this, Vera had written about getting names from them. And some of these girls had to have worked for Mrs

Pritchett. She would have seen them all day every day. How long had it gone on for? She couldn't tell the time span. The book seemed to be a generic calendar listing of notable days, not one distinct year like modern calendars.

But what did these names have to do with the hidden cell, the crypt?

She picked up the ledger. Looked again at Lady Cooper's extensive lists for parties and dinners; then the entries about a desire for a different life, one like those of the religious women who'd lived at Begars before her. How she had even contemplated a life without her husband. A life without a husband who was raping the servants. But surely her thoughts had gone further than that? Vera had been so disgusted she ran away from home. Sam couldn't understand it. How could Lady Cooper tolerate it? How could she remain so... detached? But maybe, thought Sam, that was why she had wanted to turn Begars back into a nunnery. To atone.

She looked back at the list of names she had copied out from the rusted book of hours. Eight names. Eight girls. Women. How old were they? Where were they now? She thought again about how each had been paid a different amount. £10 for Sayers. £1 for Callendwaller. What could cause the difference? Then it occurred to her. A baby. A baby would make the difference.

Maybe Roger really had gone to London, to do what the firm should've done decades ago. He was searching for Sir Thomas's illegitimate children, that he might find in London the child – now an adult – of a woman named Sayers. Or a woman named Sampson. But that seemed an impossible task, unless he had more to go on. Unless Mrs Pritchett had told him something that would help.

25

'It'll be lamb stew for dinner,' the housekeeper trilled when she saw Sam walk into the kitchen. 'Always brings a smile to your grandmother's face.'

'Are you sure about that?' Sam didn't want to play anymore. 'Sorry to be blunt. But Roger Bell. Did he come here to ask you about Sir Thomas's other children?'

'What?' Mrs Pritchett put down the pot she'd been carrying, looked at Sam in confusion.

'I know,' said Sam quietly. 'I know about the girls, what my grandfather did to them. That they were paid off. What happened to them? Do you know... did any of them have a baby?'

Visibly shaken, Mrs Pritchett fumbled her way to a chair. 'Sir Thomas has other children? What other children? What girls?'

Sam wanted to brain her. 'You said Roger Bell went to London. I'm trying to figure out why. You said he went there because of Vera, because she had gone there after leaving Begars. I think he had other reasons.'

'Oh, Miss Samantha,' the housekeeper said in a plaintive voice, rubbing at the joints of her fingers, 'those boys never tell me anything. I don't know why Roger went. I suppose he thought he could help you somehow.'

Sam shook her head. 'I think you're lying. I think you know

exactly what he's doing in London, what he's trying to find there.' She turned to leave. It was always the same dead end with this woman. 'I won't be down for dinner,' she said. 'I couldn't stomach it.'

*

Back in her room, Sam got out her mother's last diary. She used a metal nail file from the dressing table to slice apart more of its pages and then inserted hair pins to keep them from sticking back together. She set the book on a chair near the fire to keep it dry.

She washed her blouses and underwear in the bathroom sink with a bottle of shampoo she'd found. The smell reminded her of taking a shower after swimming at the YMCA. Industrial and cheap; she wished she could have found the rose-scented stuff that Ivy had used in her bath the day before. She threw more wood on the fire and lined up more chairs in front of it, draping her wet clothes over them. Finally, she picked back up the book and knelt by the hearth to try to decode its ruined words. It was hard going and didn't take long for her eyes to start aching. She decided to lie down for a few minutes; thoughts of Ivy and Twelfth Night strangely kept pushing in and before she realised it, she was dreaming.

*

She is the young lady of the house. She lets Ivy do her hair; the girl uses a curling iron and a ton of spray to force it into waves. Sam's dress is a drop-waist sleeveless black satin with a tulle skirt, her slippers a matching black satin. Double silver strands with crystal beads drape down to her navel; a smaller black onyx pendant lies against her breastbone. Ivy paints her lips red and hands Sam her gloves then runs off so she too can dress for the ball.

Sam meets her father at the top of the stairs; he is tall, broad-shouldered. She's never met him before, but somehow she knows it is him. His smile is kind and he offers her his arm. They walk into the great hall; the Norwegian spruce is too tall, its golden star crooked against the rafter. Why didn't they cut it to make it fit? Swags of evergreen are draped over the archways, the windows. Sam sees her father take the hand of a merry little auburn-haired lady, and she herself takes the hand of a young man. He's very dignified-looking; a little too dignified. They dance and at the end someone gives her a cup of punch. The fiddler picks up his bow again and the guests line up for a reel. The long table is pushed further back against the windows, its centrepiece a pyramid of oranges. The dancing begins and Sam watches the reel before her. At first she claps with the music but the beat and the dancing become erratic. She no longer sees her father. Where did he go? The night nurse, Nesta, is there, in a plain dress. The reflected light from her lantern flickers in her round glasses but the flame parts enough for Sam to see the question in her eyes.

Sam looks for Alec. He was just here, standing beside her. Wearing her favourite orange sweater, her trousers too tight on him.

She hears the sound of shattering glass, the gasps of the guests. The woman has thrown her lantern to the floor, breaking it. She's angry that Sam isn't doing what she's asked.

Sam woke up, her hair sticky with sweat, the sound of breaking glass still ringing in her ears.

Her room was pitch black and she fumbled to light the candle on the nightstand. Then she went around the room lighting as many candles as she could. Had part of her dream been real? Had the night nurse been in her room again, watching her with that lantern of hers? Hadn't she locked her door? Sam went over to check. Yes, the key was still in it.

In the distance, she heard a creaking. The same one she'd heard every night since her arrival. A window open, creaking against its casement in the wind? *Why hasn't anyone fixed it? Because there's no one to fix it.*

The creaking got louder, as if it were moving towards her. *No*, Sam realised, *it's too rhythmic to be the wind*. The sound changed. Creak-thunk. Creak-thunk. A heavy metal object, moving away now, the sound growing fainter.

She stood there, thinking. The clothes she'd washed earlier weren't dry yet, so she went to Vera's wardrobe and pulled out a silk blouse that smelled of dust and mothballs. She couldn't find where she'd thrown her ankle boots, so she put on Vera's old camouflage rain boots that had been stuffed into the bottom of the wardrobe. Then she took a lamp and went downstairs.

All was quiet. Had the sound come from the attic? Sam was loath to sneak up on Ivy again, but she was also getting pretty angry. With everything. She climbed up to the attic, taking the main stairs this time. At the top, they opened onto a large room that ran the width of the house; she recognised the skylight she'd seen earlier, and more moonlight crept in from dormer windows. A few simple wooden chairs were set against the walls, and a hip bath sat near a cold fireplace. *Just like back home*, she thought. She and Ivy were sisters after all.

She looked down the north wing corridor and saw a faint trace of light coming from under the same door as the other night. She moved closer, then stopped to listen. Ivy was awake, talking to someone.

Sam suddenly felt stupid; it was just the servants moving about at night. She had no idea what time it was, hadn't thought to look. For all she knew it was five in the morning and Ivy was awake and getting ready to start her work.

I'll ask her in the morning, she thought. She couldn't barge in on her again. She was about to walk away when she heard a sound of distress, a moan. A strangled voice, agitated, its owner at her limit.

She took a deep breath and opened the door. A lamp was lit on the nightstand and Ivy was sitting on her bed. Her head snapped up when she saw Sam; her eyes were red as if she had been crying, and smudged with black – had she put mascara on? Then she heard a rattle, and looked down. Ivy was holding a teacup and saucer, her hands shaking. Sam couldn't understand the cup – it was too fine, too dainty to be up here in a servant's room. A wreath of pink and blue roses circled the cup, and its rim and interior were painted in gold. She kept looking at the cup, puzzling over it, because she didn't want to face what else was happening in the room.

There, in front of Ivy, was Lady Cooper, writhing in her wheelchair.

'Ivy,' Sam said. 'What... what's going on? Why is Lady

Cooper up here?' Sam knelt down in front of her grandmother to see if she was okay. Despite it being the middle of the night, her beautiful twist of paper-white hair was as elegant as ever, not a strand out of place. The rest of what Sam saw was garish, vulgar. Her grandmother was wearing a thin metallic gold dress, tarnished to a dirty copper; it was loose or tight in all the wrong places, the fit against the woman's weakened body unseemly. Her eyebrows had been darkened and her eyes thickly lined, a set of false lashes added. Her cheeks were heavily rouged pink, her lips painted with a Cupid's bow, her face amply powdered. She wore diamond earrings and multiple strands of gold and diamond necklaces. On her feet were a pair of gold satin shoes, their sheen long gone. She had a teacup too, in her lap, but it had spilled. Sam reached for a blanket to sop it up – was it hot, had she been burned?

Sam was horrified. Ivy was playing dress up with her grandmother in her room. Is this what she meant about learning to be a lady's maid? She looked over at Ivy for an answer. The girl had done herself up, too. She had clipped her hair back with what Sam assumed were rhinestone barrettes and was wearing the dark blue wool dress Sam had given her, a rhinestone brooch over her breast. Around the girl's shoulders was the same pale shawl Sam had seen her wearing the other night, and with a start, Sam realised it was actually Lady Cooper's cream shawl.

'Ivy, this is nuts!' Sam almost shouted. 'What are you doing? Is this… are you pretending you're at the ball? What's wrong with you?'

Sam dropped the blanket to the floor – the tea, thankfully, had been cold; she didn't think Lady Cooper had been hurt – and grabbed the wheelchair handles and backed her grandmother out of the room into the corridor. 'Go to bed, now,' she said to the girl. 'I'll look after Lady Cooper for the rest of the night. We can talk about this in the morning.' Her grandmother was still writhing in her chair, still moaning. She seemed to be even more upset than when Sam had first walked in. Pools of blackening tears had gathered under her eyes; her slack cranberry mouth worked futilely to say something.

Out of the corner of her eye, Sam saw a movement in the shadows down the corridor. She could make out a face, a pair of round glasses. Nesta stepped forward.

'You've upset her,' the nurse said in a low, matter-of-fact voice.

Sam wanted to yell that she was fired, but Lady Cooper was twisting so much in her chair that Sam was worried she might tip herself out. She tightened her grip on the handles and bumped the chair backwards down the stairs, explaining who she was and what she was doing as she went. Telling her Vera was okay, that she was sorry she couldn't be here with her. But her words seemed to do nothing to settle Lady Cooper and Sam thought about shouting for Ivy, despite what the girl had done.

It was slow going, but Sam got her grandmother into her room. The candles were still lit, and she rolled her over to the dressing table and wiped off her make-up with cold cream. She leaned her grandmother against her and lifted her up to pull her dress up over her hips, then unzipped the back and pulled it off. Ivy had even put shimmery silk stockings and a fancy garter belt on the old woman. This was too much.

Sam checked Lady Cooper's legs for burns, but she

appeared to be fine – then opened several drawers until she found a nightgown, and put it on her grandmother. She took out the pins holding Lady Cooper's chignon in place and combed through her hair, then shaped it into a loose braid. *I know how to take care of sick people*, Sam thought, a deep, unsettled anger behind her words. *Boy, do I ever.* She pushed her grandmother's chair over to the bed and lifted her in. She held a glass of water to the woman's lips then, after a little while, was able to hush her to sleep.

26

5th January 1954, Twelfth Night

Sam didn't so much as wake up as fall out of the blue chinoiserie armchair she'd balled herself into. Unwilling to turn Lady Cooper's care back over to anyone else in the house, Sam had spent what was left of the night in her grandmother's room.

She sat up on her knees and looked over at her grandmother, then rubbed her eyes in disbelief. Lady Cooper was sitting up in bed, the cream shawl that Ivy had worn last night back around her shoulders. Her hair had been tucked back into its chignon and steam was rising from a cup of tea on the nightstand. The gold dress Sam had thrown on the floor was now on a hanger on the wardrobe door. The gold satin pumps, expectant and ready, perched beneath.

Lady Cooper craned her head forward, her right arm outstretched, grasping for something, just as when Sam had first met her. What did she want? Sam followed her sightline to the windows. Did she want the curtains open? Only one was tied back. She gave it a shot, flung the rest of them open, but Lady Cooper continued to grab at the air. Sam tried the cup of tea, but she wouldn't drink it, twisting her head to the side every time Sam touched it to her lips. She couldn't think what else to do; she felt powerless in the face of the old woman's distress. It was almost too much for her; she couldn't help Lady Cooper. It reminded her too much of how one year ago today, she had tried to help her mother and failed. Irrevocably.

*

Sam had no desire to see Mrs Pritchett. Her anger was still too close to the surface – wasn't the housekeeper largely responsible for this mess? She should have retired long ago, let them bring someone capable in. But her grandmother needed breakfast, so Sam made her way to the kitchen. Mrs Pritchett was there, drying dishes.

'I caught the maids playing dress up with Lady Cooper last night,' Sam said.

'Maids?' Mrs Pritchett gave an amused laugh. 'There's only the one.'

'No. There are two.'

'I told you, Miss Samantha,' the housekeeper laughed again, 'it's no good troubling with the ghosts.' Then she leaned against the sink and suddenly there was an angry tone to her voice. 'If you *do* see a second maid up there, send her down here! I could use the help.' She turned back to her work, picked a dish up off the drying rack. 'Storm's started up again. No one's come back. Unless they're hiding from me. I wouldn't be surprised. Now where are you going with that?'

Sam had spooned porridge from a pot on the stove into a bowl. 'To Lady Cooper,' she said roughly. The woman was splitting hairs. Ivy was a maid, Nesta was a nurse. Fine. Sam

250

had about all she could take for the moment. 'I'll take care of her today.'

'You take that to the dining room and eat it yourself,' Mrs Pritchett said, wiping a dish. 'Lady Cooper's already had her breakfast. Sent it up myself an hour ago.'

Sam stopped in the doorway. Was that possible? Her grandmother had breakfast while Sam slept in the armchair? This whole place was topsy turvy. Or doing a good job of making Sam think she was.

'Go on. You eat up.' Mrs Pritchett waved her forward with her dishcloth. 'It won't do. You're too pale. You can't run this place if you weigh no more than a willow o' the wisp.'

Run the place. Sam looked around at the kitchen: its red floor, the black range, the blue-green walls. Someone needed to. Should she? Should she stay and straighten this place up? The horrifying mess that had made Vera leave and never look back. The mess that Roger Bell had left to fester. Lady Cooper had wanted to restore Begars, in her own warped way. Sam could do it, the right way. Dig up all the secrets, hurl them out into the open. *No*, she thought. *Vera didn't want me here. I can't do that to her.*

Sam ignored Mrs Pritchett and went to the parlour and ate her porridge standing up, regretting not getting some coffee. She needed it to chase all of the bleak chatter out of her head. She had dreaded this day coming. Now it was here and she was a mess. Stuck in a mess. She hoped Alec would be here soon. She just wanted out. Her mother had cauterised so much of their lives to keep Sam away from this. And this was how Sam repaid all that suffering. But in what she prayed would be her final hours in this house, she would find out what she could.

Sam went to her room and collected Vera's map and put

on her coat and boots, then she went back downstairs and walked past the kitchen – Mrs Pritchett was still in there, humming away – to the back servants' door. She opened the sideboard and took out a torch and a hammer. Then she went to the prioress's chamber and unlocked the desk drawer. She grabbed the gate key inside by its shredded ribbon – she wasn't taking any chances – and turned and drew back the wall tapestry, knelt down with her hammer. There were two nails neatly driven at angles through each side of the beam, securing it to the wall, and someone had done a good job of it. She suspected it had been Alec, redoing whatever bent-nail, half-hammered attempt Mrs Pritchett had managed.

She wrestled the nails out and got the beam open, then turned her torch on and went down the old steps. She was going to find the cell where Vera had been kept. At the bottom, she shone the light on the iron gate... then swore. The gate was slightly ajar but now there was a heavy chain and padlock securing it to the post. Alec.

'Dammit,' Sam yelled and started wildly hammering at the gate and the surrounding walls. She stopped only when her bones ached from the rebound. She gave the chain a last, violent yank, rattling the gate, its captive bolts screeching against the rock. Then she kicked at it. Alec had done it to keep her safe. But that's not what she wanted right now.

She pounded back up the stairs in a fury. But as she crawled under the beam, she heard a scream. Sam scrambled through, and there was Mrs Pritchett shrieking; the pistol was in her hand, pointed at Sam. Sam froze, her eyes on the weapon, the shaking hand limply holding it, as if it were just another one of the housekeeper's balled-up hankies.

'Miss Samantha, you gave me the fright of my life!' Mrs Pritchett panted, putting her free hand to her heaving chest and then her burgundy head, taking great gulps of air. 'I thought someone was coming for us! Your ghastly monster! Why did you go back down there? Goodness!' She was waving the gun around in a random manner, like it was nothing more than her cooking spoon.

'Mrs Pritchett,' Sam said slowly. 'The gun. Could you please put it down?'

'What?' The woman looked down at her hand, then scowled. 'Bah, it's not loaded. Never was.'

'Well, I'd sure feel a lot better if you put it down anyway.'

'Oh how silly!' Mrs Pritchett put the pistol on the desk. 'Haven't you any sense?'

As soon as Mrs Pritchett was gone, Sam rushed over and picked up the gun. She opened the chamber. It was loaded.

27

Sam took the gun back to her room, cursing herself for not taking it earlier. She'd nearly had a heart attack when she saw Mrs Pritchett pointing it at her. Where could she put it? Where would it be safe from these nutjobs? She dragged a chair over to the wardrobe and stood up on it and put the gun on top at the back. That would do for the moment.

She took off her coat and boots, then went to check on her grandmother; she hoped she'd find Ivy with her. Had it been the girl in her grandmother's room this morning, quietly tidying her up, giving her breakfast, hanging up the gold dress? Or Nesta... The thought of either of them working in the room while Sam slept was disturbing.

But at the moment, Lady Cooper was alone, sitting in her chair, the weak daylight shining on her face as she stared out of the windows into the white nothing beyond. She was in a cream-coloured blouse and wool skirt, her face free of make-up save for a dash of powder and a bit of spring-pink lipstick. Perfectly respectable, normality restored. She looked elegant again, not a sick joke. Sam felt strangely dizzy, almost nauseous, when she saw the gold dress still hanging from the wardrobe door. It sparkled in the light of the fire, and Sam could feel its pull, beckoning her to touch its tarnished richness.

What would it feel like, she wondered, *to wear such a dress?* What powerful magic, what kind of alchemy was employed to turn cold, heavy gold into lush, liquid silk that moved with your body, instead of encasing it?

She looked again at her grandmother. The woman didn't appear to have even noticed Sam. At the moment, she seemed at peace. She was quiet, appeared content, her breathing soft – though her eyes were squinting as she stared out of the window.

She couldn't make it out – had Ivy only been trying to distract an invalid who couldn't sleep? It had to be something weirder. Why had Ivy been crying? Homesick, frustrated? Letting her hand drop away from the dress, Sam couldn't deny that this house was one of great temptation, even as shut in as they currently were. There were so many fine things. It was a house made for parties, for balls; the stairs designed for ladies to make a grand entrance and command the admiring eyes of all below. Why was Ivy expected to be content cleaning toilets and making beds?

Sam kissed her grandmother on the head before leaving. 'You bad old thing,' she whispered. 'You deserved to be punished, locking Vera in, not stopping your husband. But you didn't deserve this.' Her grandmother shifted slightly but gave no other sign of acknowledgement.

She returned to Vera's room to find the bed made and a fire blazing, the usual cup of tea on the nightstand. She instantly felt terrible. Ivy, in trouble and probably well aware she was going to be fired, but still doing her job, doing it well.

Sam took up Vera's last diary and worked at opening more pages. The centre of the book had suffered the least damage from the damp. Some of the pages only had a few phrases on them, but there was one longer entry:

24th December 1925

Left down there and forgotten. Abandoned. What they must have suffered. The hideous, agonising loneliness. The incomprehension of why they were made to suffer. Why no one answered their cries. Julia walking above them, in a frock from Paris, her golden curls scented and sprayed into place. Julia at her venerable prioress's desk, impeccably perched, so polished, so flawlessly put-together, writing her nonsense. Knowing that below her, they were pleading for their lives, for her forgiveness.

She blinds herself to her own degeneracy by giving it un nom étranger: L'Oubliette.

J'ai un nom pour toi, aussi, Maman: Le Putride.

What was *L'Oubliette*? The name for what Lady Cooper was doing, or her name for the cell? Why did Vera still refuse to say exactly what her mother had done? It was all allusions.

Sam thought back to one of the entries in another diary, when Vera had first discovered the hidden entrance behind the beam: *Who would she take into her hidden cell, with its braids of copper wire and corroded chastity belts?* The maids Sir Thomas had attacked and paid off? But that was sheer lunacy; Sam couldn't believe it. They were assaulted and thrown into an underground cell? No one would do that. Or was it done to young maids when they first came to Begars, to warn them off flirting with the male servants, or, worst of all, Sir Thomas? Or was it for other servants... or people, like her own daughter...

who knew too much and threatened to tell? This was all too extreme, Sam thought, the product of watching too many horror movies. But Vera had left, never to return. Something had happened that made forgiveness impossible. A series of rapes, being locked in a dungeon yourself, that was enough, though, wasn't it?

She continued to pick her way through several other ruined pages, and found a loose, folded paper stuck to one of them. She sliced it free and opened it – it was a map, similar to the first one she had found. Once again Begars was marked on it, along with the woods, the church ruins, and the crypt and tunnels underneath. This time, however, over one of the far tunnels was a giant X. One word was written beside it: *Oubliette.*

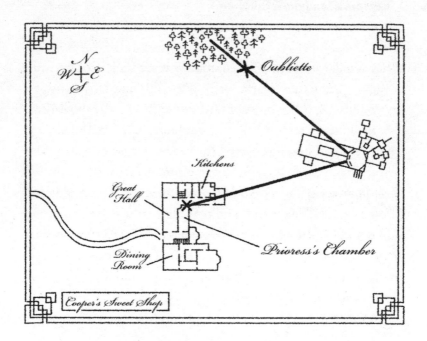

It had to be the location of the cell. Lady Cooper's name for the cell. Too many grotesque thoughts and imaginings crept around the edges of Sam's mind. These things didn't happen in real life... only they did. She groaned. It was Donna's favourite thing to read about in the New York newspapers. She looked at another page, made out the words: *cannot stand it*. Then on another ruined page: *hear them*. Further down, the writing had survived the damp somewhat better: *I hear them, the screams. They were mine. They are mine.*

Sam looked up, suddenly hearing a noise in the corridor. *What time is it?* she wondered as she glanced out of the window. The daylight was already fading, and flakes of snow bit at the glass.

'Miss Samantha?' It was Mrs Pritchett. 'There's a telephone call for you. It's Mr Bell.'

Sam jumped up; she couldn't believe it. The phone lines were working! She opened the door, ran right past the housekeeper and down the stairs to the front hall.

28

'Alec? Hello? Hello?' Sam pushed the cradle button several times, but heard only static. The line was working but the call had dropped off. She went to dial the operator, and realised she didn't know how; she needed to get Mrs Pritchett. As slow as the woman was, she had yet to make it back down.

As she headed for the stairs, Sam heard again a bow being drawn across a violin string, a long note of an accordion, a high laugh. Sam yelled over her shoulder to the ghosts, 'If you don't behave, I'll open all the windows and let you get sucked out.'

The house seemed to rock in response; another blast of wind. In the distance, Sam heard a rumble. More thunder? Or more stones falling in the ruins? Then, as she reached the first-floor landing, she heard from above what sounded like a small army of boots pounding across the floorboards. *No*, she thought, *that's nothing more than every last chimney toppling over in the wind.*

Sam climbed the rest of the stairs and, suddenly worried that she hadn't seen Mrs Pritchett yet, she ran to her room. She'd left everything out in plain sight. The door was still open, and Mrs Pritchett was inside, holding up one of Sam's blouses. Sam looked over in alarm to where she'd left Lady

Cooper's ledger, Vera's diaries. To her relief, they were still there, undisturbed. As was the list of names she'd made, resting on top of the book of hours.

'Thought I'd give you a hand,' Mrs Pritchett said over her shoulder. 'It's starting to smell like a barn in here.' She draped over her arm the blouses Sam had already washed, then picked up a skirt and some undergarments. 'I'll have these washed for you. I'm sure Lady Cooper has some nice, decent things you could borrow.'

Sam couldn't help herself. 'What about my mother's things? We were the same size.'

'Bless me, no. Those won't do.'

'Why the hell not?' Sam blurted out. *There isn't a thing about Begars she doesn't know*, she thought. That's what Alec had said. Startled by the outburst, the housekeeper gaped at Sam.

Sam stepped towards her. 'What's in the oubliette?'

'What? An eggly-et? What do you mean?'

'Down in the crypt. The hidden cell. What's in it?' she repeated.

'Oh, Miss Samantha!' she cried, almost impatiently. 'I haven't gone down there since I was a girl. On a dare from one of the older maids. Never again, I assure you.' The housekeeper looked around the room one last time, seemed to satisfy herself that everything was in order and walked to the door, avoiding Sam's eye as she went.

Sam followed the housekeeper out into the corridor. 'What's down there? I know you know. You know *everything* about this place. All its secrets. Tell me.'

Mrs Pritchett stopped at the top of the stairs, one hand on

the banister. She cocked her head like a bemused hen, then seemed to convince herself of something. She nodded and said, as if she were only talking to herself: 'Lord only knows what Vera got up to down there. It wasn't right, I told them. It wasn't right. She was a—'

Sam crossed the distance between them in a matter of seconds, and grabbed Mrs Pritchett by the arm.

'You're not feeling well. You need to rest.' She pulled the woman down the stairs, delightfully deaf to her shocked squeals of protest.

She stopped at the phone. 'Dial the operator. Ask for Alec's office.'

'Whatever for?' the woman asked.

'Because the call had dropped by the time I got down here.'

'Ahhh, I see.' She paused, then, 'Miss Samantha—'

Sam picked up the phone and handed it to her. 'Now please.'

Mrs Pritchett frowned but did as she was told and placed the call. Sam listened as she spoke with the operator, then the housekeeper sighed and said to Sam, 'The line's busy. I told them to try again. Shall I just tell them to ring us back when the line's free?'

'Please do.' When she was finished, Sam tightened her grip on Mrs Pritchett's arm and started again for the servants' passage. 'There, there, Mrs Pritchett,' Sam continued, 'I don't know how you manage to stay on those feet of yours, with all you have to do. You really are right. Too much work and too little help. It's taken a toll on you.' She opened the door to the housekeeper's bedroom and pushed her in. Mrs Pritchett had no choice; she was insubstantial in Sam's hands, a puffball. 'I'll bring you some tea. Sit down and put your feet up.' Mrs Pritchett sat down on her bed, brows knitted in dismay, as if she couldn't figure out what had gone wrong.

On the stove in the kitchen, there was the usual kettle of hot water. Sam dumped some tea leaves into a pot, and poured water over them to steep. She opened the cupboard where Alec had said the sleeping powders were. What she really wanted to do was dump four in the cup but she settled for two, poured the tea over it, then added milk and sugar and stirred. For the look of the thing she took out two biscuits from a tin and put them on a plate. Then she carried everything back to Mrs Pritchett's bedroom.

'Now, Mrs Pritchett. How will you ever recover if you don't rest?' Sam didn't wait for a response, and closed the door on the woman.

She returned to the kitchen and looked out of the window. The sky was completely dark, the snow falling harder. Help wasn't going to come. *Goddamnit.* She was going to be stuck in this freak show another night. Her head ached and her stomach was grumbling, too, but she didn't want to eat. Her throat was painfully scratchy, and she could feel two stinging sores at the back of her mouth. There was an ever-present taste now, as if someone had sewn pennies under her tongue. She was getting sick, no doubt from three nights of sleeping in that damp bed.

She took some aspirin, then forced herself to eat; she scraped the mould off a loaf of bread and found some cheese. By the time she had finished and returned to Mrs Pritchett's room, the woman was already asleep. Sam opened the door a crack; the housekeeper was flat out on her back, mouth open and snoring. Sam felt around the inside of the door; she was in luck. The key was in the keyhole. She took it and locked the door, congratulating herself for her ingenuity. If she had learned nothing else from *Rebecca*, it was that the sweet but stupid second Mrs de Winter should have poisoned the housekeeper Mrs Danvers at their first meeting. It was obvious Mrs Pritchett was disturbed. Why had Roger let her stay for so long?

Sam continued down the servants' passage to the front of the house, listening as she went. The house was fighting against the storm. She heard creaks and scrapes, felt an extreme sense of being confined, of being muffled. Like a wintering rabbit not sure if it was asleep or awake in the darkness of its burrow, or if the exits had caved in.

She took a lamp and went to her grandmother's room to check on her. It was only her fourth day at Begars and yet she had the sense that she'd lived her whole life in its gloom.

The old woman's head was sunk to her chest. A tray with a half-empty soup bowl was next to her. Her chignon was as elegant as ever, her lips a soft, pastel pink. *Ivy must have done it*, she thought. She couldn't see the glowering, lurking Nesta with a tube of lipstick in her hand – then it struck her. That's why Lady Cooper's make-up was so garish the night before. It had been Nesta applying it, not Ivy. All the loving touches – like the fur throw on Lady Cooper's lap now, her hands nestled under it. The freshly stoked fire. Ivy had done these things. Not Nesta.

The gold sheath dress was still on the hanger, shimmering, but below it, one of the gold shoes had been moved, as if it had taken a step forward. Ivy again – she probably couldn't help herself and had tried them on. It didn't matter. Ivy needed out just as much as Sam did, maybe even more so. She took the dress off the hanger and picked up the shoes. She threw them both in the fire. She knew Vera would approve.

She closed the door quietly behind her, so as not to wake her grandmother. A draught of cold air swept by, and she shivered and turned around. There, coming towards her from the main stairs was Ivy. Her eyes were downcast and she had her arms wrapped tightly around herself. Chagrin, then fury worked through Sam as Ivy moved closer and she saw what she was wearing. The girl had cleaned up since she last saw her, but she was still dressed as she had been the night before, as if she were going to a servants' ball. She was wearing Vera's navy-blue dress and her hair was neatly pinned back with the rhinestone clips. Her eyes seemed even bigger than usual – the effect of the mascara. *She's like a stubborn little girl, not wanting to change out of her party clothes!* thought Sam. *As if wishing for the ball and wearing the clothes will make it happen!*

'Ivy,' Sam called to her, 'I think you should change.'

'Yes, miss. Sorry, miss.' Ivy curtsied and turned to go back upstairs.

'Ivy, wait. Listen. We should talk. What was that about last night? With Lady Cooper?'

The girl stopped, but kept her eyes down. 'I didn't want to do it, miss. Do I have to leave here, miss?'

Sam looked at her, baffled. 'So it was Lady Cooper's idea? She rolled herself up to your room and said, "Hey, Ivy, let's have a party?"' At this, Ivy started crying. 'Look, don't make it worse. Go change.' Ivy, hugging herself again, quickly walked away.

Sam was disgusted with herself. It was like telling off a puppy. Besides, she knew Nesta had put her up to it.

One strange current after another curled around her legs and arms as she headed for her room; the wind keened through the house. Were all the windows ajar somehow? As she passed the gallery overlooking the back garden and the ruins, she saw that the snow had turned to sleet. Could she make it over to the Bagshot farm? But it was dark now, far too late. She cursed; she should have tried this morning. Asked Mrs Pritchett for directions. Not that she would've trusted them.

She heard the rumble of boots overhead, along the attic passage. She walked beneath the noise, followed it all the way to the end of the north wing and the concealed door that led to the back stairs, the ones she had taken to the attic her first night here. A chill ran down her spine as she heard the boots come pattering down the spiral staircase behind the door, the sound of someone tripping, a shout: 'Help me up.'

I don't care, she tried to convince herself.

She needed to find a way to get back into the crypt. The ruins entrance was too dangerous. She would likely get lost in the snow if she tried to find the entrance in the woods. No, she had to get down there through the prioress's chamber, through the padlocked gate. Find the cell. See what it could tell her, find all the awful secrets this place was hiding. She thought back to Vera's words: *I hear them, the screams. They were mine. They are mine.*

29

Sam got her boots and coat again, the hammer and torch. When she came back out of her room, the concealed door to the attic was open. She slammed it shut and headed downstairs.

She needed more tools to get through that iron gate; there had to be an equipment shed out back. She went out the door at the rear of the kitchens – it was so cold she gasped – and located the generator building and a tool shed; she rummaged around them until she found something useful.

Back inside, she headed for the prioress's chamber. She heard a screeching as she walked along the servants' passage; once again, the sound of a bow being dragged across strings. Then a discordant expulsion of air; the compression of the accordion.

In the great hall, the prioress's door was open. *The house is sinking*, Sam thought. The windows, the doors, all coming free as the foundations twisted and bucked in the storm.

She pulled the beam up – the bottom was already unlatched and sticking out from the wall. Faced with Mrs Pritchett and the gun, she'd forgotten to close it. Once on the other side of the beam, she turned her torch on and headed down the steps. She thought about the best way to get the gate hinges off, hoped there would be enough gaps between the plates and bolts to get a wedge in then hammer them apart. As a last resort, she'd take the sledgehammer she'd found and pound away at the weakest spot. She had no idea if she had the strength to do any of this, but it was worth a shot.

When she reached the gate she stopped, a ripple of fear spreading up from her chest. Like every other door she'd encountered in the last hour, the gate was open. She propped the sledgehammer against the wall and took a closer look. The chain and lock Alec had put on were wrapped around one side of the gate; the lock still had the key in it. She turned it, put lock and key in her pocket. *Definitely not a ghost.* Though she felt no relief. Had Mrs Pritchett woken up and come down? No, it had to be Nesta. But how on earth did she get the key? How would she have gotten it from Alec? Had he left it with Mrs Pritchett and Nesta got it from her somehow? But Alec wouldn't have done that. And why did Nesta keep coming down here? What was she looking for? How did she even know about any of this?

A bitter wind careered down the tunnel, touching everything with its mournful sigh. Sam wished she had ear plugs; it was as if it was talking to her. Words and pleas broken upon it. She could hear pain and desperation in it, the tone of a prayer that knew it wouldn't be answered. Lives wrecked, ruined, never to be recovered.

She concentrated on steadying herself as she walked; it was impossible not to be unnerved by the wispy touch of the cobwebs, the narrow field of view, the dust motes crawling through the beam of her torchlight. The cold clamminess of the rock, the crunch of the gritty floor, the mineral smell of the earth around her. The sting of damp in her nose and throat. A preview of death, the wind with its eerie dirge the only companion.

Her light caught something white on the ground ahead, something curled up in a foetal position. Sam swallowed hard as she approached. Shiny black hair, bones dripping with grave wax. Someone had moved one of the skeletons and curled it up, almost lovingly, in the tunnel. She skirted around it, flattening herself against the wall to get by, its empty eyes watching her as she passed. A raspy wail shuddered around her – the sound of someone struggling to breathe, as if each intake of air scraped the throat and lungs like jagged glass. Then a crackling, wet exhale. She instinctively looked back at the skeleton. What was happening? Was it no more than the wind? Did it enter the crypt sweet, then brush the walls, the bones, the tombs – all of the secrets buried here – and change into a poisonous miasma that soured everything? Sam stopped for a minute, her body ready to tip over into hysteria. *Cool it, Sam. Cool it.*

She entered the central chamber and pulled out Vera's second map, examined it, then stepped into the passage Vera had marked as containing the cell, the oubliette. It needed a key, one that had once hung from a key chain at Lady Cooper's waist. Each step she took, the stench got worse. From musty to something fouler, riper. Rank and nauseating. She could hear another torrent of wind rushing towards her. *It must come in from the entrance in the woods*, she thought, building speed and force as it was diverted down one narrowing tunnel after another. A spray of dingy air passed around her, followed by a small tremor, a rumble. Another stone from the ruins knocked loose, shaking the ground with its fall.

The next sound she heard was the worst yet.

'*Stay. Please. Stay.*'

The voice she'd heard before. Calling to her. The voice was weak, hoarse, but full of longing, full of pain. Was it really speaking to her? Was this all a trick?

She saw a faint glow of light ahead, then it disappeared. The night nurse and her lantern? Sam shook her head, tried to clear the headache muddling her mind. She hurried on, the piercing wind rupturing her thoughts.

'*Come back.*'

Every cell in her body resisted, willed her to turn. To get out of here before the night nurse or whoever it was got to her. She heard a series of coughs, so real, so dry and ragged it hurt to listen. Was this another one of Begars' tricks? Like the army of maids running above her in the attic? The aromas of a Christmas feast that didn't exist? The dissonant howl of a fiddler long gone?

'*Is she still here? Samantha? Is she still here?*'

Like the flick of a switch, it all changed. The fugue in her head cleared, the pain dissipated. This was real. Not a phantom. A real voice in distress. The sound of someone truly struggling for breath – the sound of her mother's flooded lungs near the end. She saw her mother's hand in hers, the fingers warm, soft... then heavy, still. She took off down the tunnel, running straight towards the voice. She flashed the light all around her as she went, looking for a break in the walls, the floor, the ceiling.

'*Help.*' Sam froze – the word came from right beside her. She whipped her torch around, searching for the source, the stench of a trapped animal all around her. There was an offshoot in the passage, an alcove barely wide enough for two people. It only went back a few feet from the tunnel.

She shone her light inside it and there, set in the floor, was an iron trapdoor, with several small slits cut in the centre. Breathing holes.

Sam screamed out as her torchlight hit a gap between the stone floor and the edge of the trapdoor. Long white fingers were reaching through the space; a single red-rimmed eye was looking straight at her.

30

'Do you have the key? Do you have it?' The voice's owner seemed near to collapse.

Sam knelt and touched the fingers. 'No.'

She put the torch down and wrapped her hands around the iron ring in the trapdoor. 'Stand back.' She pulled with all her might, kicked at the lock plate with her boots, then at the hinges. There was no give.

'Who did this to you?' She'd found it. The oubliette. Lady Cooper's oubliette. Still in use. 'Who put you in here? Nesta? The night nurse?'

The man coughed, struggled to get words out. It was a shallow, painful bark of a cough.

'Is she with you?' he asked. 'You must get away from here. Get help.'

Sam kicked again at the hinges. Tried to prise them off with the claw of her hammer. All around her, the echo of staccato breathing. The last breaths of Roger Bell. For she was sure that's who this was.

'Who put you in here? Who has the key?'

'Pritchett. Mrs Pritchett.'

Sam dropped to her knees and grabbed his fingers. 'I'll be back. Soon. I'm going to get the key.'

'No…' he gasped. 'Get the police.'

You won't last that long, she thought as she put the hammer in her coat pocket and ran down the tunnel.

*

'Miss Samantha. You can't go on like this! It's not proper. Not for a lady of the house.' Mrs Pritchett was standing in the prioress's chamber, once again looking down at Sam as she emerged from under the beam. Sam was actually glad to see her.

She scrambled to her feet. 'You're coming with me, even if I have to drag you the whole way.'

Before the woman could get a word out, Sam had wrapped an arm around her and squeezed her sideways through the narrow entrance. On the other side, she lifted up the ring of keys attached to a belt around Mrs Pritchett's waist and pulled it off.

'Is it on here? Which one is it?'

The woman only stared at her, like Sam had been replaced with an axe murderer.

'Go.' Sam nodded down the steps.

'Are you mad? I can't go down there!'

Sam took her by the elbow and forced her down.

Mrs Pritchett was crying now. 'No, no, no, no!'

Sam didn't slow down until they reached the skeleton in the passage. Mrs Pritchett howled when she saw the bones. 'What's this?' she cried, taking a step back. 'What's happening?'

Sam yanked her forward and Mrs Pritchett stumbled past the bones, her voice shaking. 'Where are we going? Where are you taking me? What did I ever do? Miss Samantha!' She tugged feebly at Sam's arm, but she ignored her, kept moving. 'Those boys,' Mrs Pritchett wailed in her high-pitched voice. 'It's all their fault! How can they not see? They've abandoned her, too!'

'Tell me what you know, Mrs Pritchett. Tell me now,' Sam said through teeth gritted at the effort of forcing the woman along. She was sweeping the passage with her torch as they went, expecting the night nurse to jump out at any moment.

Mrs Pritchett murmured through her tears, 'You were supposed to help. What happened?'

When they finally reached the oubliette Sam hissed at Mrs Pritchett to open the door.

'What? What?' The housekeeper didn't move, just wiped at her eyes with the back of her hand.

Sam pulled Mrs Pritchett down to her knees, the woman crying out in pain. 'Open it now.'

She gave the woman back the set of keys and Mrs Pritchett – with a great show of nervousness and trembling fingers – unlocked the trapdoor, saying all the while, 'How did this happen? How did this happen?'

When she heard the click, Sam got down and opened the door. She saw that the man was sitting down, his back against the wall – the hole wasn't very deep. About four feet. Not enough room to stand up. She couldn't tell how wide it was. 'That's him, isn't it?' she said to Mrs Pritchett. 'That's Roger Bell.'

Mrs Pritchett nodded, her eyes wide with fear.

'Mr Bell. Can you climb out?'

He didn't respond, but she could hear his breathing.

'Down there,' she ordered Mrs Pritchett. 'Get down there and get him out.'

'Miss Samantha, please.' She shrank away from her. 'It won't work, I can't lift him...'

Sam leaned over and pushed Mrs Pritchett's shoulders towards the hole. 'Help him out. Now. Or I'll leave you in there too.'

'You wouldn't!'

'I would,' Sam said as she got behind her and half lifted her in. Mrs Pritchett slid the rest of the way into the hole; it wasn't much of a drop but the woman still stumbled as she landed and Sam let out a slight breath when she saw Mrs Pritchett get Roger to his feet. How long had he been down there? At least a week, without food, without water. Exposed to extreme cold and damp.

'Turn him around, put his back to me.'

The housekeeper did as she was told and Sam leaned down and put her arms under Roger's and dragged him out of the hole. Once she had pulled back far enough so that he was free of the cell, she said to Mrs Pritchett, 'His briefcase. Get that too.'

'What? Where?' The housekeeper bent over to look and Sam kicked the trapdoor shut. She squatted on it and turned the key in the lock. This much was clear: the housekeeper had known which key unlocked the oubliette.

She put one of Roger's arms around her shoulders and helped him out into the tunnel, tuning out Mrs Pritchett's pleas for her to come back.

Roger was as hot as a furnace, on fire with fever. He struggled against her. 'No. No. We can't leave. Alec. We must get Alec.'

'He's not here.' Sam kept her voice low, calm. The fever had made him delirious. 'He's in York. It's okay. He's gone for help.'

'No, no. No. He's here. He's here. Please.'

Sam halted in disbelief. 'Where? Here? In the crypt?'

'You must get him. Get him.'

Sam leaned Roger against the wall, then helped him slide down to the ground. 'How? Where?'

'Over there.' Roger pointed vaguely, his eyelids closing.

Sam looked around, feeling half crazed. She pulled out Vera's second map. Another cell? She looked closely at the map, the large X over the entire passage. Could there be more than one oubliette here? A series of them, like a real dungeon? Had Alec never left, but somehow been trapped down here too? No. Roger had to be wrong, seeing things. She hurried back down the tunnel, searching. There, a few feet past where she had found Roger, was another opening, another alcove; this one on the opposite side. She dropped her light down and saw another metal door in the floor. But there was no begging eye peering out. No fingers reaching through a gap. She got down on her knees and could hear a shallow, pained breath; she called out, but got no response.

Jesus Christ.

31

Sam fumbled for the key, cursing herself that she hadn't paid attention to which one it was. There were at least thirty keys on the ring. She looked for the biggest, the oldest. Her mind became blank, her fingers disconnected from her body. She felt the jolt of release, heard a click, looked down to see her hands pulling on the iron ring, lifting the heavy door up. She watched as she stepped down and lifted the figure under the arms; the scent of stale tobacco. She hated the smell and she loved it.

She heaved Alec up out of the hole and onto the floor of the alcove. Mrs Pritchett was nothing but air; he was heavy as death.

How would she get both of them back to the house? Alec was over six feet tall. Roger had been down here longer and had to be the worst off. But he was conscious, talking. Alec, even as she slapped him hard on the cheek, wasn't responding. She dragged Alec down the tunnel to where Roger was leaning against the wall.

She took off her coat and cardigan and covered Roger with them, stuck the hammer in her waistband and the ring of keys in her pocket. 'I'll be back. Ten minutes. I am so sorry.' He nodded for her to go.

She let Mrs Pritchett out of the cell. She had no choice.

'You're going to help me carry Alec back to the house.'

Mrs Pritchett didn't say a word, and Sam liked this even less than her shrieking. What was she plotting now?

They slung Alec's arms around their shoulders and began the slow process of getting him out of the tunnel.

*

Back in the kitchen, Sam and Mrs Pritchett lowered Alec to the warm tile floor in front of the range. Sam looked at the housekeeper. What should she do with her? She made her go with her to the front hall, the woman silent but limping in pain, then asked her to dial the operator.

As soon as she heard a voice join the line, Sam took the phone from Mrs Pritchett. 'We need an ambulance. Right away. Begars Abbey. Two brothers, Roger and Alec Bell. They're extremely sick, they're having trouble breathing. And we need the police too. They were locked up against their will by one of the servants. She's still here,' she said, eyeing Mrs Pritchett.

She heard the operator put a hand over the phone, then muffled, worried talking on the other end. She knew why. The storm.

'How long?' she asked. 'How long before they can get here?' Her throat constricted at the reply: an hour or two. If at all.

'There's a farm nearby, Bagshot's I think? Can you call the farmer? Does he have a phone? He has a tractor, he could get them out. Call him, please. I need help.'

She hung up and sat down right there on the floor. Mrs Pritchett stood before her, rubbing the joints of her hands. Still saying nothing.

Sam looked up at the housekeeper for a few moments. There hadn't been time for Roger to tell her much down in the tunnel, but he had said Mrs Pritchett had the key. Sam would be a fool to think she wasn't involved somehow. 'I'm sorry, Mrs Pritchett,' she said. Then grabbed the woman by the calf and brought the hammer down on her toes.

*

It took almost as long to get Roger out as Alec. The movement made his cough worse and Sam had to stop every few feet when he was seized by a coughing fit; she was afraid he would collapse before they reached the stairs. He walked in a stupor, yet he tried to make himself understood as they went. That he needed to tell her now, because soon, he might not be able to.

'She said they'd be there.'

'Who?'

'I became terrified of her. Her face, her skin... dissolving.' He doubled over coughing, fought for air. 'She came to me many times. I don't know how often. Sat with me. Said she'd let me out. That she forgave me. Forgave my father. But she never did.'

'Mrs Pritchett?'

'No. The maid.'

'Which maid?'

'That poor girl. Can you imagine such cruelty?'

'Why didn't she let you out?'

'She's dead.'

'Please. Mr Bell.' His fever was too high, he wasn't making sense. 'Please. Who locked you down here?'

'Mrs Pritchett.'
'Mrs Pritchett?'
'Yes.'
'Are you sure?'
'Yes.'
'Who said she'd let you out?'
'The maid.'

32

Sam propped up Roger next to where Alec was lying on the floor. She didn't allow herself to check if Alec was still alive. Not yet.

She went upstairs and ransacked several empty bedrooms, returning to the kitchen with a pile of pillows and blankets, yelling for Ivy as she went. Mrs Pritchett was nowhere to be seen, and Sam regretted stopping with the woman's toes.

She mixed two glasses of sugar and warm water and gave one to Roger, telling him to take small sips, and helped him swallow some aspirin. She dissolved more aspirin into Alec's glass and poured little sloshes into his mouth, massaging his throat to try to get him to swallow. She couldn't understand why Alec was so much worse. What had happened to him? She wrapped both men in the blankets, made sure the range was well fuelled, then took the sharpest knife she could find.

'*Who locked you down here?*' she had asked.

'*Mrs Pritchett.*'

But someone else had known he was there... someone, it seemed, who he thought was even more terrifying than Mrs Pritchett, someone who had sat with him, taunted him. He had said it was a maid, and talked about her face, her skin dissolving. How could that be? What a strange thing to say.

But it had to be Nesta. Ivy wouldn't do that; she wouldn't taunt a man, leave him locked underground. But then, Roger had also said, '*She's dead*.' It made no sense. Perhaps he was referring to someone else at that point? Vera?

As she ran through the great hall, Sam wondered if she was dead, too. Through a veil she saw two fiddlers, an accordion player. A giant spruce topped with a crooked star. Men and boys hovering in corners, freshly shaved and skin red from scrubbing. Their eyes drawn to the long table laden with a Christmas feast. She passed through a swarm of girls, finding herself accosted once again by the nauseating scents of lily of the valley, lilac, tea rose. Were they there? Or was she the one trapped and feverish in the crypt, hallucinating? She pushed forward through the crowd; real or not, they looked back at her, annoyed at her haste. She didn't stop to ask them for help; she knew they wouldn't.

*

Sam climbed the stairs, shouting again for Ivy, and turned towards her grandmother's room, hoping she might find the girl there. Lamps blazed all down the corridor; she'd never seen the passage so bright and Lady Cooper's room was just as radiant. The fire burned high, every candle and lamp was lit. Her grandmother's delicate jasmine perfume filled the air.

But Ivy wasn't in the room. Nor was Lady Cooper. A pendulum clock on the wall chimed nine. *No*, she thought. *Not again*. The scene before her flicked and jumped with each strike of the clock's bell. *Ivy would be crazy to do it again*.

Sam ran upstairs and into the attic, then burst into Ivy's

room. The girl was there, sitting on the bed. She hadn't taken off the navy-blue dress, but she looked just as upset and dishevelled as the night before. What had happened since she'd last seen her? It had only been a few hours. Why hadn't she changed? Ivy's hair had fallen loose from its clips and her mascara was once again smudged. Her lips were red and raw, and she was looking down at the floor, tears silently streaming down her cheeks. Lady Cooper's cream silk shawl was wrapped around her shoulders, and her fingers were slack around another rose teacup; she seemed oblivious that it was about to slip from her hands.

Lady Cooper was in her chair, facing Ivy. The diamonds in her hair, the gold thread of her dress glittered in the light of a lantern. Sam's jaw dropped in shock and she stepped closer, touched the scorch marks on the dress. Parts of it had been burned away – she could see her grandmother's undergarments through the holes. It was the dress that Sam had thrown into the fire that afternoon.

'A cup of tea, miss?' Sam's heart stopped when she looked over. Nesta was sitting on the twin bed across from Ivy, partly hidden in shadow. She was holding a rose teacup as well.

Sam had never been this close to her before. Nesta wasn't tall, about the same size as Ivy, but whereas Ivy exuded the fluid vibrancy of youth, Nesta looked brittle, broken. Gone. Her bones seemed to sag under an unseen weight; the skin of her face was cracked and peeling. The hands holding the perfect little cup were rough. She looked at Sam through her round lenses, her dark eyes preternaturally large, unmoving.

Sam blinked. Turned away from the ghost.

'Ivy? Why are you doing this?'

The girl didn't respond, didn't move her gaze from the floor.

Sam went over to her, took the cup and saucer from her hands before they fell. Gently shook her, tried to break her stupor. Had she been drugged? Ivy looked up at her for a second, long enough for her eyes to fill with tears again, then she looked away.

'Sit with us, miss,' the ragged woman said. 'Go on, it's Twelfth Night. You're allowed.' She leaned forward and put her hand on Lady Cooper's arm. Sam thought she saw her grandmother tremble. 'It's your granddaughter, m'lady. Lovely, isn't she? Has your eyes. Those high cheekbones, that cool look. But that's Sir Thomas's mouth, isn't it? Unfortunate, that.'

'Who are you?'

'Nesta, Lady Cooper's nurse.'

'Ivy, who is this woman?'

Nesta held out the teacup for Sam. 'Drink up, miss. It's time we got back down to the ball. It'll be over soon. Ten sharp, right, m'lady? That's when you ordered it to end. We're not to have too much fun, are we?'

'There's no ball.'

'Did you hear that, Ivy? She says there's no ball.' Nesta looked at her incredulously. 'But there is. Do you not hear it, miss? The servants' ball. We have it every year, whether we want it or not, don't we, Ivy?'

Sam grabbed the handles on her grandmother's chair; the woman was shaking, locked in with an emotion she had no way to communicate.

'I'll take her back downstairs and put her to bed. Ivy, will you be all right?'

'Will you be all right, Ivy? Did you hear that?' Nesta said softly, looking straight at the girl. 'No, I don't think she will be.'

Sam started to back Lady Cooper out of the room. Nesta smiled at Sam. 'Lady Cooper hasn't had her tea yet. She must have it.' She bent over and held the cup to the woman's lips. Sam's grandmother jerked away. 'Last time. I promise you. Then you can rest. You want to rest don't you, m'lady?'

Lady Cooper was moaning now, an awful sound, like a donkey braying. Sam ripped the cup out of Nesta's hand and flung it against the wall.

'Now why would you do that?' Nesta stood up, feigning shock. 'You're just making it harder on her.'

'Making what harder?' Sam was trembling now, too. How could a ghost hold a cup? What else could she do?

'Look at our Ivy. She's tired. She's had enough. She wants to sleep. Let's leave her, shall we? Here, let me do that.' She grabbed the handles of Lady Cooper's wheelchair from Sam, her skin cool to the touch. 'It's what I'm paid for. Mind you, it's not what I wanted, m'lady,' she said in a low, calm voice, leaning down to speak into Lady Cooper's ear as she turned the chair into the corridor. 'It would be more fitting to do for you as you did for Ivy. Have a nice cup of tea. Then take you down and drop you in the hole.'

Nesta turned and looked at Sam. 'What I don't know is – did they kill Ivy before they put her in that hole? Or did they leave her there to die? Do you know?'

Sam took a step forward, her hand tentatively reaching towards her grandmother's chair.

'I thought Miss Samantha might help us,' Nesta said to

Lady Cooper. 'I tried to talk to her. I'd go into her room, look at her there, sleeping, and I just couldn't tell. Was she like Miss Vera, or was she like you? And then you'd start in with your tricks, mewling and crying – upset that I'd left you in the attic to have a bit of tea with Ivy. Lord, what a fussy old thing you are!

'Then I found her down in the crypt. I thought she'd come looking for Ivy. So I showed Ivy to her, but she only ran off.'

'Ivy...' Sam stammered. 'Ivy... get out here. What's going on?'

Nesta smiled. 'Our Ivy. A sweet thing. We all loved her. Sir Thomas loved her too, didn't he? But oh that's right.' She stroked Lady Cooper's hair as she spoke. '*You* didn't love Ivy, you wicked old goat.'

She looked back at Sam. 'You wouldn't have recognised the place that night. So many people packed in, made it as warm as a summer's day. They kept the electric off and lit all the candles and lamps. You couldn't tell the difference between the servants' ball and the one they held for the rich folk. Well. That's not true. But it was something. To be a young girl and standing in the great hall, in your best dress, a cup of punch in your hand.' Nesta rolled Lady Cooper slowly down the corridor towards the main staircase.

'Ivy helped me with my hair. She helped everyone get dressed that night; she had such a touch, didn't she? A real natural. Old Sekett wouldn't lift a finger to help – do you remember her?' she asked Lady Cooper. 'She was your lady's maid at the time. Just as foul as you were. Almost. It should've been our Ivy. She was far better. Far sweeter. Too sweet. Sekett left you didn't she? Left you cold within a week.'

Sekett. Sam had seen that name, in Vera's last diary. Alec had been right. Vera had gotten names out of her, names of the girls who'd been attacked.

'Ivy did her own last,' Nesta continued. 'She shone brighter than everyone, even as borrowed as she was. Them cheap rhinestone hairclips. That old day dress Miss Vera had thrown to her.' She laughed, a dark, heavy laugh. 'Still. You looked like a plucked old turkey in your gold dress, next to her. You knew it too, didn't you?'

Nesta had reached the top of the stairs and turned, began to walk backwards down them, carefully bumping Lady Cooper's wheelchair down in the same way that Sam had done the night before. Sam stayed close to her, desperately trying to figure out how to get Nesta – whoever she was, whatever she was – away from her grandmother.

'Your grandfather died with his cock up Ivy, miss,' Nesta said, as they reached the first-floor landing. 'Did you know that? Got her into his study. Died right there on top of her. And what does your grandmother do? She blames our Ivy.' She leaned down to Lady Cooper again. 'But you were a wily one, weren't you? Smooth as a snake. Had Pritchett take our Ivy to her room. Kept her out of the way. When I came up for the night, Mrs Pritchett told me that Ivy had got some bad news from home, and that I should go and share a bed with one of the other lasses. I couldn't say no, could I? I didn't want to be a bother, did I? Not on that night, when so much seemed to be going wrong. But I didn't know, not yet.

'Then once it was quiet and the fuss was over, you came up to see her, I think,' she said to Lady Cooper. 'Gave her your beautiful cream shawl to take the chill off, the one I always see

Ivy wearing now. Had Pritchett bring up some tea, served in your best cups. Next morning Pritchett told us Ivy'd gone, had to leave just like that, a situation at home. No one ever saw her again, not alive anyway. Girls were always disappearing like that at Begars, weren't they?

'She left behind a teacup,' she said to Sam. 'That's how I knew. Found it in Ivy's bed that next morning.' She sighed, turned back to Lady Cooper. 'But we still see Ivy, don't we? Every night. Wearing your shawl. Holding that cup. Did you put anything in it?' Then she leaned over and hissed in Lady Cooper's ear, 'Did you kill her before you put her in the pit? Or did you leave her there to die?'

Sam stepped closer to Nesta, put a hand back on Lady Cooper's chair. Nesta smiled at her; it was almost a friendly smile. Then she said lightly, 'Do you want to do it? Your mother would've liked that.'

'Do what?'

'I think Miss Vera meant to kill her, not just hurt her. And I think she'd want you to finish it.'

Sam grabbed the chair more tightly. 'What in hell are you talking about?'

'Vera knew. Knew what Sir Thomas did. And what Lady Cooper did after.'

Nesta saw the look of confusion on Sam's face, and nodded. 'Sir Thomas didn't care what happened to them. Couldn't be bothered. They were just little dolls he broke and tossed aside. Then Lady Cooper, she picked them up and punished them for it.'

'Punished them?' Every word from Nesta felt like a punch to the chest.

'It was the day after he died and Ivy had disappeared. All the other servants were downstairs working, but I was in my room. Our room, the one I shared with Ivy. No one came looking for me – they knew I was upset. I was up there, and I heard m'lady and Miss Vera arguing and I thought I'd come have a listen, things had been so strange. As I came close and spied over the rail I saw them down here, and I saw Miss Vera give her a great shove and watched as Lady Cooper fell down the stairs. Then Miss Vera walked away, towards her room. Cool as you like.'

Sam looked down the staircase to the front hall below, then at the terrified, shivering woman in the wheelchair. Her eyes were squeezed shut, her mouth working. How desperately she seemed to want to talk. To scream for help.

Sam had a vision of Vera, standing right where Sam stood. Knowing how easy it would be, because Lady Cooper would never expect it. A great shove, and then it would be over. Vera hated her that much.

Just then, she heard an ear-shattering shriek from the hall below.

'Get away from there, Vera! Leave her be!' Mrs Pritchett was limping up the stairs. One hand on the banister, the other pointing a gun at them.

Sam should've known. That was what the housekeeper had been doing in her room earlier, after sending Sam to answer a telephone call from Alec that he couldn't possibly have made. Searching for the gun. *Goddammit.* And clearly the housekeeper had fully lost her grip, calling Sam by her mother's name.

'Nesta! Girl! Stop her! Vera, don't!' the old woman cried.

Sam heard a gentle sob behind her and turned around. Ivy was walking down the steps. 'Ivy! Please!' Sam shouted.

Ivy came down to the landing and walked right past Sam and Nesta, towards Mrs Pritchett and her gun. Lady Cooper's cream shawl had fallen from her shoulders and trailed along the ruby-red carpet behind her.

'Ivy, wait, no!' Sam shouted, then stood stock-still, astonished, as the girl vanished before her eyes.

Sam looked at Nesta, her eyes frantically searching the woman's face for an explanation. Then she realised Nesta had already given her one. So had Roger. Nesta was alive. Ivy was dead.

Nesta smiled. 'Two birds with one stone. Shall we?'

'What?' Sam asked.

And in that second, when Sam's mind had turned inward to try to reconcile what she had just seen, what she had just been told, when she loosened her grip on her grandmother's wheelchair ever so slightly – Nesta pushed the chair with all her strength and sent it flying down the staircase.

It seemed to last an eternity; the chair still upright, bumping down the first steps, then crashing into the wall of the small landing. The chair rocked sideways and tipped over, her grandmother rolling down the rest of the steps, her body as light and helpless as spilled apples, meeting the hard stone floor at the bottom with a terrible sound of snapping twigs.

Mrs Pritchett threw herself towards Lady Cooper to break her fall – but was too late. As Sam stumbled down the stairs to pick up the gun from where the woman had dropped it, she watched the housekeeper pull Lady Cooper's lifeless body into her lap and cradle her like a child.

33

Julia Cooper was dead. Her oldest and most loyal of servants stroking her hair, begging for forgiveness, praying for her soul. Sam watched them, watched Mary Pritchett cry genuine tears of anguish.

She put a hand softly on Mrs Pritchett's shoulder; she knew that soon the housekeeper's tears would be for herself, because the only life she had ever known was over.

Nesta had come down to the small landing to survey her work. As Sam watched, the woman's smile of satisfaction faded, to be replaced by the same pained and weary expression she had worn before. The relief afforded by her revenge had been transitory. Nothing had been fixed. She turned and climbed back up the stairs. Sam didn't care where she went; the woman would be dealt with soon enough by the authorities.

Sam stood motionless for a moment, the house silent and cold. No sound of fiddles or laughing, no smell of a feast from years before. The house still shuddered in the wind, but whatever had been here before was gone.

There came a sudden pounding on the front door. Sam opened it, and saw a group of people on the doorstep, bundled up against the cold. 'Bagshot,' said a craggy-faced older man.

'Here to help.' It was the farmer and his wife, accompanied by two daughters and a son. *Thank god.*

'Alec and Roger are in the kitchen. Hurry,' Sam said. No one moved, struck dumb by the tableau at the bottom of the stairs. 'Lady Cooper is dead,' Sam said. 'We can't help her now. But please, the brothers, they're really sick.' That seemed to work. The family rushed ahead of her, she came slowly behind.

The farmer's wife took charge, ordering the others to bring two armchairs into the kitchen and lift Alec and Roger into them. Pots of water were put on every available surface of the range, its belly stuffed with coal.

'Steam, that's what's wanted,' said the farmer's wife. 'It'll help the poor lads breathe.'

The farmer and his son took on the grim task of carrying Lady Cooper's body to her bedroom. They then secured Nesta and Mrs Pritchett in separate rooms until the police could arrive.

'Jasper, my eldest, he's got the tractor. Clearing the way for the ambulance. We'll get the lads out of here soon enough,' the farmer reassured Sam. 'They've got new pills these days, don't they? Anti-botics. Took 'em myself once. Don't worry, lass. They'll make it.'

Sam left the family in the kitchen and walked outside; she wanted to feel the cold on her face, the brush of snowflakes on her eyelashes and cheeks.

In the distance, she saw lights slowly moving towards her. A tractor in front, followed by an ambulance and a police car.

It took a lifetime for them to climb the drive, but eventually they drew up in front of Begars. When the vehicles' occupants approached the house, Sam stepped out of their way and started walking down the drive. She walked past the ambulance, where a man was still pulling equipment out.

'Miss, you'll catch your death out here. Best get back inside.'

Sam slowly turned around, looked up at the house. 'Inside?'

The man stood up. He was burly, around Sam's age. He took her by the elbow, his eyes taking in her clothes, her lack of a coat. *He's going to tell me I've turned blue. That I'm already frozen. He's right.*

'A good cup of tea will sort you out. Or a drop of whisky,' he added, seeing her frown.

Sam thought of Ivy. All the times the girl had nervously swept Sam's full cups of tea from the room. Ivy didn't want her to have them. Who had put them there then?

She stared up at Begars, the lone rise of smoke coming from the back kitchen chimney. As she stared, flickering lights twinkled from one room to the next, starting on the ground floor, then moving upwards. Were the police searching the house? Why? Both Nesta and Mrs Pritchett were locked up. Weren't they?

Sam groaned. On the roof, above the south wing where Lady Cooper and Sir Thomas had their rooms, she saw movement. A shape came into focus. The ambulance man saw it, too. He yelled and ran towards the house. Sam shut her eyes. Waited for the crack, the thud.

She'd seen this before. Heard it before. Her mother throwing herself off the roof of their apartment building in Brooklyn. Her mother had insisted on leaving the hospital. Said she wanted to die at home. Sam had thought she meant in her own bed…

Twelfth Night. Vera had chosen that date for a reason. The

night of the servants' ball at Begars Abbey. The night Ivy was raped by Vera's father then murdered by Vera's mother. Perhaps Vera thought she was somehow responsible, had blamed herself, too. She had known what her father was doing, that her mother then made a hellish situation worse. But always this much worse? Was that possible?

Twelfth Night. Begars Abbey. Four words that hadn't crossed Vera's lips in twenty-seven years. Knowing why didn't make it better. Sam wished everything was different. She wished her mother were still here.

Sam sat down in the snow and cried.

34

It was Nesta who had thrown herself off the roof. After it happened, Sam had walked straight to the ambulance, got into the cab, and waited. Four short days. That was all it had taken for Sam to want to leave Begars Abbey and never come back. Her mother had survived seventeen years there. Had endured its demons – living and dead – for another twenty-seven. Sam had thought Vera didn't tell her about the cancer until it was too late because she didn't want Sam to push her to get treatment they couldn't afford, didn't want to leave Sam with that debt. Now, she had a different view. Perhaps Vera had held on as long as she could, satisfied herself that she had made Sam safe. That she had protected her and knew Sam could make it on her own. That Vera, as damaged as she was, would now only hold her back. So Vera chose to leave. To rest.

That day, 5th January 1953, Sam's office had shut early because of a coming storm. She still had her job at the port authority then and was making a little bit of money. She stopped at the grocer's on the way home; she'd wanted to make dinner for her mother. She was going to roast a chicken, then make a soup for Vera from the bones – she had hoped her mother could tolerate it. They'd made it through Christmas and New Year's and no matter how gaunt her mother looked, Sam refused to believe what the future held. The grocer had given her the chicken for free, the carrots, the celery, the onions. He knew what was happening at home.

It wasn't even five-thirty when Sam had reached her block but it was already dark; a thick snow had started to fall. She had just turned the corner when she heard Donna, her new baby in her arms, shout, 'Ms Cooper! Ms Cooper! Vera, don't!' A crowd had gathered, all staring up at the top of Sam's apartment building. The bags dropped from Sam's hands.

*

The burly ambulance man brought out wool blankets and a whisky for Sam. He told her that the police needed to talk to her. Sam had trouble hearing much of what he said. She was surrounded by a wall of white noise, trapped in a loop. She saw the same thing over and over.

Eventually the farmer's wife joined her in the cab of the ambulance. She put her arm around Sam's shoulder, holding her as Sam relived her mother's death, mourned her all over again.

You're wrong, Sam thought. *You were wrong. I still need you. I could've helped. With all of it.*

The window was fogging up and Sam suddenly felt claustrophobic, her mind flashing to the oubliette. Vera trapped in there. Ivy dying or dead in there. She rolled down the window, then wiped at her eyes – she saw her mother coming towards them.

Vera had her head down, her hands buried in her pockets and her thick hair was swirling in the snowy wind. She didn't look at Sam this time as she neared, just walked straight by the ambulance, but close enough so that Sam could see those familiar, unflinching eyes. She thought back to what Nesta had said as she watched the ghost of her mother fade away. *'I think Miss Vera meant to kill her, not just hurt her.'*

Yes... that's right, Sam thought, proudly, bitterly. *That was my Vera.* A young woman who had witnessed the vile and abhorrent actions of her parents, and refused to look away. *My Vera,* she thought again as the tears streamed down her face.

At that moment, Sam realised she knew the answer to Nesta's question: *'Did they kill Ivy before they put her in that hole? Or did they leave her there to die?'*

The girl had been put in there dead. Vera wouldn't have left Begars without her otherwise.

35

16th January 1954

On a bitterly cold morning, Alec drove her once again down a country lane near York. This time, they were going to see Roger. Both brothers had spent several days in hospital after their ordeal, but were now on the mend.

Roger lived in the house that had been his father's and his father's before him. It was newer and more modest than Begars, yet older and more lavish than almost any other home Sam had been in. It was made of grey stone, not the tawny stone of Begars, but Sam still felt nauseated as she stepped through the doorway; she'd had enough of these places. The nausea became worse when a smiling older woman greeted them. Sam was about to turn around and run – she'd had enough of housekeepers, too – when Alec caught her arm. 'No, Sam, it's my sister Josephine.'

The nausea eased slightly and Sam followed them towards Roger's study. Another difference she noticed: someone had gone to the trouble of crowding the house with as many plants as possible. There were great tall palms and squat pots of ferns in all the corners and bordering the windows.

'Our sister,' said Alec, when he saw her take note.

'Josephine?'

'No. Theodora. She did the same thing to my rooms in town.'

'They look after you,' Sam said quietly.

'I suppose.'

'It's nice, Alec.'

'You're right. It is.'

Roger Bell stood up when they entered his study, but not without some effort. Alec's condition had been the more acute, despite only spending two nights in the oubliette, due to the shoddy condition of his smoker's lungs, the doctor had said, but Roger was older and had been captive much longer; his recovery had not been as swift. He was a tall man like Alec, but stooped. He had the same features, too, but they were even sharper, if possible, because he had lost considerable weight during his week in the crypt. His cheeks were sunken and his eye sockets hollow, giving him the look of an old soldier. His manner was subdued and cautious; he had none of Alec's air of constant agitation and restlessness.

Roger sat down in a tall-backed armchair by the fire; Josephine arranged the throw over his legs and took a seat nearby. Sam took a seat opposite and noticed, gratefully, that no one was offered tea.

Roger Bell stared at her for a few moments, taking her in. She knew what he was doing. Looking for Vera.

Finally, he said, 'I let her down. Terribly.' There were tears in his eyes.

'Was she in love with you?'

'No.' He looked at her in surprise, then exchanged glances with Alec. 'No...'

'She thought about marrying you.'

'No, it was only foolish talk.' He tried to wave his hand dismissively. 'But we were friends. Great friends. Once.'

'Then why didn't you come? Why didn't you help when she asked you to search the crypt with her?' Sam refused to be merciful, not after all that had happened.

'I thought she was mistaken. I was a rather proud young man and she was a rather headstrong young woman. I had thought that in absence of all the facts, she was exaggerating things. About her family. Those girls. My father – he had thought they were *all* sent away, paid off. That that was the end of it. It wasn't right, he shouldn't have allowed it. But I am sure he did not know the whole truth. He did not know about the young maid. I was even there that night. I did not know. He... Sir Thomas... was fully clothed by the time I reached his study. His head was down on his desk, a brandy in his hand. She... Lady Cooper... had staged it well.'

'But you never wondered all these years how she was doing in New York? How she was getting by?'

Roger looked down at his hands. 'I thought if she needed help, she would ask. I assumed she had done well enough for herself. She was always so resourceful.'

'You didn't think it was strange that she left so soon after Lady Cooper's...' Sam struggled with how to phrase it, '... fall? It didn't seem unusually cold-blooded to you? Vera was gone by the next day. Didn't you wonder?'

Roger hesitated. 'I did. I didn't understand. Two horrible tragedies had just struck the family. It was all quite unfathomable. The only reason I went to Begars that night, the night of the servants' ball, was because Vera had asked me to come. She wanted a friend there.' He reached for his glass, his hand shaking. 'But I failed her.'

'After she left, you didn't try to find her? Ask her what happened?'

At this, Roger's voice faltered. 'I… assumed she hated me. Because I wasn't as strong as her, because I didn't believe her. I knew how she felt about her mother. And I had some idea about Sir Thomas, particularly after his behaviour towards my sister. I told myself she had simply wanted to leave it all behind, that she was not willing to spend her life a nursemaid to a mother she thought cruel.'

'Vera didn't leave any of it behind. It killed her.'

He turned his face away and sat silently for a few moments, wringing his hands so hard she thought he was trying to break them. Then at last he said in a faint voice, 'I was wrong. So very wrong.'

Sam let out a long, low exhale and a sense of quiet filled her: there was someone other than herself who had known her mother well and cared deeply for her, and who missed her. Sam stood up to leave, nodded at Alec.

Roger looked up at her suddenly and said, 'It wasn't foolish talk at all, the marriage business. She had wanted to protect me, thought I might need it. It was such a silly thing…' His voice broke again. 'She was always so strong… too strong.'

He looked away once more and she wondered if he would ever recover from the regret of leaving Vera to go it alone.

*

306

Sam told Alec she wanted to be someplace loud and crowded, so he took her to a tearoom in York. She ordered a ginger beer and a ham sandwich and told him to order the egg mayonnaise in case she decided to eat both their lunches. As they waited for their food, he started to light a cigarette and she took it from him. 'Not in your condition.'

Alec rolled his eyes, but relented.

'Why did Roger go to Begars then?'

'We shouldn't talk about this here.'

'Yes we should. No one's paying attention.'

Alec took out a handkerchief and coughed into it, then started fidgeting with the salt shaker. 'I spoke to him in hospital. He hadn't thought there was any mystery when he went out right after Christmas. He only went to tell Mrs Pritchett that she would need to retire shortly, and that Lady Cooper was to be moved to York. He knew he had let things slide for too long. But now an heir was returning. It was time.' He looked around at the white-haired ladies and young mothers. 'The rest I refuse to tell you here.'

'They're not listening.'

'They are.'

'Just tell me this then. What is an oubliette? What does it mean?'

Alec took a deep breath, coughed again at the effort.

'A room that's meant to be forgotten.'

*

They finished their lunches and Alec took Sam to a bench near the minster.

'When Roger told Mrs Pritchett that she would have to leave, he said she agreed, said she understood.' Alec slouched down on the bench, stretched his legs out before him. 'He said she served him a rather nice tea and seemed to take the news surprisingly well. Told him she was satisfied that she'd done her duty to Lady Cooper and she fancied a holiday somewhere, a trip to the seaside.' He coughed and rubbed his chest. 'Then she said there was something he needed to see before he left. Told him that if you were coming, there was something he should know about Vera. She planted the idea in his mind, just as she did with you, that Begars' secrets were Vera's. Not Lady Cooper's. Not hers.

'She took him into the prioress's chamber, under the hidden beam and down the stairs, telling him what had happened on Vera's last night at Begars. What Vera had done. Apparently he started to feel unnaturally drowsy in the tunnel, but thought it was just late-afternoon fatigue. She took him to one of the oubliettes and told him to climb down inside, to see what Vera had left there. He told me that he was quite fuzzy-headed at this point; besides he had no reason to expect such deceit from her. He climbed down, and before he could stop her, she'd closed the door and locked it. She told him to rot in hell with his father and left him there.'

'Lady Cooper's trick,' Sam said quietly. In the back of her mind, she heard a voice ask, *Who taught it to Lady Cooper?*

Alec nodded. 'At first Roger thought she only meant to keep him there for a few hours, revenge for telling her she had to retire. As the hours went on, then the days, he realised she meant him to die.'

'My god. She wanted him to suffer. She wanted him to die slowly.'

'Yes.' Alec took out his lighter and started flicking the top open and shut. 'I used to think she was just a mad old turtle. But she really meant to kill him. She was that far gone...' He coughed, and pulled his coat collar tighter. 'She took his car over to a nearby train station, to make it look like he had gone to London.'

'She did the same to you, then—'

'Yes, though she changed the story slightly. After you had gone to bed, she came to find me. Said she wanted to show me what she'd shown Roger. What sent him running to London. And she put the sleeping powder in his tea.' He gave an angry laugh. 'Mine she put in a whisky. She said I'd need a stiff drink – two, actually – to prepare me. The doctors think she put something else in there too, part of the reason I went under so fast,' he said, rubbing at his chest again. 'I did briefly think about what Lady Cooper had done to Vera. But I thought, *Mrs Pritchett isn't that clever*.' He gave Sam a rueful smile. 'Showed me, didn't she? But Roger had a far worse time of it than I did.'

'Because he was kept prisoner for so much longer?'

'Not just that. This is where Nesta comes in. She would come to visit, sit next to the trapdoor and drink tea or eat her lunch to torment him as he starved. And she would tell him about Ivy. About what really happened.

'She said there had always been rumours among the staff, that all those servant girls who'd suddenly left without saying goodbye, they were really buried in the crypt. Murdered by Sir Thomas. Nesta said the servants didn't actually believe Sir Thomas had killed anyone, and that she had seen Ivy alive in her room after he was dead. But then she found that teacup in Ivy's bed, and she couldn't leave it. She told Roger she got into the crypt through the entrance at the woods; the boards were already half off. She walked the passages and called for Ivy, but no one answered and so she left, dismissed it all as nonsense. Then she went back a week later, this time out of a plain old curiosity about the place. But as soon as she got in the tunnel, she knew it was all over. There was a smell that hadn't been there before. That was how she found the cell – she followed the stench.

'She described that moment over and over to Roger. How she'd shone a light into the slits cut in the door and seen the rotting corpse. She'd finish her story and say that as soon as Roger agreed to tell her the rest, she would let him out. She kept repeating, "Who else knew? Who else knew and did nothing?"

'He couldn't tell her – he hadn't known – and so she would leave, then return a few hours or a day later and it would start all over again.'

Sam stuffed her hands deeper in her coat pockets and buried her chin in her collar, felt a numbing whirr creep into her brain; she pinched herself hard to snap it away. 'Why didn't Nesta call the police?'

Alec shrugged. 'Sir Thomas was dead and Lady Cooper was paralysed; it wasn't known if she would even live. So Nesta left, never intending to come back. She tried to put it all behind her, like your mother did, but she told Roger she hated herself for it. Felt she had betrayed Ivy. At least Vera had tried to kill Lady Cooper, and even if she had failed, the woman was imprisoned for the rest of her life. She would sit in that chair, day after day, slowly rotting from the inside out. And what had Nesta done? Nothing. Wandered from one job to the next, never able to escape. Until she decided to come back to Begars and finally stand up for Ivy.

'They needed a night nurse – no one wanted the job or stayed very long. But Nesta stayed. Told Roger she fed Lady Cooper cup after cup of tea, saying, "Did you put something in Ivy's tea? Do you think I've put something in this tea?" Late at night, she'd dress Lady Cooper up in the gown she'd worn to the servants' ball, then wheel her up to Ivy's room and replay that night over and over. She'd remind her of all the vile things Sir Thomas had done, then would ask her what she did to Ivy. Nesta never harmed your grandmother physically, but she tortured her in every other way she could.

'But like Mrs Pritchett, like Roger – she knew that with your arrival she had little time left. That she would be fired and replaced with someone more qualified, or that Lady Cooper would be transferred to York. She told Roger that he would have company soon. That one night, she would bring Lady Cooper down to the crypt to join him. Alive, if possible. Dead, if not. She would leave him with one last cup of tea, though. Full of rat poison. Enough to kill them both. To drink whenever he was ready.'

'Did she know you were there too, in the other oubliette?'

'Yes. She really was quite horrid, but let's leave that for now.' Alec's hand was trembling as he put the cigarette to his lips. Sam gently took it away.

They sat in silence for a while, watching mothers pushing their babies across the snow-covered green, messenger boys passing by on bikes. Everyone in a hurry.

'The other girls? Do you know? Did my grandmother kill them too?'

'Mrs Pritchett denies all knowledge. But the police think there would have been an outcry if so many girls had gone to Begars and never come back.'

'But the skeletons out in the centre of the crypt chamber... there were six of them.'

He looked at her grimly. 'I know. The police are working to identify them, but they suspect most of the bones are far too old. Hundreds of years old.'

'But the one with the hair. Is that Ivy?'

'Yes. Nesta had gotten Mrs Pritchett tipsy on sherry one night, stolen her keys and opened the oubliette door. She took out poor Ivy's bones and arranged them in the crypt. She hadn't wanted her to stay in her prison.'

'But why Ivy? What did she do that Lady Cooper thought was so much worse than all the others?'

'I don't know. I suppose she blamed Ivy for her husband's death.'

'Of course,' said Sam, repulsed. 'If Ivy hadn't tempted Sir Thomas, he might have lived to rape another day.'

Alec put an arm around Sam's shoulder and she slumped against him. 'It really is a far more wretched story than I ever thought,' he said.

In a way, it seemed Ivy had made Lady Cooper's dream possible. With Sir Thomas dead, Lady Cooper could have retired into a solitary community of ladies. Why kill Ivy instead of thanking her? Sam watched a fat pigeon waddle across the gravel, pecking about. Ivy was the sacrifice. Ivy the martyr. The new patron saint of Begars. Lady Cooper's penitence.

Sam shook her head and muttered, 'Not bloody likely.'

36

5th February 1954, York train station, England

The train whistled in the far distance; it would be here soon. Sam stood by a tobacconist kiosk, stamping her feet against the cold. She bought some gum and a postcard to send to Donna. She looked at the cigarettes, but refused to buy any for Alec.

She was on her way to London. She had a list of names with her: the women her grandfather had raped. One of them was known to be dead, her bones eventually to be buried in a little churchyard near Kirkbymoorside.

Ivy Goforth, born 1911, died 1926.

Alec and Roger were now working to trace the rest of the girls. Two had been found and they had addresses for them in London. Sam wanted to talk to them, to see what could be done. To see if they had any children.

The preliminary inquiry into Lady Cooper's death was over; both Sam and Mrs Pritchett had made statements to the police that Nesta had pushed the woman down the staircase.

With Nesta, Lady Cooper and Vera all dead, there was no way to prove the housekeeper's involvement in any crime regarding Ivy Goforth twenty-eight years ago. But Mrs

Pritchett would be tried for the attempted murder of Roger and Alec Bell. Most likely she would be sent to a home for the criminally insane for the rest of her life. An ending that was too good for her.

Sam was as alone now as when she had left Brooklyn. *Well,* she thought, as she stepped away from the kiosk and looked over, *there might be a possibility there.*

She walked out onto the platform, tilted her chin towards the high vaulted ceiling. She wanted to feel the Yorkshire cold on her face one last time. As the train pulled in, it brought with it a gust of gritty wind and she closed her eyes. A scene came forth, unbidden. The one that had kept her awake most nights since her grandmother's death.

*

Vera is seventeen. She's wearing a black silk sheath threaded with metallic green and gold, and she smoulders in the candlelight. She sees her father Sir Thomas dancing a little too closely with a beautiful young maid. She shivers as a chill runs down her spine. It's about to happen again.

Ivy stands in the corner, a cup of punch in one hand, her eyes brighter than any light in the room. But she sees the young lady who has been so kind to her, who has given her the navy-blue dress she is wearing tonight, the shiny black pumps on her feet, the rhinestone clips in her hair; she sees her frown and shiver. She thinks Miss Vera is cold and runs upstairs to fetch her a shawl. Ivy wants to be her lady's maid someday.

Vera glares at her mother, who has just finished dancing with the first footman. Lady Cooper throws her head back

314

in delight, her laugh rich and infectious. She is golden, she is worshipped.

The butler comes over to Vera, does his duty. Asks her to dance; she can't refuse. Then the second footman sweeps her up. She doesn't notice that Ivy has left and not come back. That her father has left too.

Now Roger Bell approaches. He takes her hand, and puts the other on the small of her back. She wants to hit him. He's left this all up to her. But she softens for a moment, puts her head on her friend's shoulder. When the dance is over, she looks around and sees Pritchett, her eyes pinched and worried, her lips wet and quivering as she whispers something into Lady Cooper's ear. Watches as her mother's face falls, then hardens to stone. Vera's soul shatters. She let her guard down, forgot for the length of a few dances. This time, it was her fault.

*

Sam dug her nails into her hands to free herself from her trance; through the clouds of steam from the waiting train, she saw Alec frowning at her and waving for her to hurry up. She smiled at his impatience, then pretended to check the back of her nylons for a run, just to annoy him more. He blew out an exasperated sigh, and pulled the brim of his fedora down even further over his dark brow. *Poor guy*, she thought, still smiling. *He wants a cigarette.*

He put a foot up on the carriage step and waved her forward again. He looked so very angry it made her almost laugh. She thought, *I'd like to kiss him. Maybe. Some day.*

'By god, if you don't…' he hissed through his clenched jaw.

She danced a slow little two-step towards him and at last gave in and reached to take his outstretched hand.

He finally broke into a smile. 'Not bad,' he said admiringly, as he pulled her closer.

'I didn't think you were the dancing type—' She stopped cold. Behind Alec, down the platform, Sam saw a young woman running towards them. Her wool coat was plain, like Sam's; the navy-blue dress underneath was not her own. She was radiant, her cheeks were full, her eyes glowing – what Sam could see of them, for when the girl reached them she stared shyly at the ground.

'Miss, may I come?'

Sam stood there, unable to speak. Then, out of the corner of her eye, she saw another figure approaching.

A woman wearing round glasses, holding a lantern.

Acknowledgements

The architecture of Mount Grace Priory near Northallerton, Yorkshire, is a partial inspiration for this book. The monastery there was founded in the fourteenth century and was home to a Carthusian order of monks; it was surrendered to Henry VIII in 1539 as part of the Dissolution of the Monasteries. The prior's house still stands and is the present-day manor house. The walls of the medieval church and the cells where the monks lived in solitude also remain; today Mount Grace is owned by the National Trust.

There once was a medieval priory in Yorkshire named Begar, though it also has been referred to in historical records as Begger or Begare. It was located near Richmond and was an offshoot of an abbey called Bégard in Brittany, founded in the twelfth century. But unlike the fictional Begars Abbey, this Yorkshire priory was home to Cistercian monks, not nuns.

While *Begars Abbey* draws inspiration from these places, the characters and story threads in this book have no basis in Mount Grace or the original Begar Priory. Those ideas came from another place...

*

Three years into this coronavirus pandemic, what is top of mind for me is gratitude. A huge thanks to the most fantastic editors, Miranda Jewess and Therese Keating, for taking on this book, and to all of the incredible Profile Books/Viper team – Graeme Hall, Drew Jerrison, Hayley Shepherd, Flora Willis and Lucie Ewin. And thank you Sam Johnson for yet another stunning cover design and Steve Panton for your maps!

Thank you forever to my fearless agent Victoria Skurnick at Levine Greenberg Rostan, and to Anna Carmichael at Abner Stein.

Thank you to Jennifer Ryan for your never-ending generosity and taking the time to read early versions of Begars; and to Alison Richards for being so brilliant and always there for me.

Thank you to Pia Harold and Tracey O'Halloran – the two of you are always front and centre when I write.

I wouldn't get anywhere in this world if it weren't for Sonya Artis (who is the best companion for a visit to the Met or NYC's Tenement Museum), Gisele Grayson, Eliza Barclay and Michaeleen Doucleff. And these days, especially, if it weren't for Lin and Callie.

Anthony and Manny, more adventures, please! (And thank you Mr Manzanares, for sharing your memories of growing up in Queens.)

To my mom and dad, for allowing me as a child to read or visit any scary thing I could; they are responsible for the imagination that makes my novels possible. But, also in the case of Begars, I thank them for the stories they've told me about their families in 1930s and '40s America. The story of the kid nicknamed Boots in this book is actually a true story about my grandfather.

And never last, always first, my Sylvan Cat. Boy oh boy, I agree! Cancel work! Cancel school! Play!

About the Author

V.L. Valentine is a senior science editor at National Public Radio in Washington, D.C., where she has led award-winning coverage of global disease outbreaks including Covid-19, Ebola and the Zika virus. She has a master's in the history of medicine from University College London and her non-fiction work has been published by *NPR*, *The New York Times*, the Smithsonian Channel and *Science Magazine*. *Begars Abbey* is her second novel; her first, *The Plague Letters*, was published by Viper in 2021.